THE NIGGER FACTORY

GIL SCOTT-HERON

THE NIGGER FACTORY

CANONGATE

Edinburgh · London

First published in Great Britain in 1996
by the Payback Press, an imprint of Canongate Books Ltd,
14 High Street, Edinburgh EH1 1TE

First published in the United States of America by
The Dial Press, 1972

This edition published by Canongate Books in 2010

Grateful acknowledgement is made to Abeodun Oyewale and
Douglas Communications Corporation for permission to quote
from the song 'Gash Man'.
Copyright © 1970, Douglas Music Corporation.

British Library Cataloguing-in-Publication Data
A catalogue record for this book is available upon request
from the British Library

ISBN 978 1 84767 884 3

Typeset in Minion and Serif Modular by
Palimpsest Book Production Limited,
Grangemouth, Stirlingshire
Printed and bound in Great Britain by
Clays Ltd, St Ives plc

www.canongate.tv

this book is dedicated to:

Sister Jackie Brown
Brother Victor Brown
Brother David Barnes
Brother Brian Jackson
Brother Eddie Knowles
and
Brother Charlie Saunders
whom I met on the assembly line

Contents

Author's Note

Black colleges and universities have been both a blessing and a curse on Black people. The institutions have educated thousands of our people who would have never had the opportunity to get an education otherwise. They have supplied for many a new sense of dignity and integrity. They have never, however, made anybody equal. This is a reality for Black educators everywhere as students all over America demonstrate for change.

It has been said time and time again that the media makes the world we live in a much smaller place. It is no longer possible to attend Obscure University and be completely out of touch with the racist system that continues to oppress our brothers and sisters all over the country. Black institutions of higher learning can no longer be considered as wombs of security when all occupants realize that we are locked in the jaws of a beast.

Change is overdue. Fantasies about the American Dream are now recognized by Black people as hoaxes and people are tired of trying to become a part of something that deprives them of the necessities of life even after years of bogus study in preparation for this union. A college diploma is *not* a ticket on the Freedom Train. It is, at best, an opportunity to learn more about the systems that control life and destroy life: an opportunity to cut through the hypocrisy and illusion that America represents.

New educational aspects must be discovered. Our educators must sit down and really evaluate the grading system that perpetuates academic dishonesty. The center of our intellectual attention must be thrust away from Greek, Western thought toward Eastern and Third World thought. Our examples in the arts must be Black and not white. Our natural creativity must be cultivated.

The main trouble in higher education lies in the fact that while the times have changed radically, educators and administrators have continued to plod along through the bureaucratic red tape that stalls so much American progress. We have once again been caught short while imitating the white boy. While knowledge accumulates at a startling pace our institutions are content to produce quasi-white folks and semithinkers whose total response is trained rather than felt.

Black students in the 1970s will not be satisfied with Bullshit Degrees or Nigger Educations. They are aware of the hypocrisy and indoctrination and are searching for other alternatives. With the help of those educators who are intelligent enough to recognize the need for drastic reconstruction there will be a new era of Black thought and Black thinkers who enter the working world from colleges aware of the real problems that will face them and not believing that a piece of paper will claim a niche for them in the society-at-large. The education process will not whitewash them into thinking that their troubles are over. They will come out as Black people.

Wednesday Night

1

Seven p.m. Phone Call

Earl Thomas was wiping shaving cream from under his chin when the telephone rang. He waited, thinking that his neighbor Zeke might answer, but when he heard a second shrill jingling he opened the bathroom door and released the receiver from its holster.

'Earl Thomas,' he announced.

'Thomas?' A bass voice boomed. 'This is Ben King. I called cuz I wanned t'tell you 'bout this meetin' we had dis afternoon wit' the studen's.'

'Meetin'? What meetin'?' Earl asked. He was afraid that he already knew the answer to the question.

'MJUMBE had a meetin' wit' the studen's this afternoon 'bout fo' thutty. We had drew up some deman's fo' Head Nigger Calhoun an' we had t'fin' out 'bout hi the people felt 'bout things ... I called you befo' but I got a bizzy signal.'

'Zeke,' Earl muttered.

'What?'

'Nuthin'.'

'Anyway,' King continued, 'I wuz callin' befo' cuz we were gonna like confer wit'choo befo' we handed the shit to the Man, but when I couldn' get'choo we cut out over t'the Plantation,' King laughed. 'Calhoun wudn' home so I called agin.'

'Yeah ...'

'We figgered you might wanna be in-volved,' King added.

The sarcasm that dripped through the receiver as King slowly drawled his way through the monologue was beginning to grate on Earl's nerves. Something very screwy was going on; something that Earl felt an immediate need to pinpoint. But too many ideas were dashing through his head. There was no real way to slow down the thoughts that were turning him into a huge knot. What were the demands? Why hadn't he heard anything from anyone? Faster and faster the questions came, obscuring the words King breathed slowly through the telephone.

'What did you say?' Earl asked. 'I missed that last part.'

'I ast you hi long it's gon' take you to git down here.'

'Down where?'

'Well, we in the frat house on the third flo'.' King said.

'I guess I can be there in 'bout twenny minnits,' Earl calculated.

'Right on!' King laughed. 'We'll be waitin'!'

The call was terminated. Earl felt for the first time the beads of sweat that had been sprung loose from wells at his hairline. Blood was circulating again in his left ear now that the phone had been unclamped. A very sick smile was spread over his face.

There was nothing he really felt capable of doing or saying at that moment. It was sixth grade all over and he was watching his girl being walked home from school by someone else. Everyone in the world was waiting, watching to see what he would do. There was nothing that could be done. Odds had warned him. Lawman had warned him. The pulse of the campus had told him. 'MJUMBE is up to something!' the messages read. But Earl Thomas was not a hasty young man. He had been drawing up a list of demands and researching every item carefully with the Board of Trustees and members of the administration. When he went after Calhoun he was going to be damn sure that everything was perfect. Now the whole thing was shot to hell.

'Where the hell is Victor Johnson?' he asked out loud.

Victor Johnson was the editor-in-chief of the Sutton University *Statesman*, the campus's weekly newspaper. Earl often referred to Vic as the editor-in-everything because the bespectacled senior seemed to be the only one who ever did any newspaper work on campus. Wasn't a coup newsworthy any more? Wasn't the story of the president of the Student Government Association being shot down worth the print? They printed shit like the ZBZ sorority's news.

Earl slumped heavily on the side of the bathtub. See! See! he heard stumbling through his head. Here you sit inna damn bathrobe splashin' aftershave on yo' mug while some two-faced muthas run 'roun' an' pour freezin' damn water down yo' goddamn back! An' you can' rilly even ac' su'prized cuz evybody tol' you . . .

Earl started counting backward. He was trying hard to remember the various dates he had marked on his political calendar; still searching for that one elusive idea that felt so important but could not be captured. Today was October 8th. School had opened on September 9th. He had been elected the previous May and had taken office on June 1st. He had promised the students then that by the end of the coming September he would have a list of their prime grievances drawn up and ready for their approval. It had taken longer than he had thought it would. The old bylaws and old Student Government constitution hampered everything that he wanted to do. He found himself struggling like a man in quicksand; the harder he fought the deeper he sank. It had been as bad as Lawman had predicted: 'It's impossible to move faster within the system than a turtle with two busted legs.'

The truth was that it was his inability to make any headway that was really upsetting Earl about King's call. The message meant that MJUMBE was running head on into Ogden Calhoun, the university president, with nothing to back it up. MJUMBE's act might have been courageous, but it was definitely unwise politically. Calhoun hadn't lasted at Sutton for nine years for no reason. He knew what could and could not be allowed. He had kicked more student reformers out of school than the presidents of any other five schools combined.

Earl switched off the bathroom light and flip-flopped in his shower shoes down the second-floor hall to his room. He strode past the room of Zeke, the handyman, with the record player playing Mongo Santamaria full-blast, and past Old Man Hunt's room, where absolutely nothing was ever going on.

'So the great Sutton revolution has finally begun,' he muttered sarcastically, flinging his door open. 'And Earl Thomas has been kicked the hell out.'

At that point another real question arose. Why had he been called? To hell with why Lawman and Odds, his best friends, had *not* called. Why had Baker let Ben King call? Earl Thomas and Ralph Baker, the MJUMBE leader, were political enemies. Earl had defeated Baker for the post of SGA president. What was going on?

The chain of events that had wired Earl for the phone call were at that very moment wiring others to the fuse slowly smoldering on the campus of Sutton University. The meeting. Phone call. Busy signal. Calhoun not home. Second call. Earl speaking. A million possible combinations were spiraling across a background of human skin; dominoes that stretched out and were nudged, forced to collapse into one another until a whole line of white dots drilled into black rectangles stumbled jointlessly through a massive collision and lay silent.

Earl pulled his pants on hurriedly. He wasn't sure how much he could do. Maybe nothing. There would be little sense in his asking MJUMBE to halt plans that were off the ground. No one would wait. There would be little point in his explaining to the MJUMBE leadership how much work he had done to get things together. No one would wait. At least he was involved. That was something that would allow him a little say-so. It was much better to be invited in than to have to control the situation from outside. The students would be watching very carefully to see what happened between him and MJUMBE. MJUMBE would doubtlessly be watching to make sure he didn't get away with anything. Everyone would be watching him.

'Ice. Ice. Ice.' He muttered to himself. 'I got to be very cool.'

The train was moving, gaining speed as it left the comparative safety of the yards. The first stop would be a funky frat room on Sutton's campus. Earl knew that if he wasn't cool the train might go no further. He wondered if he could take it. Baker and King laying down the rules. Earl Thomas caught in the middle. He definitely did not dig the plot. But he realized that he had no real choice. He was not the train's engineer. He was a passenger.

2

MJUMBE

Mjumbe is the Swahili word meaning messenger. On the campus of Sutton University, Sutton, Virginia, it was also the identifying name for the Members of Justice United for Meaningful Black Education. MJUMBE.

The name was chosen by Ralph Baker, a six-foot two-hundred-pound football player who had organized the group and served as its spokesman. Baker sat in the third-floor meeting room of the Omega Psi Phi fraternity house waiting for the results of Ben King's phone call to Earl Thomas. He was also reliving the day.

The day had really started for Baker at four o'clock that afternoon. He had left a note in the frat house lounge after breakfast notifying the four other MJUMBE chieftains of a four o'clock meeting. When he came into the lounge at four the others were waiting.

'Brothers,' he had said, 'the time has come.'

'Right on!' Ben King had said, sitting up.

Baker placed a stack of one thousand mimeographed sheets on the battered card table. Each man took one.

'We been layin' an' bullshittin' too long,' Baker commented as the men read the paper.

'Fo' hundred years,' Speedy Cotton mumbled.

'Thomas said when he was elected that by the enda September he wuz gonna have everything laid out like a train set ... I don' need ta tell nobody that iz October eighth an' we ain' heard from the nigger yet. He ain' nowhere near organized an' ...'

'He a damn Tom!' King said. 'I tol' yawl he wuz a Tom!'

The members of MJUMBE all nodded. Baker glared down at them as though they were to blame. Ben King and Speedy

Cotton sat on the same side of the table as usual, a set of diagrammed football formations in front of them. Fred Jones, Jonesy, tapped a deck of cards on the side of the table. Abul Menka, the only MJUMBE member who was not a football player, sat in the corner of the room with his feet propped on the window ledge.

'So na',' Baker went on, 'it's pretty clear t'me that if anything gon' get done, we gon' do it!'

'Right on!'

'I wanna know what yawl think 'bout the stuff,' Baker said gesturing to the paper. 'We gotta have it t'gether 'cuz we gon' be meetin' wit' ev'y man, woman, an' chile on this campus in 'bout fifteen minnits.'

'That wuz the meetin' we heard bein' announced?' Speedy Cotton asked.

'That wuz it!'

'Then this las' deman' means Calhoun gon' get these deman's t'night?'

Baker smiled. 'I think you catchin' on.' Baker, King, and Cotton shared a loud laugh.

'What 'bout practice?' Jonesy interrupted. 'We s'pose t'be at practice at fo' thutty.'

'No practice today.' King snorted. 'We gon' be bizzy.' He laughed.

'Why today?' Jonesy asked. All four men knew that Jonesy was the worrier. He was never comfortable until he was on a football field where all he had to do was knock hell out of anything that moved.

Baker ran a big black hand over his bald-shaved head. 'I figger we got a surprize fo' Calhoun. He been in Norfolk for two days an' he ain' gittin' back 'til 'bout six t'night. By then we be done had our meetin', ate, come back an' wrapped everything tight . . .'

'What 'bout Thomas?' King asked.

Baker frowned. 'I'm gittin' to that . . . if Thomas ain' at the meetin', an' he may not be . . .'

'Why wouldn' he be there?'

'Look. Lemme say the shit. All right? . . . Thomas ain' got no classes on Wednesday so he don' be here. All right? So if Thomas ain' at the meetin', after we come back an' git our shit right, we gon' call 'im an' tell 'im to come over here an' do somethin' fo' us.'

'We gon' blow his min' this time,' Cotton laughed.

'Him an' Head Nigger if shit work out.' Baker laughed louder.

'We gon' have him take Head Nigger this list?' King asked waving the demands.

'I wanned to s'prize Thomas.'

'It'll s'prize a lotta folks,' Cotton remarked.

King, Baker, and Cotton enjoyed another good laugh. Jonesy simply frowned and Abul Menka, as usual, did nothing.

'What if Thomas don' dig bein' out the driver's seat?' Cotton asked, getting serious.

'Either secon' or nothin',' Baker said setting his jaw. 'From now on we runnin' shit!'

Baker continued to go over the afternoon in his mind. The four o'clock prompting for the MJUMBE team had set the stage for the four-thirty rally with the students. The five of MJUMBE had left the meeting room together. They had strode across the Sutton Oval that was set in the middle of the campus to the Student Union Building. They crushed the dead grass beneath their feet and quickly scaled the thirteen steps that led to a balcony overlooking the crowd of students that had already begun to gather. All five were dressed in black dashikis. All except Abul Menka were heavily muscled athletes who had shaved their heads when the coach complained about bushy heads not allowing helmets to fit tightly enough. All five were intent and stern-faced, silhouetted by a fading red disc that had darkened their bodies during an early-autumn heat wave. All bad. All Black.

The student response to Baker's demands had been greater

than even he expected. He had thought there might be some question as to his authority. Nobody had even mentioned Earl Thomas. The students seemed very unconcerned as to who actually became the leader for the change the campus needed so badly. All they wanted was action.

Baker had been in his world. He bathed in the light of the handclapping, whistling, and shouted support heaped upon him and his comrades. It seemed that with the reading of each demand the support grew. He had said everything he could think of about Ogden Calhoun, the Head Nigger, and the members of the administration. When he finished, the five men marched through the crowd that still stood chattering like monkeys. All Baker could hear was:

'Do it, Brother!' and 'Right on with power!'

There was little they could do now but wait. Wait and think. Baker knew that the support had been good, but he also knew that Ogden Calhoun had a reputation as a destroyer of student dissent. The Sutton president had been asked recently how Sutton had escaped the student disruptions that had rocked other Black campuses. Calhoun had replied to the interviewer: 'I have a saying for students on my campus. It says: "My way or the highway!" In other words: "If we can' git along, *you* goin' home!"'

So the lines were drawn. Calhoun had no room in his plans for student disruption. MJUMBE had no plans for going home.

Baker's mind drifted. After the afternoon meeting his plan had started to become shaky. Just at the point when his name was on the lips of every Sutton student, he was knifing himself in the back by having Earl Thomas notified. He hated to think of turning the least credit over to a man he considered an enemy, but there was really no way out of it. While running for Student Government president he had preached Black collectivity; all political factions putting their heads together. And there was no denying that Earl Thomas was a smart politician. The election had proven that. Then too, if Earl endorsed Baker, another bloc of students would fall easily into line.

In late August when Jonesy had arrived for summer football training Baker had started talk about MJUMBE. 'If you ain' out fo' nuthin' but revenge on Thomas fo' beatin' you,' Jonesy had said, 'forget it.'

'I ain' lookin' fo' nothin' but progress,' Baker had sworn. 'I think MJUMBE can serve a two-way purpose. First, Thomas gon' move if he know somebody lookin' over his shoulder. Second, all the athletes would be down to back Thomas up if we wuz organized an' spoke fo' him.'

The possibility that MJUMBE might give Earl its backing was what had sold Jonesy. And now that the time had come Jonesy had not objected to any of Baker's arguments about why MJUMBE should cast the first stone. But Baker knew well enough that Jonesy would pull out if he felt as though the group spokesman had lied about his intentions. Earl had been called.

That's when things started fuckin' up, Baker thought.

Earl's line had been busy. Baker decided on a second's notice that since Earl couldn't be reached MJUMBE would deliver its own mail.

'It's six thutty,' he said when King notified him of the busy line. 'Calhoun was s'pose to git home 'bout six. He prob'bly got wind a the deman's already. We can' give 'im too much time to pull no fas' stuff on us.'

They had started out. Five men in black dashikis crunching through the dead leaves across the quadrangle behind the fraternity house, across the football field to the big white house Sutton students called 'the Plantation.' Calhoun wasn't home.

Calhoun's absence implied several things to Baker. It indicated that Calhoun knew nothing of the demands. God knew he would have been setting up some counterattack had he heard. It also meant that MJUMBE might have *peaked* too soon.

As a football player Baker knew a lot about peaking. A team

is built up by a good coach to reach its emotional and competitive *peak* just before the charge down the shadowed runway; when the only sound to be heard is the thunderous clacking of forty pairs of cleats grating against the rough-grained concrete. The team tears down the ramp ready to tackle a moving van. Every inch of your body would be choking with the smell of forty men, practice jerseys, wintergreen, urine, and the sweaty jocks that lay in a corner hamper. Your heart strait-jacketed in your chest, climbing up bony columns of your throat, tightening you into a gigantic ball.

Baker had been a bad coach. He knew now that he should have called the Plantation before he and his cohorts started out. There had been an emotional letdown when there was no one at the Calhoun residence to accept their papers. They had stood on the threshold with hearts the size of a football, ready to slap all authoritative danger in the face. The silly old maid seemed to mock them, though she knew nothing. The air had been let out of them.

Now they sat. Thinking and waiting.

'Thomas will be here in twenny minnits,' King said barging through the partially open door.

'Good,' Baker said without conviction. He took a look at his watch. In twenty minutes it would be seven thirty. It was getting late.

The MJUMBE spokesman reread the sheet he had handwritten and practically memorized. He would take everyone through their parts again before Thomas arrived.

He looked at his comrades closely; looking for signs of panic or fear; looking for things that he might feel if they were indicated anywhere in the room.

Baker started with the man he knew best. He had grown up in nearby Shelton Township, Virginia, with Fred Jones. Jonesy was a plodder, a man of few words who checked things out very carefully before getting involved. Since their elementary school days Baker had always been the outspoken, active leader and Jonesy the quiet, steady henchman who did his leg work and faithfully stuck by him. Everything about the smaller man signified concentration and determination. Baker knew that as long as he, Baker, kept his word there would be no problems.

Baker had met Speedy Cotton during their freshman year at Sutton. Speedy was a coal-black, West Virginia miner's son who had been a second-string high school All-American at halfback. They had spent quite a few nights together going over football plays in Baker's room when they started playing football together and had become even faster friends when they pledged for the fraternity. College was not really of primary interest to Cotton. He wanted to play football and perhaps go on to play professionally. Baker supposed that his political involvement was based solely on their friendship, but the wiry six-foot-two speedster wasn't afraid of anything and Baker knew that he wouldn't back down.

The MJUMBE spokesman shifted his attention to Ben King. When it came to courage there were few legends that he could recall that did Ben justice. During their junior year at halftime in the last game Ben had come limping off the field. Pain had been chiseled into the deep creases around the young giant's mouth and eyes. Baker had watched King conscientiously avoid Coach Mallory and the trainer as he grimaced in the corner of the locker room during the intermission speech. Twice he asked King if someone shouldn't be notified, but was put off with a frown. Only after the game did the huge tackle permit himself to collapse from the pain. X rays taken that night showed that King's right ankle had been fractured, but somehow he had played on, had virtually held up the left side of the Sutton line, and insured the hard-fought victory.

The question in Baker's mind was whether or not Ben could or would keep his mouth shut. The big tackle had a notoriously bad temper and had been expelled from the track team for tearing up the training room during a fit of rage. It had been all Baker could do to avoid a fight between King and Thomas when Thomas, speaking the day before the election, said that 'certain bullies would not be able to threaten anyone into voting against their wishes.'

Baker knew that there was also a great deal of hatred and animosity between King and the university president. Calhoun had been the one to put King on the carpet after the training-room explosion. Baker nodded thoughtfully, thinking that he would have to watch King as closely as he watched Thomas.

In the dim light of the meeting room a flare ignited in the darkest corner where Abul Menka lit still another cigarette and attracted Baker's attention. If ever there was a man who puzzled the MJUMBE leader, Abul was that man.

When Baker arrived at the first pledgee meeting of Omega Psi Phi during the spring of his freshman year, the only man present he did not know was introduced by the Dean of Pledgees as Jonathan Wise. Baker had seen Jonathan Wise (who later began calling himself Abul Menka) driving around campus in a new Thunderbird with women hanging all over him, and he could not have imagined the man as fraternity material because the style-conscious New Yorker from the Bronx already had everything. And the perplexing thing was that during the two-month pledge period Abul had done nothing to indicate why he was there. Even during 'Hell Week,' the last week of the indoctrination schedule, when their line, 'The Jive Five Plus One' was not allowed to sleep, Abul never complained, never reacted even in private to the paddlings they were receiving or confided in the others during their restless nights in the 'Dog House' when they waited nervously for Big Brothers to come in and deal with them.

Baker had asked Abul to join MJUMBE as a matter of course because of their common interest in the fraternity, but he had been a little surprised when he accepted. Baker had seen him frequently in the frat lounge with a Black history book or reading material relating to the Black struggle, but the man had never expressed an inkling of political consciousness in the way he spoke. But there was little question of Abul's dedication to the organization. He was on time for every meeting and faithfully carried out every duty assigned to him.

'He ain' got a nerve in his body,' Baker decided. 'He'll go with us all the way.'

The roundup had given Baker a little more confidence in his co-workers, but his personal confidence was slipping. The thought of working with Earl Thomas did not appeal to him. Even if everything looked good. He compared himself to Thomas critically. Earl was six-two, perhaps one hundred and eighty pounds. He had a broad chest and wide shouders like a boxer. Next to him Baker looked like a powerful Black barrel. Football had developed Baker's arms, neck, and chest until he resembled a tree trunk. Baker's eyes were deep set and his nose was African flat. Earl was a bushy-browed Indian-looking man with a wide mouth and two inches of kinky hair. The MJUMBE leader rubbed his bald head thoughtfully. When football ended he would grow it again.

Sitting in the half-light of the MJUMBE meeting room, the massive strategist was slowly turning new facts over in his mind. He had been so let down by Calhoun's disappearance that some aspects of MJUMBE's move had slipped by unseen. Now, with time to think, new evidence was focusing on his mental screen.

First of all, Earl Thomas was going to be his pawn. He felt very good about the position the SGA president was in. It didn't matter if the students saw Earl puttering around in connection with MJUMBE demands. They knew who the real leader was. But second and best, Calhoun didn't know who was in charge. He would identify Earl as the leader of the detested militant faction on campus because Earl would present the demands. Earl couldn't do anything to stop MJUMBE. The students would construe any negative move as jealousy. The deposed SGA leader would be a *Mjumbe* for MJUMBE. Pleasure at his own play on words almost capsized the chair in which Baker sat, back-tilted.

Gone was the animosity he had felt the previous April when

told that some skinny, ostrich-looking nigger from Georgia had defeated him for the SGA post. Gone was the bitter gall he tasted when told forty minutes before: 'Mr and Mrs Calhoun returned from Norfolk, but they are attending the theater this evening. They are expected to return about ten o'clock.' The small, wigged maid who delivered those lines had stood in the Calhoun door-way like a reject from a Steppin' Fetchit movie wiping her greasy hands on a napkin and trying to sound like a fancy British bitch.

Baker laughed out loud. He could imagine Thomas sitting helplessly in front of him like a jackass with an Afro.

'Did'joo, did'joo hear that bitch?' Baker asked when he realized everyone was watching him. 'Did'joo hear that funky-ass maid callin' the Sutton moviehouse wit' wall-to-wall rats a thee-ate-uh?' He told them that because he knew what Jonesy would say if he told them why he was really laughing.

Evidently everyone had heard because a faint smile choked through their clamped mouths. They smiled because they needed to. No one really thought that it was very funny. The crooked grins bounced off the dimly pulsating light bulb and skipped nervously out through the window. The room then returned to its tomblike silence.

Baker felt grimy. Sweat had stuck his underwear to his crotch.

Jonesy was visibly worried.

Speedy Cotton and Ben King were tired and nervous. They sat directly beneath the bald, waxy wattage that illuminated itself and little else. They tried to convince themselves that the tightness in their groins came from too much beer, too much football, and too little sleep. Their eyes wandered about the room but they saw very little.

Abul Menka remained cool. It was impossible to conclude exactly what was on the man's mind. Baker called him 'Captain Cool.' He sat in the corner, feet propped, smoking a cigarette. In truth, Abul Menka was very seriously thinking about cutting out. He would have been gone had he not known that his motives would be misinterpreted. The MJUMBE men would have thought he was leaving because he was afraid of Calhoun.

'Fuck Calhoun,' he thought sullenly. Abul did not care if Sutton's Head Nigger had *eight* strokes and *ten* heart attacks, outdoing all of the other university presidents who were cracking up as a result of student demands. No, Calhoun was no problem. But Abul Menka was not anxious to see Earl Thomas.

3
Earl

There were only three tenants at Mrs Gilliam's boarding house on Pine Street. The three men lived on the second floor of the white three-story structure. It was not for lack of applicants that the third floor was empty, but because Mrs Gilliam was very particular about her roomers.

Earl had always considered himself highly fortunate when he thought about how quickly Mrs Gilliam had taken him in. At the end of the previous school year he had decided not to leave Sutton, but to take a job as a mechanic at the nearby computer factory. All at once the dormitories were closing for the summer and he was without a place to stay. It was then that he remembered Zeke, the Black handyman, who had often mentioned his room at Mrs Gilliam's, where he also took his meals. With three days remaining before school closed Earl had gone to see her. The two of them had hit it off immediately.

Mrs Gilliam was sixty years old. A short, gray-haired, thickly built matron of a woman who had lived in Sutton for thirty years. Her husband had been a conductor on the ICC railroad, making runs from Miami to Chicago on the Seminole, when she met him. She was a waitress at a coffee shop in Kankakee, Illinois, and after having seen the big, raw-boned Black man twice a week over a six-month period, they married. The railroad rerouted Charles Gilliam soon after, and his route carried him through Sutton and other parts of southern Appomattox County in Virginia. He bought an impressive three-story frame home on Pine Street and started his family. He had been working for the line nearly twenty-six years when he died of a heart attack.

His wife, Dora, thrived on company. She was a cornerstone

at Mt. Moriah A.M.E. Church and the head of her sewing circle. Soon after her husband's death she began to take in tenants, mostly for the companionship it provided.

Earl had made Mrs Gilliam break one of her cardinal rules. She had vowed never to rent rooms to college students. For the most part she considered them to be impolite, disrespectful young men with no idea of the meaning of the word responsibility. Earl was somewhat different. In the first place he was working his way through school and intended to add his summer's earnings to a partial scholarship. Secondly, he was as polite and mannerly a young man as Mrs Gilliam had ever met. And he had looked so let down when she told him, quite gruffly, that she didn't rent to college students, that she had had no choice but to invite him in for a cup of coffee to better explain her position. Somehow over coffee the word 'college' came to mean more to her than it had meant before. It took on the meaning of her dead husband's unfulfilled dreams. She found it very easy to overlook the fact that Earl was a student. She even rationalized her decision by pointing out the fact that he wouldn't be a student during the summer, but when September rolled around there was no mention of Earl moving out.

As Earl combed his head of thick hair his mind ran through the maze of emotions that gripped him, identifying first one and then the other. Jealousy? Fear? Anger? Anger was the most predominant. He felt as though he had been betrayed. Not betrayed by friends, but by that insidious 'Brother' term. MJUMBE subjugated the entire campus into one giant malignancy and classified all constituents under the heading of 'Brother.' The word seemed to have less meaning every day. Long ago he had decided that he would not be a part of the group that criticized the hypocrisy without an alternative. Who was sure how it felt to be Black? Maybe running your tongue over the word 'Brother' a thousand times a day was a step in the right direction.

Earl felt the muscles at the hinges of his mouth tightening

to form knots of energy. He looked like a cracker ballplayer on the Baseball Game of the Week with a quarter package of Bull O' the Woods chewing tobacco poking his mouth out a foot and nowhere to spit.

He knew he must not allow himself the luxury of rage. He knew he could never accomplish anything that way; barging into the MJUMBE meeting room and screaming, 'Just what the fuck is everybody tryin' to pull?' He decided to play it New York-style. Be cool. They had him by the balls. Everybody knew that. But if he acted as though he didn't know it or didn't care he might be able to jive them into a mistake. Then what? He didn't even know if he wanted them to make a mistake. He couldn't decide which side of the fence he was on.

He thought about the election that had taken place the previous spring. When March rolled around and the first signs about nomination procedures were pinned on dormitory bulletin boards he had thought little of it. He had never run for a school office and often thought that the only reason he had been a high school basketball captain was because he was the only returning letterman his senior year. But one afternoon after a heated argument between him and his Political Science teacher he had been halted in the hall by a classmate he knew only by sight.

'Excuse me, brother,' the other had said. 'My name is Roy Dean, but people here call me Lawman. I was wondering if I could talk to you for a minute.'

'Sure,' Earl had replied, caught off guard. 'I'm Earl Thomas.'

'I know,' Lawman said as they started walking. 'I couldn't help but know you after all the hell you raise in Poli Sci.'

'The man bugs me.'

'Me, too . . . where were you goin'? You got a class? . . . how 'bout a cup of coffee in the SUB on me?'

'All right,' Earl said a bit hesitantly.

'Poli Sci is my major,' Lawman said, going on. 'Everybody calls me Lawman because I'm thinking seriously of going into law . . . we used to have a thing called 'The Courtroom' when we were freshmen. If somebody on our wing of the dorm did something questionable, like trying to steal another cat's woman or something like that, we would have a mock trial. I was a laywer for the defense.'

'You win a lot of cases?'

'It was just a joke, but I pulled a lot of fast ones on the jury. Most of law is just semantics anyway. You can say a thing one way and make it sound entirely different from the way it appears if you rearrange a few words.'

'I guess so,' Earl agreed.

'But what I wanted to talk to you about was your political thing,' Lawman continued.

'My political thing?' Earl laughed. 'I don't really guess I have one. Just trying to be Black, I guess.'

The two of them walked on toward the Student Union Building, leaving Washington Hall where liberal arts classes were taught, Carver Hall, the science building, Adler Annex, and the mini-square referred to by students as the 'quadrangle,' where students sat and studied and talked on the benches.

'Sutton is fucked up,' Lawman began as they entered the crowded Student Union Building. 'A lotta in quotes Black schools are fucked up, but they seem to be gettin' something done about their problems. If Sutton is doing anythin' it's digressin', you know what I mean?'

Earl nodded.

'This school was founded in eighteen eighty-three and for all intents and purposes it's still eighteen eighty-three here, because there hasn't been much progress.'

'What about the things the Student Government president, Peabody, planned to do?' Earl asked as they left the service area with their coffee.

'Peabody ain' nuthin' but a lot of mouth,' Lawman snorted. 'What I mean is that the man is disorganized. He's spent the whole year havin' Calhoun twist his mind around like a rubber band . . . he goes to Calhoun and sez: "The students want this and that." Calhoun laughs and sez: "So what?" You dig?'

Earl nodded for Lawman to continue.

'So next month *ther's* gonna be another Student Government election and something needs to be done . . .'

'What are *you* planning to do?' Earl cut in.

Lawman laughed uneasily. He wasn't sure how to handle Earl, how to handle the question he was fed.

'I personally can't do very much. I can't dedicate the kind of time you need to give to the Student Government job to run for office 'cause I have an outside job that pays for my schooling. The point of this conversation is to find whether or not you'd like to run.'

'What?'

'You care, don'choo?'

'Yeah. I do, but . . .'

'But what?'

'But I'm a transfer student. This is just my second semester here. I don't think I know enough about the place to . . .'

'You mean,' Lawman cut in, 'that until I mentioned it you hadn't had one thought about the kinda things that might be happ'ning if you had anything to do with it?'

'I suppose I had some thoughts . . .'

'What did you decide you would do?'

'It didn't matter since I wasn't the president,' Earl said.

'Give it some thought,' Lawman suggested. 'You've got a good political mind. Anybody who can hold his own with old man Mills has to have a good political mind.'

'What about the two guys I've seen listed as candidates already?'

'Worthless,' Lawman spat out. 'Hall is a "egghead" dude from Boston or somewhere. He spends about thirty hours a day in the library reading Emily Dickinson and shit like that. He's a brown-nosed jackass as far as I'm concerned. I go to the SGA meetings sometimes and see him rapping. He's a junior class senator. Calls himself filibusterin' when he gets up with a little Robert's rule book on parliamentary procedure and starts hangin' everything up with points of order . . . thass what democracy has done for niggers. They lay in that idealistic crap all day and smell like shit all night.'

'What about Baker, the football player? He's runnin'.'

'Yeah. So what? He's a maniac as far as I'm concerned, although he'll prob'bly win unless you or someone like you goes against him. I never heard a sound political thought come from his direction. Him and King go through political issues like they're runnin' an off-tackle play. Everything that they don't like is wrong. I can't . . .'

'I understand,' Earl said thoughtfully.

'Good!' Lawman said as he got up. 'You give it some thought, brother, and I'll be talkin' to you.'

That was the beginning. Earl and Lawman talked about it again the next day. Earl admitted that he had often thought about things that would be done differently if he were president. Somehow it had never gone any further than that. Together, the two men constructed a platform for Earl to run on. Odds, Earl's best friend, was drafted as a campaign manager. They were on their way.

The memory of all the things he had been through with Odds and Lawman brought still another question to the surface. Why hadn't either one of them called to say anything about the meeting with MJUMBE and the students?

Earl came out of his bedroom and locked the door behind him. He checked his pocket for the keys he needed. Door key and car keys were there. It was then that his light sweater and slacks almost collided with Zeke's khakis and T-shirt.

'You got troubles?' Zeke asked.

'No,' Earl lied. 'Why?'

'You in such a durn hurry yo' leavin' shavin' cream stuck behin' yo' ear,' Zeke pointed out.

Earl wiped at the spot and Zeke nodded.

'Dumplin's t'night?' Earl asked mischievously.

'Naw, but we'da had'um if I'da wanned 'um.'

'Yeah. You an' Miz G. runnin' a game on me an' Ol' Hunt.'

'Shit!' Zeke waved. 'Mosatime you ain' here an' Hunt could be eatin' cobras an' drinkin' elephant piss fo' all he know. May as well have chicken an' dumplin's since I lak 'um.'

'Naw,' Earl laughed. 'That ain' it. Tell me, man, whuss happ'nin' wit'yo' kitchen thing?'

Zeke played the game. He looked both ways down the narrow hall and then lowered his voice in a conspiratorial tone. 'I shouldn' be tellin',' he admitted, 'but since you an' me s'pose to be boys . . . I, uh, sneaks down to the galley wit' Miz G. every other day o' so an' we gits high on Barracuda wine. Then I starts talkin' 'bout hi' I been all over the worl' an' still ain' dug nothin that tastes as good t'me as her chicken an' dumplin's. Jus' lak that they out there on the table. Same as when you talk 'bout banana puddin'.'

'Without the Barracuda wine.'

'Wit'out that.'

Earl laughed aloud. Zeke maintained a straight face somehow, but the thought of Mrs Gilliam drinking anything stronger than iced tea was too much for him. Zeke was notorious for drinking anything that could be classified as liquid and Earl had often met the handyman at O'Jay's, a local bar, but Mrs Gilliam? A pillar of Mt Moriah? Sacrilege!

'We love dem grapes!' Zeke said as Earl scurried down the stairs.

'Right!'

Zeke was a good man as far as Earl was concerned. The older man had never had a family or a real home until Mrs Gilliam had started renting rooms. There was nothing that could be described as his real profession either. He mowed lawns or shoveled snow or worked on cars at Ike's garage and come the first of every month he always had his rent money and he rarely missed a night at O'Jay's. At forty-five he was a slightly built, balding man with a coffee complexion and a contagious sense of humor.

Mrs Gilliam was stirring the evening stew when Earl rushed

through the kitchen with a quick 'Good evening.' He was halfway to the back door when she stopped him.

'Where might you think you goin' this evenin' befo' you eat yo' dinner?' she asked indignantly.

'I got a meetin' to go to,' he said. 'It jus' came up.'

Mrs Gilliam looked at him fondly for a second. With purpose she clamped the lid down on the stew pot and wiped her hands on the red trim apron. She took Earl by the arm and led him to the kitchen table where she sat him down.

'Let me tell you something,' she began. 'I've been in Sutton a long time. A long time to realize certain things. When I got here Sutton University was sittin' right where it is today. My husban' went to Sutton fo' a year at night … why you runnin' yo'sef into a fit fo' them? They ain' never been organized. Why you think you got to do so much to organize 'um? Why you got to be there every blessed minnit? No, I take that back. You ain' over there half as much as my daughter was. Laurie was there all day an' wuzn' no studen' … how she got away wit'out havin' one a them men's babies is still beyon' me. Go on, chile, do what you think you got to do.'

Earl nodded constantly during her monologue as though he understood all of the things that she was trying to say. But as he reached the porch he was more sure than ever that he didn't understand her and he wanted to go back and tell her to talk, say everything that was on her mind.

'Earl,' she called, 'I don' wanna hear you ramblin' 'roun' in my kitchen at no thousan' o'clock like las' night. I know you gon' be wantin' some a this somethin' t'eat, but you can' have it so if you don' git it na you won' have it.'

'Yes ma'am, I hear you,' he said.

Zeke heard Earl leaving as he came down to the kitchen. Mrs Gilliam still sat resting her elbows on the kitchen table as though she was tired. It was always a strain for her to deal with her youngest tenant. He never seemed to think twice before agreeing to skip a meal to attend something on campus. She personally didn't understand why so many meetings demanded his presence.

'Earl ain' eatin' again,' Zeke surmised.

'That boy gonna run hisself to death,' the landlady commented getting up and walking back over to the stew pot.

Outside, Sutton was just feeling the first kisses of autumn. The wind was a baby chick wiggling inside an egg beneath its mother. Evening came gliding down early to chase the sun and bring in Father Night with a blanket of black air to cloak the dying leaves. Though not a moment had passed since Earl's hasty exit, both Zeke and Mrs Gilliam heard the footsteps on the back porch. Earl reentered the room allowing the screen door to slam behind him.

'Uh, it's not too cold now, but I think I'm gonna need my coat later,' he announced looking around. 'Uh, where is it?'

Zeke smiled and Mrs Gilliam put on her sternest face.

'Iss hangin' in the hall closet, but I oughta not let'choo have it 'cause it was layin' 'cross the kitchen table when I got up this mornin'. You mussa lef' it here when you sneaked in las' night tryin' t'git somethin' t'eat ... I'm tellin' you Zeke, ain' he somethin'?' They exchanged glances. Earl smiled.

Earl grabbed his jacket off the hook in the hall closet and went back outside. His car was parked and the motor hummed a throaty tune. The night held a tingle of expectation. When Earl thought about the things that lay ahead for him there was a feathery tickle in his stomach. The sidewalk yawned up at him. The lawn was speckled with leaves of a thousand shades, dead or dying. At the side of the house Earl spotted Old Man Hunt pawing the ground with a toothless yard rake. They exchanged waves.

Earl's car was a '64 Oldsmobile; a gift from his father two summers past. It had been just the sort of thing he had come to expect from his father. The car had been in an accident and the left side had been caved in near the driver's door. The owner had been asking three hundred dollars for it, but after a brief conversation with John Arthur Thomas he had been willing to let it go for half that price. The elder Thomas said nothing about the purchase to his son, but kept the car parked in a garage and presented it to his son as a going-away present after Earl's graduation from the two-year Community College.

'It ain' but a small thing,' John Arthur Thomas declared struggling for words. 'It ain' like what I really want you to have, but I knew you wuz gon' need a car to git around in.'

There was a stiff handshake and a rugged smile from the older man. Everything had been warm but awkward, sincere and yet limited. Earl had wanted to ask if his father had talked to his mother or seen her but had been afraid. The subject was a sore point; a constantly aching tooth that one became used to after awhile.

When he had been fifteen and his mother and father had been apart for almost a year, Earl had asked his father outright why the couple didn't live together any more.

'Yo' mama's a good woman,' John Thomas had said softly. 'She a independent woman by nature, but I convinced her when we wuz seein' each other that she could depend on me an' be a woman for a while. I knew that wuz what she wanned to be. But I wasn't a good provider for her. Everything wuz workin' out bad for me an' her. We wuz damn near at razor's edge when we found out you wuz comin' ... I guess that saved our marriage if you can call what we ended up havin' somethin' worth bein' saved. We said we wuzn't gon' bring you out without some people lookin' after you. So we tried to keep things together, but we stopped talkin' to one another an' really stopped havin' anything for one another exceptin' the fact that you were a link b'tween us.'

'I'm s'pose to be grown now?' the fifteen-year-old Earl had asked.

'Grown enough to understand, I reckon,' his father had replied.

'I really don't,' Earl had confessed.

'Whoa!' John Thomas said laughing a bit. 'Neither do yo' mama an' me. Folks don't never really understand themselves, but they always rely on havin' someone that they love under-stand. Thass what we wuz doin'.'

Earl pulled away from the curb thinking about his father. He would have to write the man a letter and admit that he had received some valuable information. Things were happening in his life that he didn't understand. Yet he was the only one who could be held responsible for them.

In the rear-view mirror Earl caught sight of a black Ford that seemed to be trailing him. He was brought back to the present, hoping that the car was the Ford supplied by the school to members of the Sutton newspaper staff who had to travel to get their stories. Just as he was about to pull over and allow the Ford to draw abreast of him, the trailing car pulled off down a side street.

But now Victor Johnson was on his mind again. Somewhere at that moment he knew Vic was working on a backbreaking story against him. The move by MJUMBE would probably be built up as a great blow against the Sutton establishment, which included the SGA. It didn't matter that Earl hated the establishment as much as any of the rest of them or even more since he knew exactly how it sucked in Black students and warped their minds. It only mattered that during the course of the election none of Earl's speeches had made reference to faculty members as 'racist bastards' and that he hadn't filled students' ears with militant denunciations of Calhoun or the administrators. To many narrow-minded students anyone who didn't carry out the flimsy, outraged rhetoric of a television revolutionary was a Tom. It was just circumstance blown up out of proportion to truth. Earl could already picture the front-page story in the student paper asserting that his inactivity had spurred MJUMBE's movement.

'Shit!' he swore loudly.

Earl's mind was busy trying to organize strategy. It was too late for any of the moves that came readily to mind. He was now *under* the eight ball. The only thing that he could do was wait.

'One more week,' he grumbled again without conviction. 'Johnson would have had the story of his life. There would be no way for any demands to be turned down!'

MJUMBE COUP D'ETAT! the headline would scream.

'Goddamn hick bastard Johnson,' Earl breathed. 'Goddamn hick bastards! I need a damn drink!'

4
Lawman and Odds

When Earl Thomas arrived on Sutton University's campus for the very first time he had in his pocket a letter that he had received over the summer from a junior named Kenny Smith. The letter was actually a mimeographed note from the Dean of Admissions office designating Kenny as a student orientation assistant who should be looked up when the newcomer arrived; he was the person who would help the incoming student find his way around campus.

Kenny Smith had been easy to locate. Earl found him sitting in the Admissions Office reading a copy of the special *Statesman* that welcomed freshmen and transfer students. The thing that immediately warmed Earl to his orientation assistant was the young man's dress. Kenny was wearing a pair of low-cut sneakers, no socks, cut-off blue jean shorts, and a Sutton sweat shirt. He was a world apart from the other orientators lining the walls dressed in slacks, shirts with collars; even a suit and tie or two could be seen.

'My whole wardrobe is odds and ends,' Kenny told Earl when the transfer student pointed out the contrast.

It had become understood between the two young men, who hit it off immediately, that Kenny could not be held to tradition and conformity of any description. Kenny did not seem to care in the least what any other students did, thought, wore, or acted like. He was his own man and described himself as the odd one even in his family circle. The nickname 'Odds' became quite natural between them.

At approximately the time that Earl was leaving Mrs Gilliam's boarding house for his meeting with MJUMBE, Odds was just learning of the day's political activities. Earl's campaign manager had been in bed all day with a cold and had managed to sleep through the afternoon MJUMBE announcements in his room. Only a trip to the bathroom and an open dormitory door gave him any inkling of the ingredients that were bubbling in the political cauldron.

'Wonder why Thomas let Baker take over?' someone was asking as Odds passed the open door.

'Aw, bruh, c'mon,' was the reply. 'Thomas ain' lettin' Baker do nothin'. Thomas ain' never been nowhere. Baker just dug that we was gittin' ready to have another bullshit year an' did his thing. The bullshit intellectuals voted for Egghead Hall, the brothers voted for Baker, and the bitches put Thomas in office from the col' ass jump.'

Odds tried to place the voices and couldn't. He wanted to hear more about the 'takeover' they were discussing and he didn't particularly like being referred to as a bitch. He had voted for Earl.

'Ya gotta be tough to deal wit' Calhoun, man. You know what happened to Peabody las' year,' the voice went on. 'He bullshitted an' Tommed jus' like Thomas an' in the end didn' nuthin' git done.'

'As usual,' someone added.

'An' Baker's gonna mess with Calhoun?' Odds asked entering the room.

'Whuss happ'nin'? ... Fuckin' right!' The speaker went on. He was a tall, bearded boy wearing sunglasses. 'Baker'll git over.'

'Kin I git a match?' Odds asked.

'Yo, bruh. I got one,' a second student with sunglasses offered.

'Did'joo see the thing today when MJUMBE got it together? They came out on that platform bad wit' capital letters!'

'I didn' dig it, man,' Odds admitted. 'What happened?'

'Man,' came the enthusiastic reply. 'You missed a helluva thing. Lemme tell you. All day long they was announcin' this meetin' for fo' o'clock in fronta the SUB, right? Nobody knows who's callin' it or what it's about. So at four bells damn near the whole school is millin' 'roun' in front a the platform steps leadin' t'the SUB, but the only thing there is a mike. No people. Up through the crowd comes Baker and King an' them. They all dressed in black dashikis with gold trim. All five of 'um got bald heads except my man from New York, whuss his name? Abul. Abul Menka. You know that dude wit' the big 'fro an' the T-bird? ... well, they read out this list a deman's, grievances that they got t'gether for the Head Nigger an' they say they gonna lay the shit on 'im t'night. That mean this muthafuckuh gonna be jumpin' in the mornin,' Jim.'

'Or not,' Odds said. 'What did Earl Thomas have to say?'

'Nuthin', man. I didn' even see him. What could he say? Iss all true. Most a the shit is stuff he been sayin' he wuz gittin' t'gether, but he ain' done nuthin'.'

Odds already knew where Earl had been. Chances were that Baker had known too. Earl seldom came on campus on Wednesday since he didn't have a class. For a second Odds was tempted to point this out to the students in the room, but he decided that there would be little reason. He wanted to tell them that Earl *had* been trying to get things together too, but his association with Earl would have made everything sound like a mere cop out.

'Later,' he said, sliding back out into the hall. Echoes of the discussion followed Odds back into his room, but his mind was far away. What should he do? Call Earl? No. Earl probably wouldn't be at home by now. What time was it? Just past seven his watch told him. The best thing would be to try and find Earl and get something started. Started? Ended? Stopped?

It was at that moment that Odds thought of Lawman. Lawman was a good friend. He was surprised, as he thought about it, that Lawman had not called him. If ever there was a guy who could sort out a political mess it was the ever-serious pre-law major.

Odds grabbed a dime from the top of his desk and padded back out into the darkened hall. Quickly he uncradled the receiver and dropped a dime into the pay phone. He turned the dial seven times and waited. The phone rang twice.

'Hullo?'

'Hello. Lawman?'

'Yeah.'

'Look, brother. This is Odds. We got problems. Have you heard?'

''Bout what?'

'As near as I can tell Baker an' his knuckleheads took over Earl's program this afternoon an' s'pose to be goin' to Calhoun's t'night.'

'Goddamn!' Lawman breathed. '*When* did this happen?'

'This afternoon. Were you on campus?'

'I had a one o'clock class. I went to it an' then I split.'

'You didn' hear?'

'Nuthin, man. I met this bitch over here at two. She was talkin' 'bout calculus, but you know better than that.'

'Yeah. I know 'bout what got calculated ...'

'Where were you?'

'In bed. Man, I had me a ass-kickin' chest cold all week.'

'You sound like it. Where's Earl?'

'You got me. Out makin' like a hero I guess.'

'Tryin' to carry it by himself too. He didn't call me.' Lawman was thoughtful. 'Whew! Man, this is too much. I can hardly get this shit together.'

'I know.'

'Where you at?' Lawman asked.

'In the dorm.'

'Let's get together an' talk this over. I was jus' sittin' down to eat when you buzzed. You want to come over here and have a bite to eat?'

'No grit, man. I figger with a half-gallon of Esso Extra or something I might be able to deal ... why don' you meet me at O'Jay's 'bout eight o'clock?'

'All right,' Lawman agreed. They hung up.

Odds scuffled back down the hall to his room and prepared to wash up and brush his teeth. He was no longer concerned with the nagging cough and chest cold that had kept him in bed.

The Lawman turned back to a small pot of soup and the slices of ham that rimmed his plate. His small one-room apartment was a mess. Records were scattered all over the floor near his record player. The books he had been attempting to deal with when the young woman arrived earlier in the afternoon were still open and loose-leaf notes from his notebook had blown onto the floor. His small army cot in the corner was a disarranged mess with the stained sheets from three hours of love-making tangled up at the foot of the bed. He stepped over to the sink next to the hot plate and rinsed his mouth out and splashed his face with a double handful of cold water.

'Rraugh!' he snorted as the water shocked his circled, reddened eyes. He felt around the wall for the wrinkled towel and rubbed his face roughly when he ripped it from the rack.

'Fuck!' he cursed out loud. Then he sat down to eat.

5
Confrontation

Earl's green Oldsmobile wheeled through the open gates at the mouth of the university. The arch stretching between two twenty-foot-high stone pillars announced: SUTTON UNIVERSITY. A small wooden plaque nailed into one of the columns noted that the arch had been donated by the class of 1939.

Fifty feet from the gate was a huge oval flower bed, containing now, in autumn, only dead reminders of the blazing color that had decorated the front of Sutton's administration building from early spring until late summer. An arrow in front of the flower bed pointed all traffic to the right, around the famous circle that emptied into a large parking lot.

Earl drove slowly past the Ad Building, Washington Hall, the remodeled Student Union Building, Adler Annex, Paul Lawrence Dunbar Library, and Simmons Hall which housed almost six hundred men. To his left, the old science building, Carver Hall, Garvey Plaza for freshmen women, Mallory Hall for upperclass women, and the three-story fraternity house which had once been for home economics (before Adler Annex) completed the other half of the oval.

Earl parked in the ample lot, took a look at himself in the rear-view mirror, lit a cigarette, and got out. The newborn wind whistled at him. Smoke came from the chimney atop the small wooden hut that housed the security guard in the corner of the area. He saw through the naked branches of trees a pale-eyed, unblinking moon that hovered low in the sky like an oval of cold, shadowy clay.

Jonesy was standing on the steps of the frat building. The stocky MJUMBE chieftain, who played linebacker on the football team, was dressed in a black, short-sleeved dashiki and dark trousers.

'Niggers always rather be hip than warm,' Earl thought as he contemplated how strongly the wind was whipping against the short-sleeved African shirt.

Jonesy looked as though he wanted to say something, but noting the cold indifference on Earl's face he merely nodded. He led the way into the building.

The first floor was in total darkness. Earl could hear couples positioning themselves in the dark. It was against school regulations for women to be in the frat houses unless there was a chaperoned dance or some other university-sanctioned function going on. The frat men gave little attention to what school regulations stipulated. They unscrewed the first floor lightbulbs and did as they damn well pleased.

'Upstairs,' Jonesy mumbled.

The two men took the stairs quickly and entered the thirdfloor meeting room where Baker, King, and Cotton sat around a square card table. Abul Menka sat in the corner staring intently out of the window. Earl took the chair directly opposite Baker. Jonesy stood by the door and folded his arms, looking over his shoulder out into the hall from time to time.

'Happ'nin', Earl?' Baker asked.

'Nothin' much,' Earl replied lightly. He hated bullshit like this, but he had expected a great deal of it. 'I could use a run-down on the score.'

'Yeah,' Baker said as though bored. 'We got a lista shit t'gether fo' the Head Nigger.' He grinned and continued to look through a pile of papers in front of him. 'We figgered maybe you could take 'um over there if you wanned to.'

Here we go, Earl thought as he took the list from Baker. If I wanted to.

There was a tight feeling in the pit of the SGA president's stomach. He could feel his pulse vibrating and drumming an uptempo solo next door to his brain. He lit a cigarette and left the pack on the table. He could feel the pairs of eyes drilling holes into his forehead. Though he noticed that Abul Menka had not looked up when he entered, he felt that even the notorious Captain Cool was tense, watching and waiting.

'Yeah,' was all that Earl said when he had completed his reading of the list.

Ben King snorted like a bull. Earl cast a glance in the black giant's direction and the returned stare blazed dislike. He met the look head-on. He was by no means intimidated by the huge football hero, though he had no eagerness to test the myths that had been built up pertaining to the larger man's strength and ferocity.

'So, uh, this is the score,' Baker stammered uneasily. 'We decided that perhaps, uh, things might be working out a little slowly for your office. We know how hard it is to get organized since we're always tryin' to organize things in the frat ... we thought maybe you could, uh, use a little help to get the ball rollin' an' get people behind you.' Baker was choosing his words very carefully. 'Uh, it was shapin' up like another one a them years like las' year.' The tension in the room could be felt as Baker dragged on. Earl did nothing to ease the pressure. He did not move or frown.

'So we got things off the ground!' King said suddenly.

Earl chose to ignore King and did not even look to his left in the challenger's direction. He wondered how much more he would be told about the things that were lying beneath the surface. He didn't buy what Baker was saying for a second and the lie was infuriating him more than the overall maneuver. Everything was too hazy, but Baker was waiting for Earl to start the name-calling. Earl would have to force any direct split that became visible between the two groups. Baker could then go back and report that he had tried to work with the SGA leader without success. Ice. Ice. Ice.

'Everybody knows the problems around here,' the MJUMBE spokesman said slowly.

Earl almost laughed. He could see that he was rattling Baker instead of the other way around. Baker had wanted to see him squirming, nervous, and uneasy in the unfamiliar position of follower. Earl's deadpan composure was reversing the pressure and anxiety was crawling deeper and deeper into Baker's eyes.

'We got the same pains in the ass that they had here forty years ago if you read back issues of *The Statesman*. But whenever it comes time for a direct confrontation the students shy away. They so concerned wit' a fuckin' piece a bullshit paper that they refuse to pull their heads outta the fuckin' groun'. Who cares if they spent four years in hell and lived like pigs in a sty? Thass why I sed: "if you wanted to get involved." I don't know how concerned you are about graduatin' on time.' Baker leaned back.

'You may git in trubble,' Ben King baby-talked. 'We wudn't wan' anything like that.'

'Look aroun',' Baker injected. 'We all seniors. Fo' uv us are on football grants that they could snatch in a minnit, but ain' no *man* s'pose to sit fo' alla this shit! We cain' live with a pipe up our assholes, can we?'

He was talking to keep Ben King quiet. Ben was spoiling for an argument with Thomas. He had been told to lay cool. They had everything on their side. Earl had nothing. But the SGA leader's apparent calm was unnerving.

'What do you expec' Calhoun t'say 'bout these?' Earl said, fingering the demands.

'He has 'til tomorrow noon. We don' expec' him t'say anything in particular t'night. When you take him a copy a the things, you need not even ask what he thinks. We'll wait 'til tomorrow when the new copy a *The Statesman* hits. We boun' t'git some readin' out befo' he does. Then we'll be in good shape wit' trustees, faculty, all the resta the bullshit artists ... what we want 'um to see is some laid-out thought 'bout whuss happ'nin'.'

'That's short notice,' Earl commented. Baker's last lines about *The Statesman* had let him know that Victor Johnson was lined up with MJUMBE.

'Shit! We too damn late!' Speedy Cotton snorted.

There was a pause and the only sound that could be heard was the tap-tap-tapping of Jonesy's foot on the hollow floor.

Earl was glad that shadows cloaked most of the room. He knew that a smile was creeping into his face. If he stayed there much longer he was a cinch to blow everything.

'Waddaya think?' Baker asked suddenly.

Earl almost laughed. If anyone had ever told him that Ralph Baker would ever ask his opinion on anything he would have called them absolutely insane.

'I couldn't say,' Earl breathed. 'Like I sed: thass pretty short notice.'

The room stirred. Something was going on in the doorway behind Earl. He didn't bother to turn around.

'What, man?' Baker asked someone.

'Dude name Johnson downstairs t'see you.'

Baker watched Earl. No reaction.

'Tell 'im ta wait. I be there.' Baker snorted.

'What time is Calhoun comin' home?' Earl asked.

''Bout ten,' Cotton said. 'From the thee-ate-uh.'

'Ol' bag bitch!' King cursed, recalling the maid.

'Does he know about these?'

'I doubt it,' King said. 'The firs' thing you do when people start plottin' on you' shit ain' goin' to the movie.'

Earl got up. 'I'll be goin' over there 'bout ten.' He turned toward the door. He could feel that heat rising to his head. Somehow he could feel that Abul Menka was looking at him for the first time since he entered the room. He turned and caught the stare head on. Yeah, he thought. I got alla these muthafuckuhs shook . . . thass good. But it's not time fo' you yet, Captain Cool. Or you, unfriendly Giant, as he thought of King. Time *will* come though.

'You can wait here!' King exclaimed on the verge of rage. Earl confidently estimated that he had upset King more than any of the others.

'No. I missed dinna, man. I'm goin' to O'Jay's for a bite befo' I go to the Plantation.'

'Yeah,' Baker mumbled.

'Later,' Earl said, leaving.

When Baker next looked up Earl had gone and the only reminder of his presence was the echo of Ben King hammering the already battered card table time and time again.

6
The Plan

'Jonesy? Do me a favor and go down ta git Johnson.'

'He in the lobby?'

'Somewhere down there.'

Jonesy exited. The four remaining young men in black dashikis sat in silence. Baker ran his hand over his hairless head. Speedy Cotton, the lithe, coal-complexioned halfback, yawned broadly. Ben King sat frozen in his chair. Abul Menka looked out of the window.

Jonesy came back in, followed closely by a short young man of medium build who wore thick glasses and a blue business suit. He carried a pad and a pen under his arm.

'Hi, brothers,' he said emitting a smile that looked like a cracking mirror. He was extremely nervous and uncomfortable with the five MJUMBE chieftains and they were all aware of it.

The three seated members vaguely acknowledged his presence. Abul Menka remained silent. Johnson didn't notice. He fidgeted with the pad, looking through it for notes that obviously did not exist. He wished he hadn't allowed Baker to talk him into this situation. He had wanted the details for his story over the phone, but he had been bribed. Baker had promised him an inside seat and the real detailed story Victor wanted in return for two promises. One, that Earl Thomas not be interviewed until after Calhoun had been served with the papers. That demand had not bothered Johnson. He didn't like Earl and had never received any real cooperation from his office. But the second point was a sore spot with him. Baker was asking to see the story before it was printed. That went against a lot of things. It went against professional ethics, objective standards, and everything else. Baker sounded intent on having his way however. So what could Victor Johnson really do? Nothing. He sat there, knees rattling.

'Did'ja bring them numbers I ast for?' Baker questioned, breaking the silence.

'I, uh, already knew those numbers,' Johnson smiled weakly. Naturally he wanted to be cool.

Ben King was already on edge. He was tempted to reach across the table and slap the sniveling muthafuckuh! Those goddamn glasses and that bitch's voice. Shit!

'I'll take 'um down. What are they?' Cotton asked.

Johnson handed Cotton the pad and pen.

'Uh, *Portsmouth Bulletin* – TU 6–3090. Uh, *Roanoke Tribune* – UL 9–6200. What were the others? I forget?'

'The *Norfolk News* and AP and UPI county offices.' Baker snapped.

'Yeah. Uh, *Norfolk News* – LO 2–0000. AP and UPI news services can, uh, be called through the *Norfolk News*. Extension six-nine-nine for AP. Extension eight-two-two-three for UPI. Uh, I donno what county this would be for.'

'You got 'um?' Baker asked Cotton.

'Uh-huh.'

Baker hoisted himself upright. He never talked to the group sitting down. He needed his hands and arms to gesture.

'Everybody know what to do?' he asked.

No one commented.

'All right then. One more time: Speedy, you an' me go wit' Johnson. While we gittin' the paper t'gether you gonna be callin' them people tellin' Calhoun been served wit' deman's on Sutton University's campus. Tell 'um tomorrow we expectin' a answer. At that time we gonna respon' to his responses.'

'Right on.'

'Ben? You ready?'

'You know that,' King said.

'What you gon' do?'

'When Calhoun come out tuhmaruh, if he don' say we gittin'

what we want, me an' the guys gon' start closin' shit down fa' the boycott.'

Johnson's eyes popped. 'Boycott?'

Baker laughed. For a minute the tension was knifed, stabbed, and floating melodramatically to the floor. Everyone except Abul smiled at the grotesque look of horror that masked the editor's face and the awkward, choked question that had slid from between his tightly closed teeth.

'Yeah,' King growled. He was especially dramatic for the benefit of their visitor. 'Tuhmaruh if shit don' go right we callin' off classes an' we stop eatin' inna cafeteria an' alla resta that shit. People who don' dig it can come see me. I'm gon' be the complaint department.'

'Jonesy? You ready?' Baker asked.

'Yeah. I got it done . . . the statements you want released to the press and whatnot been typed up by some sistuhs in the dorm. I kin git 'um anytime I need 'um.'

Baker smiled. He felt better. 'We'll want 'um t'night, okay?'

Everybody laughed.

'Abul?'

Abul Menka swiveled away from the window with exaggerated slowness. The eternal question was in his eyes. Baker laughed again.

'Captain? Captain, why you *so* damn cool?' Baker almost choked on the words. 'Johnson, why is this man so mutha-fuckin' cool? Goddamn! This is the iceman an' what have you.' He turned to King. 'Benny? Why?'

'I donno, brother.'

'I swear. Captain Zero! Ha! Tell me, captain, hahahahaha, iz you or iz you not ready?'

'I iz, suh,' Menka drawled *slowly*. 'Tuh-ma-ruh afternoon iz in my con-trol. When I heard you needed a bit a my help I immediately stole the white boys' quickes' steed an' hopped nimber-ly into the saddle. I iz gonna pass out copies a yo' statements to the faculty hopin' alla while ta pull a few insomnia cure-ahs ovuh to our way a thinkin'.'

Johnson's mouth fell completely open.

'You the cooles',' Baker said.

'Ultra cool,' Jonesy chimed. Baker almost collapsed. Whoever heard of Fred Jones saying something without being asked?

'Uh, what 'bout my story?' Johnson asked, trying to capitalize on the upsurge of good spirits.

'Ha! Baker, did this cat ast you somethin' or am I gone completely outta my head?'

'Vic, my main man an' campus Waltuh Cronkite, I'm gonna give you a story to take the salt outta the shaker. After this muthafuckuh thay givin' me a gig writin' fo' the *Secret Storm*. Ha!'

Everyone was thinking the same way. 'To hell with Thomas! To hell with Head Nigger Calhoun! We gonna step out there with a program God hisself cain' do nuthing with. We bad! We Black! We MJUMBE!'

7

O'Jay's

Earl found Odds and Lawman engrossed in conversation when he joined them at a back booth in O'Jay's, the most popular off-campus hangout. He slid into the booth casually.

'Earl!' Lawman exclaimed. 'What in hell's happ'nin'?'

'A whole lotta bullshit,' Earl said disgustedly. 'Lemme get a beer an' I'll fill you in . . . where the hell yawl been?'

'Nowhere. That's the point,' Odds grumbled, picking up his glass.

A waitress came over with a pad and pencil.

'Black Label,' Earl said.

'I'll take one mo',' Lawman told her. She didn't bother to write the orders down.

'C'mon, man. Whuss up?'

'MJUMBE iz up. My gig iz up. The jig iz up.' Earl replied smiling wryly.

'Start at the beginnin',' Odds said impatiently.

'That iz the damn beginnin'!' Earl said raising his voice irritably. 'The beginnin', the middle, the . . . Look, uh,' he paused to light a cigarette, 'I jus' hit campus a l'il while ago, right? I don' know shit.'

The waitress arrived with two bottles of beer and one glass. Odds put a dollar on the tray. The waitress pulled thirty cents out of her apron pocket and laid it on the table.

'I got a call 'bout seven,' Earl continued. 'It wuz King from MJUMBE. He sed they wuz havin' some kind a meetin' an' they wanned me t'come over to the frat house.'

'Thass where you were? We jus' called an' Zeke sed you wuz gone.'

'Well, I wuz.'

'What happened?'

Earl was making patterns from the circles left on the rough-grained surface of the table by his beer glass.

'This,' he said sourly, 'is what happened.' He pulled a mimeographed sheet of paper from his pocket and placed it before Odds and Lawman.

We, the student body of Sutton University, request that:

(1) The Pride of Virginia Food Services, Inc., be dismissed.

(2) Gaines Harper, present Financial Aid Officer, be dismissed.

(3) The head of the Chemistry Dept. be dismissed.

(4) The head of the Language Dept. be dismissed.

(5) The men of the present Security Service be forced to leave all weapons (clubs, guns, etc.) inside the guardhouse while making their rounds.

(6) The supervision of the Student Union Building be placed under the auspices of the Student Government.

(7) The book store be placed under student control.

(8) The Music and Art Fund for Visiting Artists be placed under the auspices of the Student Government.

(9) A Faculty Review Committee be established consisting of students and the heads of the remaining departments (exceptions being Chemistry and Languages) to review the performances of the present faculty. This committee's findings would be honored by the university and all decisions forthcoming would depend on their decision.

(a) A Faculty Interview Committee be established in order to carry out whatever necessary changes be recommended by the members of the aforementioned Faculty Review Committee.

(10) A Black Studies Institute be formed at Sutton including courses in Racism, Black Literature, Black History, and Negro Politics. The head of this Institute would be hired by the committee mentioned in request 9a.

(11) The Comptroller, Financial Aid Officer, Treasurer, Music and Art Department Head (of funds), Maintenance Staff Coordinator, and Student Union Director be forced

to open their books to an auditor hired by the Student Government Association with Student Government funds.

(12) The present medical staff be reorganized and made larger in order to facilitate the Black people within the Sutton University Community.

(13) These demands be responded to no later than noon tomorrow.

Lawman whistled and turned the paper over after reading the demands through. Odds slapped himself.

'Noon tomorrow?' Odds asked aloud.

'In black and white.'

'Thirteen demands,' Lawman said to no one in particular.

'How many of these things had you done research on?' Odds asked Earl.

'All of them and more. These are practically my words. I had a few more things jotted down with notes, but the whole damn thing is like a muthafuckin' gypsy turned them on to my shit.'

'A gypsy?'

'Hi 'bout a gypped-up bitch?'

Odds's question smacked Earl in the face. 'I donno,' he coughed.

'D'you think whut I think?' Lawman asked, swallowing half a glass of beer.

'I donno what in hell you think,' Odds squirmed, 'but I think that lazy bitch in Earl's office turned Baker on to all the shit we had been tryin' ta get together. I think that!'

Odds's voice was carrying like unleashed thunder. All three of the men seated in the booth turned to see who was watching and perhaps listening to their conversation. There was no one in the black half of the bar with them except the waitress who appeared to care less what happened.

'Yes – it must have been Sheila,' Earl said softly.

'What'choo doin' when you leave here?' Odds asked nervously.

'I'm s'pose t'be goin' ta Calhoun's wit' these,' Earl said shaking the paper.

'I think it might be hip if you ... look, when wuz the las' time you wuz in yo' office?'

'Monday night,' Earl said.

'Did you check the papers we had written out?'

'No.'

'When wuz the las' time you took a look to see if everything wuz in order?'

'What?' Earl lit another cigarette irritably. 'Man, I don' check on no goddamn papers every day. I ain' got time fo' that kinda shit! I'm runnin' aroun' this deserted muthafuckuh like a chicken wit' no goddamn head already ... I saw the papers las' week. They wuz all there.'

'Las' week when?'

'Las' Thursday or so. Yeah, las' Thursday.'

'So, fah all you know Baker an' MJUMBE could a had yo' work since las' Thursday? Right?'

'For all *I* damn know, longer than that. They coulda been makin' copies a all the shit fo' a month.'

The friends fell silent. Questions were appearing from nowhere and going nowhere. If Baker and MJUMBE had gotten to Earl's notes inside the SGA office there was no telling how much of the information they had. Earl, Odds, and Lawman had been placing pieces of information in a filing cabinet in the SGA office since the beginning of September. There were five keys to that office that Earl knew of. Odds had one. Lawman had one. Earl had one. The maintenance staff had a fourth. The fifth key belonged to Sheila Reed, the SGA secretary. The demands listed by MJUMBE resembled so closely the things that the three men had been working on that they could not help but suspect that they had somehow been betrayed.

'What about MacArthur?' Odds asked.

'Naw, man. Not Mac. He couldn' let nobody in. That job iz all he got.'

'So if Mac didn' do it, it wuz Sheila.'

'We're jumpin' to conclusions,' Lawman said. 'We seem to be assuming that MJUMBE got inta our files.'

'Listen to Mr Law Major,' Odds said, pointing a crooked finger at Lawman. 'Whatta hell it look like ta you?'

'Fuck whut it looks like,' Lawman exclaimed. 'How do we know that they been in the files?'

'Go check?' Odds asked.

'What good would that do?' Earl asked. 'If they got in to take the stuff, they could git in to put it back.'

'Somehow we got to know whether or not they been in there,' Lawman realized. 'We gotta know whether or not they got all our info or what.'

Earl got up stiffly. 'I gotta make a call,' he said. 'I came in here ta eat, but I don' feel like I could take a bite without throwin' up all over this joint. Matter of fact,' he added, 'when I dug this list I almost upchucked then.'

'I bet'choo did,' Odds laughed.

'Get another round a beer,' Earl said dropping a dollar on the table. 'I'll be right back.'

O'Jay came by. He was a big man with a charcoal tan. His face was battered by the six years of professional fighting he had endured. O'Jay had been the fighter's fighter. In thirty-nine fights he had never been knocked out. He had lost sixteen, but all of them had been by decision. He was very proud of that. Though he had never been ranked or made anything that resembled a main event, he had been in demand because he came to fight. He was never one for much cute, tricky punching. It was all or nothing for him. When he had acquired enough money and enough beatings to feel that his call was elsewhere he gave up the ring and bought himself a tavern.

'Hi iz it, brothuhs?' he drawled as he made his way toward the oval bar in the front of the tavern. He was hassling with an apron string that was frayed at the end and difficult to make stretch around his rather imposing stomach.

'Better for us than you, Orange Juice,' Odds laughed. 'Na it ain' but so much you kin ask of a damn apron.'

'Iss gon' fit,' O'Jay chuckled.

'Look like a rhino inna bikini,' Odds retaliated.

The four men all howled. O'Jay, at length, tied the apron around himself.

'Gonna have a good weeken'?' Lawman asked.

'Wuz goin' fishin' tuhmaruh,' O'Jay said scratching his head, 'but the way I hear it, alla yawl may be livin' wit' me come the weeken'. I heard people tryin' ta git some things done 'roun' here.'

'Tryin' to.'

'That means who ever doin' the tryin' bes' be packed. Calhoun ain' noted fo' playin' that young man revolution shit. HAHA!'

'We'll see.'

'Yeah. Lemme run up here an' help out at the bah.'

'Right on!' Earl said as O'Jay made his way between the rows of tables.

'Hey!' Earl called, 'when you gonna git some new furniture. I'm back here gittin' splinters.'

'Where at? In ya elbows?'

The three students laughed again.

'Lemme make this call,' Earl said.

'Hello?'

'Shorty? This iz Earl.'

'Shorty? I like your nerve.' The tone became softer. 'How are you? I heard you've had some trouble.'

'No real trouble. Not yet.'

'You comin' to see me?'

'Thass what I called 'bout. I got a few things to do. I'm, uh, s'pose t'be the one who lays the deman's on Calhoun. I'm goin' over there in 'bout an hour or two. Hey! You still there?'

'Ummm. Uh-huh. I was asleep when you called.'

'Were you? I'm sorry.'

'No. I need to be up. The place iz a wreck. Bobby had Peanut over here playin' cowboys an' Indians . . .'

'What time iz it?'

'Must be close to nine.'

'Well, I'm goin' over to Calhoun's at ten,' Earl said. 'Can you have me somethin' t'eat when I git by there?'

'By where?'

'By yo' house, baby. Wake up now.'

''Bout ten thirty?'

'Uh-huh.'

'I imagine I can do that. But you cain' keep me up all night like you did las' night.'

'Okay.'

'You promise?'

'No.'

'Good . . . Earl, I love you.'

'You mus' still be sleep. Bye, baby.'

'Bye.'

The beers were arriving at the booth when Earl got back.

'S'cuse me, Miss Pretty Legs,' Earl said. 'Will you tell Ellen to come back here, please?'

'Ellen, the waitress?' Earl nodded.

'Sure,' the booth waitress replied, smiling.

The three men sat in silence sipping beer. Ellen, the waitress from the front of the bar, came back. She was a student at Sutton as were most of the young women who worked at O'Jay's. The owner seemed to realize where his interests were. His clients were students. His employees were students.

'Can I help anyone?' she asked the trio.

'I jus' wanned a better look at that smile,' Earl said. 'An' perhaps . . .'

'I knew you wuz lyin',' Ellen said, mocking irritation.

'. . . a bit of information.'

'About who?' Ellen said. She took a furtive look up front and then slid into the booth next to Odds.

'About SGA's secretary, Sheila Reed,' Earl said.

'You mean you cain' get it?'

'Well . . .'

'You better start winkin' at some a these wimmin,' Ellen smiled.

'Who is Sheila's boyfriend or man or whatever?' Earl asked. Lawman and Odds leaned forward. All at once they knew what Earl was getting at. Sheila would definitely give the key to the office to her boyfriend.

'Oh really?' Ellen asked. 'Lawd, Sheila's been goin' wit Che Guevara. You better get busy.'

'Che who?' Lawman asked.

'The Revolutionaries!' Ellen giggled. 'She been goin' wit' Ralph Baker from MJUMBE.'

The three men looked at each other. Truth is light.

8
The Head Nigger

Earl pulled up in front of Ogden Calhoun's huge white home at exactly ten o'clock. The house had been built for the president of Sutton College in 1937. Since then it had changed hands eight times, had been destroyed almost entirely by fire in 1940, was remodeled twice, but remained a landmark in the area. Two years before it had been remodeled for Mrs Calhoun, and now it stood like a sentinel of southern history, a replica of the label the students applied to it – the Plantation.

The lights burning on the first and second floors told Earl that the Calhoun household was not completely asleep. He had been here on other occasions as representative of the SGA for various meetings. He realized at a glance that the first-floor lights were shining in the living room and Calhoun's den and home office.

He was surprised when Mrs Calhoun met him at the door.

'Good evening, Mr Thomas,' the president's wife said, smiling politely. 'How are you?'

'I'm fine, ma'am. How have you been?'

'Just a bit run-down,' Gloria Calhoun said with a hand at her forehead. 'Won't you come in? I'm sure you're here to see Ogden. Is he expecting you?'

'No, ma'am,' Earl replied smiling. He commented to himself that he certainly hoped that Calhoun was not expecting him.

'I'll run back and see what he's doing,' Mrs Calhoun said. 'We haven't been here for the past couple of days and our maid was very busy. When I came home from the theater this evening I told her to go right to bed.'

Earl smiled lightly and Mrs Calhoun made her way across the spacious living room toward the den. There was no question in the young SGA leader's mind but that Gloria

Calhoun was indeed tired. As far as he could see she was always on the run; speaking on a Woman's Day program at somebody's church, helping to raise money for a drive of some description, or just appearing with her husband at a university function.

Earl admired her. Not only because she had been married to Ogden Calhoun for almost twenty years, which put her in line for sainthood, but because throughout all their brief encounters she had impressed him with her sincere interest in community problems and genuine concern about the issues confronting Sutton students.

She emerged from the den having given Earl just enough time to light a cigarette.

'My husband will see you now,' she said with a pleasant smile. It seemed to Earl that Gloria Calhoun was always smiling. He considered it quite a tribute to her that she could continue to do so after living with the grouchy, grumbling Calhoun for so long a time. 'By the way, how is Dora Gilliam? You do have a room with her, don't you?'

'Yes, ma'am,' Earl replied. 'She's fine.'

'I must have a chat with her soon. She's such a fine woman. I've been thinking about having her return a favor and speak at my church's Woman's Day next month.'

'I'm sure she'd enjoy that,' Earl said.

'Good ... well, do give her my regards. I've got to run along now.'

'Good night.'

'Good night.'

The president of Sutton University sat in a leather swivel chair behind his desk, smoking a pipe, with a pair of bifocals perched on his nose. Ogden Calhoun was fifty-seven but didn't look a day over forty-five. He was dressed in a silk bath robe with a pair of maroon silk pajamas peeping from beneath the robe. As Earl entered the room Calhoun put down the sheets of paper that he had been studying. He stood and shook hands with Earl rather stiffly and then sat back again. He ran a hand through his thick, silver head of hair.

'How are you, son?' he asked Earl.

'I'm fine. Yourself?'

'Good,' Calhoun boomed.

Earl looked around. The working den was well decorated. An oaken bookcase against the wall to his right was stacked with thick volumes on law, a multi-volume encyclopedia, textbooks, and pamphlets that proselytized for Sutton University. Behind Calhoun was a sliding door that led out onto a glass-encased patio where sat yet another desk, plus a round patio-table with an umbrella, a glider, and a couch with plastic cover. In the corner directly to Calhoun's left was a lamp that seemed to grow out of an expensive-looking jade vase. The illumination was detoured by a rose-patterned lampshade. The thick green carpet was wall-to-wall here in the office. There were several chairs in the room: a captain's chair, a reclining easy chair that resembled a leather throne, and another plastic-covered couch.

'Sit down!' Calhoun boomed, sucking on the pipe. 'An' tell me what I can do for you.'

Earl offered the mimeographed sheet of paper. 'I have a list of requests here from the students,' Earl said choosing his words very carefully. 'They're for you ta take a look at.'

Calhoun adjusted the glasses across his nose and took the copy of the demands. He read them, lost deeply in thought for a moment. Then his head snapped up. There was a crooked grin on his face.

'Requests?' he asked. 'There's nothing here that I'm requested to do. These seem to me like threats! It says here that I'm to respond to these by noon tomorrow. Is that right?'

'Thass right,' Earl agreed.

'What's requested then? These are intimidating. This is an intimidating document . . . never mind,' Calhoun tried to lower his voice, 'it sez by noon tomorrow. What if I don't reply by then?' There seemed to be real amusement in the president's voice at this time.

'I suppose I'll jus' have to wait until then,' Earl dodged.

'For what?'

'To see what the studen's have to say.' Earl replied evenly meeting Calhoun's eyes.

'Meaning that *I'll* have to wait until then too?'

'Thass right.'

Calhoun backed down a bit at that point. He took another look at the paper. Earl had half-expected to get kicked out.

'This is a short-time thing you have here,' Earl was told.

Earl said nothing.

'I doubt seriously,' Calhoun went on, 'that I kin do anything excep' reread these damn things before tomorrow noon.'

'Do what you can,' Earl said icily.

Calhoun blazed at that remark. 'Look!' he said almost shouting, 'I have asked students over an' over again to talk 'bout whatever the hell it is they want in them various meetings that students are a part of. If this isn't enough for them I will not be intimidated by a piece of paper tellin' me what *I* have to do by tomorrow noon or no time soon! I will make a call or two. I'm gonna have a meeting to ask the people on them various committees what they have been doing if and when these suggestions came up. Chances are none of *these* things have been brought up. Students generally don't appear at the meetings even when they have elected positions to serve on various functioning committees that we have. Now you come in here with a piece a paper telling me to put students in charge of damn near all the money that this institution spends within a year! Telling me that I will allow students to check books behind the people that I have appointed to take charge of various funds. And telling me that I, meaning the university, will pay for it? I think that you think I must be outta my mind! I don't respond to this sort of thing. Ha!' Calhoun sat back in the chair and puffed the pipe forming a cloud of the sticky-sweet cherry blend tobacco over his head. 'I will call this meeting! I will tell the students when these issues will be open for student-faculty-administrative discussion. That is all I will do.'

'All right,' Earl said. Calhoun appeared not at all prepared for that response. He regained his composure very quickly.

'Then I'll see you tuhmaruh?' Earl asked.

Calhoun cautiously fielded the question. 'I'll try an' call a meeting in the morning,' he said, getting up to see Earl to the door.

'I can make it out,' Earl said holding up his palm as a restraining gesture. 'I'll see you.'

Ogden Calhoun had not allowed the sound of the closing front door to die entirely before he picked up the phone on top of his cluttered desk. He dialed seven hasty numbers. Calhoun sucked at his pipe, but the flame was dead. He didn't like the tone of voice or the sarcastic glint in Earl's eyes. He didn't like the way Earl had gotten up to leave.

'Hello. Gaines? This is Ogden. I jus' had a visit from that boy Thomas. Uh-huh. The transfer that the students elected. Uh-huh. He brought over a list of *requests* from the students.'

Calhoun listened for a minute. 'You weren't there, but you heard about it? What?' The president sat bolt upright in the chair. He reached for a lighter and set his cherry blend on fire. 'Can you come over here tonight? Good. I'm going to call Miss Felch and a few others and see if I can't get to the bottom of this thing right away ... I said Miss Felch, my secretary ... One more thing. I suppose you must not have heard everything because request number two is that Gaines Harper be dismissed. ... What am I going to do? I don't know.'

9

Wheels in Motion

Ogden Calhoun came down the carpeted, spiraling staircase from his bedroom wearing a blue suit, white shirt, and tie. The tie was a bit loose at the collar and the jacket was a touch wrinkled, but the president had a stern policy of never holding any official university business when not dressed for the part. Consequently when he heard the bell ring he knew that Miss Felch had arrived and he came quickly down the stairs to meet her.

The maid, up and around at Calhoun's request, showed Miss Felch in. She was a tall, willowy, white, matronly-looking woman with pinched features and thin rectangular glasses squatting on a razor-sharp nose. She was dressed in a navy blue, two-piece suit and carried a matching handbag plus a corduroy zippered satchel with papers and note pads. The expression on her face was one of severe annoyance. She had been upset when the call interrupted her movie, when the cab driver tried to take a long route to increase the fare (thinking perhaps she didn't know the Black section of Sutton), and when she got out of the taxi realizing that she had forgotten her lipstick in the rush and looked like absolute hell. She pushed a lock of dirty-blond hair away from her eyes.

Calhoun stepped on the first-floor carpet like a man walking on eggs. He glided up to Miss Felch with his most gracious smile intact.

'I'm terribly sorry, Miss Felch. I've had a real emergency situation arise in the last hour and I've had to call a rather hasty meeting. I thought it would be appropriate if you were here to take notes and keep things in some sort of order ... As only you can.' The compliment bounced off Miss Felch's unpainted face. 'Louise, could you get Miss Felch coffee. Cream, no sugar. Right?'

Miss Felch attempted a smile and nodded. Louise began her exit.

'And Louise, I'm going to be in my den. I'll need a few of the light folded chairs from the back. Use the big coffee pot because I've invited quite a few men and we'll probably be keeping late hours. I hope you don't mind. This emergency, y'know.' Louise made her exit. Calhoun and Miss Felch entered the den.

'What makes you think this iz so much different from the las' time when Peabody woke everybody up in the middle of the night?' Vice-President Fenton Mercer was asking Calhoun in a corner of the den while the others who had been called were gathering. 'I saw the meeting, but I didn't even go out to investigate.

'Maybe you should have,' Calhoun told him. 'There should have been a note on my desk when I got here.'

'Most of the faculty members and administrators were gone. I was talkin' to the man from that Kentucky Graduate Program an' happened to look out the window . . . I thought it might've been a prep rally for the game on Saturday.'

'It wasn't,' Calhoun said, keeping his voice lowered. 'And I *don't* know if it's any different from Peabody.'

'Then why are we here?'

'I just didn't like Thomas's attitude when I questioned him about certain things. He looked . . . smug. That's the way he looked.'

'Like he had it in hand, huh?' Mercer chuckled.

'Yes. Like that.' Calhoun walked away from Mercer and stood next to his desk. It seemed that everyone who had been called was present. Calhoun made a quick head count. Yes, eight people.

'Harrummph. Uh, I'd like to get this over with as quickly as possible,' he said. 'If everyone will be seated I'll, uh, get things going. Most of you have some idea as to why this meeting was called. I had a visit tonight from the president of the Student Government Association, Mr Earl Thomas. He presented me with a list of what he chose to describe as "requests." Miss Felch?' Calhoun turned to the secretary, who nodded. 'Miss Felch has made everyone a copy.' Miss Felch passed the stack of papers around and handed Calhoun the original folded print.

There was a slight buzzing and mumbling as everyone read the list. Calhoun sought out particular facial reactions from various individuals.

Mercer, the chuckling vice-president, wasn't chuckling any more. Gaines Harper, the sallow-faced, flour-colored whale of a Financial Aid Officer was catsup-red and coughing. Cathryn Pruitt, the Dean of Women, was biting her right index fingernail. Edmund C. Mallory, the stocky, mustached football coach frowned and continued to sip his coffee. Arnold McNeil, head of the History Department and chairman of the Student-Faculty Alliance was nervously smoking his cigar and rubbing his balding head.

'As you can see,' Calhoun continued drily, 'there are several issues covered in the document here, but I wanted to ask for a few comments from the people present here before continuing.'

'You have your mind made up?' Mallory asked, fingering his mustache.

'Not entirely,' Calhoun hedged. 'Every president at every university has a different way of dealing with lists of in quotes requests. I have my particular way of dealing with them and may well do what I generally do ... tone is important, Ed. I've been doin' quite a bit of running here and there trying to align things for Sutton. I wondered what the tone was; what the feeling was that the group of you had gotten and then I would, quite naturally, proceed from there.'

'I don't think it's good,' Mrs Pruitt chirped. She never thought anything was good. 'The girls have been coming to me talking constantly about things.'

'*These* things?' Calhoun asked surprised.

'Many things. Primarily social things like curfews and late time and visiting time . . .'

'These issues are not listed,' someone reminded her before she went into one of her tirades about being handicapped at her job. They had all heard it before.

'But it's an indication,' she continued. 'It indicates the unrest.'

'We live in an era of unrest,' Calhoun said flatly. 'Mallory?'

'Yes, well, I would say that there are some things here worth investigating. I went to a meeting last week that Arnold was having and . . .'

'Right,' McNeil said rising. 'Ed was at last week's meeting of the Student-Faculty Alliance. Right in the middle of one of our discussions a student came in and started shouting loudly about our committee being the, pardon me ladies, "Bullshit Squad". He went on about us never handling the *real* issues at Sutton. Who was that Ed?'

'I didn't know him. The students called him "Captain Cool" or something,' Mallory laughed.

Calhoun leaned back against the desk. He struck an imposing figure. He was over six feet tall and his complexion was burnished leather. The silver hair gave him an air of importance and command.

'And "Captain Cool" disrupted your meeting,' Calhoun said, with the proper exaggeration applied to the use of the nickname.

'In a sense,' McNeil stated. 'But then he left. Just like that.'

'And this was not . . .'

'No. I didn't report it.' McNeil rubbed his balding head again. He was, along with Mallory, the only under-thirty-five-year-old present. 'I didn't report it because I wasn't sure what the complaint was.'

Calhoun was shocked. 'You didn't . . .'

'Allow me to finish,' McNeil said, waving a calming hand.

'The implication was that our committee wasn't really doing anything ... it isn't.'

Gaines Harper looked up. He and McNeil were the only two white men there. McNeil was turning red. 'I mean,' he continued, 'I became the head of the Student-Faculty Alliance because I thought it would give me a chance to more closely associate myself with the students and become a part of some of the meaningful change that my classes are always speaking of as necessary ... we have hassled over the price of a new score-board for the football field. We have handled a few minor disciplinary problems about curfews and violations of visitation, but we haven't *really* done anything.' He sat down.

'Are you suggesting that we go along with these?'

'I'm not suggesting anything!' McNeil said, raising his voice. 'I said that I didn't report the man who interrupted my meeting because he was absolutely right! The damn committee *has not* done a damn thing! The things that are listed on this paper are the things that students come into the meetings to hear discussed. Instead the agenda is full of crap like the allowance for decorations at various dances and allowances for the Homecoming Committee to prepare for the Homecoming Dance!'

There was absolute silence in the room. Everyone, except Miss Felch who continued to jot things down in shorthand, was looking at Arnold McNeil who was self-consciously trying to pretend that he was unaware of their scrutiny.

'Then I can gather that there is a mood of dissent,' Calhoun said through a cloud of smoke from his pipe.

'I think so,' Mrs Pruitt chirped.

'Looking at this list I would say that there are several alternatives left open for us as administrators and faculty members.' Calhoun was fingering the paper carefully. 'We can tell the students that this is a list of things that we will look into ...' There was a dramatic pause. 'Or we can tell them that this is a document of intimidation and that the university will continue to work on the problems which face the institution as a whole as we have done in the past.'

'What about the remark about noon tomorrow?'

'That's when we'll tell them.'

'I think we should hold a meeting in the morning and discuss this with the whole faculty and everybody else on the nonstudent level,' Mercer said.

'Why?' Harper asked.

'Because there are going to be faculty members who do not want to be associated with the administration,' Mercer replied.

'Thank you,' McNeil commented, head down.

'We've all been grouped together by the students,' Calhoun boomed. 'They all realize full well that within this paper is a question of faculty solidarity. There is a deep professional question here for faculty members. It is a question of professional allegiance.'

'It's a question of whether or not a man is doing his job too,' Coach Mallory stated.

'I think there should be a meeting too,' Mrs Pruitt said thoughtfully.

Heads started to nod all around the room. Calhoun squirmed. He knew that he could take charge and pull the rug out from under all of them and make it appear that he was just doing his job as he saw fit. That was not what he wanted to do however. This was an opportunity for him to take a good look at the people he had working around him and find out exactly where everyone stood. No matter what happened in the meeting he could always take over and say what he felt should be said.

'Take this down please, Miss Felch,' Calhoun said, striking a thoughtful pose as he leaned against the mahogany desk. '"To all faculty members and administrators. There will be a general meeting in the small auditorium tomorrow morning at ten o'clock. There will be a meeting of all department heads directly after this meeting." Put a copy of that in every mail box in the morning. Post in the Student Union

Building and cafeteria that there will be no classes in the morning.'

'Ten did you say?' Mrs Pruitt asked in her singsong.

'Ten,' said Calhoun.

10
Angie

Angie Rodgers had been dealt most of the blows people have in store for them in life by the time she was twenty years old. Her mother had died when she was born. Her father's death had occurred when she was eighteen. The young man who had spoken to her of marriage had run off when she became pregnant, leaving her to raise her son alone. Now, at twenty-three, she lived alone in the home that had been her father's one achievement in life aside from his daughter. She had been lonely in the little red brick house with only her son Bobby as company. She had even gone so far as to invite her father's unmarried sister to share the three-bedroom house with her, but she learned that her relatives felt that her unmarried pregnancy had contributed to her father's death. In a bitter scene on the steps of Angie's home her aunt had called her the Sutton whore and university tramp, unworthy of the love her father had given her.

Earl Thomas was the nicest thing that had ever happened to Angie. She trembled when she realized how she had nearly never met him, and even after their meeting had almost turned him away with her bitterness and icy reserve. He was so good to her. She felt so safe with him. And best of all, he got along well with Bobby.

Her relationship with Earl had not started off well. She had considered him just another application for a summer job when he applied for work at Sutton Computers, where she worked as the employment secretary. Her son's father had been a Sutton student and nothing in the world meant more to her after her father died than saving enough money to leave Sutton and the rest of Virginia far behind.

But it hadn't been that simple. Though her father had paid

for the house, after the funeral expenses and lawyer fees to close out all responsibilities to the hospital and the doctor, what little insurance there had been was exhausted, and what with car payments on her second-hand Volkswagen, and living expenses for herself and Bobby, there was no money to move and no time to do extra work to save any money.

She had been approached several times by the younger Black men at the factory, but she always felt she could detect a sneer behind their eyes because she was the mother of an illegitimate child and would supposedly have hot pants. At times she felt herself near tears because she was lonely but so far she had not found sincerity in any of the eyes that coolly surveyed her across her desk or over a cup of coffee in the lounge.

Once or twice when tossing restlessly, unable to sleep, she had even considered giving in to some of those inquiries, even though she knew it would only mean a fleeting chance to hold a man in her arms and later facing up to the bitter humiliation. She never tried to convince herself that she was a strong woman. She had missed Don, Bobby's father, terribly, and even when she sat up late at night trying to balance her small budget, she never claimed that anything other than love for her son was making her so firm.

But Earl had surprised her. The first time he stepped into the front office she had been there. She gave him a cool 'How are you?' and handed him an application, pointing to various lines where specific information was required. When he had finished she took the form from him and said very formally, 'Mr Egson will see you now, Mr Thomas.' Earl passed through the gate, into the secretarial area, and on into the back of the office where Mr Egson waited.

She had thought about him only briefly. She considered him handsome. He was tall, well muscled across the shoulders and chest. He had a thick head of hair, but it was trimmed and neat as was his mustache. He had been dressed in a short-sleeved sports shirt, open at the throat, and a pair of slacks. His eyes were serious, almost sad, but he had a strong chin and his nose was just right for the soft, but firm lips. The only point that she readily did not approve was the fact that he smoked and his index and middle fingers on each hand were stained yellow, clashing with the smooth amber of his hands, arms, and face. She had been tempted to ask him if he was Indian or of Indian descent, but that would have been definitely out of character.

She nearly forgot about him. Her position in the front office rarely brought her into contact with the mechanics who worked on the assembly line. It was almost three weeks later when she next saw him. He had come into the air-conditioned personnel department mopping a handkerchief across his forehead, dressed in a faded sweatshirt and work jeans with an oil-stained mechanic's apron tied around his neck and waist. He had marched straight over to her desk.

'I'd like to take you out this evening,' he said quite suddenly.

'I'm sorry,' she stammered trying to recover from his matter-of-fact approach. 'I go directly home from work ... I don't even believe I know your name.'

'Then you haven't been nearly as interested in me as I have been in you,' he replied quietly.

'Really?'

'Really.'

'Well, I'm sorry, but I can't go out with you.'

'What about a movie sometime?'

Angie had looked furtively around the front office. The other secretaries and workers didn't seem to be paying the least bit of attention to her. Earl propped himself on the corner of her desk and lit a cigarette.

'Mr Thomas,' Angie had exclaimed. 'I'm ...'

'"... a liar,"' Earl cut in. '"Because I said I didn't know your name, but I do and though I can't have dinner with you this evening I would love to have you drive me home after work because I didn't bring my car in today."'

'How did you know I didn't bring my car in?'

'We mechanics get here early,' Earl said, brightly smiling for the first time. 'And if we saw a good-looking woman taking her car in to LeRoy's the night before and happen to wonder whether or not she got it fixed, we look out the next morning to find out how she arrives. Never can tell when you might get a chance to drive somebody home.'

Angie was unable to control a smile. It had felt good smiling at him and with him that first time. She still felt warm when she remembered the way he sat on her desk in front of everybody as though he didn't have a care in the world about being spotted by the boss and fired or reprimanded.

'I'll meet you by the punch-out clock at four-oh-five and if you work late I'll wait.' Earl had smiled a bit shyly then and left her sitting with her mouth open at the desk.

They had been dating now for almost five months. They stopped going out so often when he started back at Sutton, but Angie didn't mind. She was a good cook and loved to cook for him. He always acted as though he were starving and as if she were the best cook on earth. And she loved the feel of his arms around her. He was strong and masculine. She liked to rub her hands over his shoulder blades and feel the muscles rippling under his skin. She loved to have him crush her and then revive her with a kiss when she was almost breathless. She loved Earl Thomas.

She was sitting alone in the kitchen at nearly eleven o'clock having a second cup of coffee when she heard a car pull up outside her house. Seconds later she heard a car door slam and steps trotting up the brick path that led from the curb to her front door. Then there was a knock.

'If it's not the late Mr Thomas,' she said smiling at the door.

Earl kissed her on the forehead and stepped into the living room. 'If it's not the lovely Miss Rodgers,' he said. She took his coat and hung it on a hanger in the closet next to the front door. Earl was looking out through the curtains at the darkness of Maple Street. She bent over his shoulder and pecked him on the cheek. He turned to her and embraced her and kissed her mouth.

'You've just got to tell me everything,' she exclaimed, remembering the day's activities. 'Louise called me an' told me just enough to drive me out of my mind. She said that nobody knows the full story but you and Baker and Calhoun. The rest of the campus is in a frenzy, I suppose.'

'Everything's fucked up,' he said gruffly. 'Where's the eats? I think I jus' may starve.' He wrapped a long arm around her waist and walked side by side with her to the kitchen.

In the kitchen he sat in the corner and leaned back sighing. She watched him close his eyes as though he would go to sleep. He yawned a big yawn and stretched his long frame, finally exhaling while pounding his chest.

Angie took pride in her kitchen. It was, as was the rest of the house, spotless. Earl often marveled at how she managed to keep the place so clean, especially in the wake of the 'Black Hurricane,' which was his nickname for Bobby. Bobby had a tendency to lose baseballs and guns under beds and sofas and there were times when he had the entire Santa Fe railroad in miniature lined up to make stops all over the house.

She took a minute now to set the table with dishes that had been arranged across the drainboard. The pot was on the stove atop a low flame. When the lid was removed the kitchen was filled with the aroma of tomato sauce and Angie appeared to have a halo of steam around her head.

'We had spaghetti for dinner and I added some for you and some meatballs,' Angie commented without turning around.

'Good,' Earl said.

'Uhl! Uhl, I knew you wuz here!' Bobby's head had appeared at the door and he was taking a flying leap into Earl's arms. Earl caught him with a big laugh and placed the youngster down between his legs and held his giggling captive a prisoner between his knees while he tickled the boy lightly under the arms.

'Bobby Rodgers if you don't get back in that bed,' Angie said, coming to the table and reaching for her son with mock anger. 'Earl, don't tickle him. You know he won't go back to bed.'

'Bobby? Will you go back to bed?' Earl asked continuing to tickle him while holding the lad away from his mother's reach.

'Can I have a soda?' Bobby wondered. 'I'll go back to bed.'

'No soda,' Angie stated firmly. 'You know he almost drank a whole thing full of Kool-Aid by himself.'

'You can have some of my beer,' Earl said. 'Get me a beer out of the refrigerator.' He let Bobby go and the youngster bounded away. 'They gotta be makin' four-year-old giants nowadays. I was seventeen befo' I was as big as he is now.'

'Earl, you oughta stop,' Angie said going back to the spaghetti.

'Here go,' Bobby said climbing into Earl's lap. Earl gave out with a muffled 'Oof!' as the boy plopped a slippered foot into his stomach.

'Bobby, Earl may not want you climbing all over him. Earl has been busy today and he's tired.'

'You tired, Uhl?' Bobby asked unbelieving.

'Little bit, my man,' Earl said. He had poured a couple of ounces of the beer into a glass and handed it to Bobby.

'Cheers!' Bobby said, imitating what Earl said when they drank anything together. Angie laughed.

'Cheers!'

Bobby downed his beer thirstily in one gulp.

'Good man!' Earl said. 'Now off to bed.'

'Do I . . .'

'You promised me,' Earl reminded him. 'But tell me something. Where you get them pretty eyes?' he asked the boy, pretending to reach for Bobby's eyes.

'From my momma.'

'And where'd you get that big ol' smile?'

'From my momma.'

'And where you get them plump cheeks?' Earl pinched a cheek. Bobby started laughing again.

'From my momma.'

'And where you gonna get a spankin' if you don't head for the sack?'

'From you!' Bobby cried wrenching away. He ran to Angie who stood laughing. She appreciated the routine that Earl and Bobby had worked out during his late visits.

'G'night, Momma,' Bobby said, holding her over for a kiss. She kissed him and he returned to Earl. 'G'night, Uhl.'

'G'night, my man,' Earl said allowing himself to be smacked soundly on the jaw.

Bobby ran out of the kitchen and the couple heard his muffled footfalls on the stairs leading to the bedroom upstairs.

'This spaghetti seems to be good,' Angie said heaping Earl's plate. 'Bobby ate two plates full.'

'Doesn't have to be too good for Bob,' Earl laughed. 'Thass a big-eatin' rascal.'

Earl dug into the large pile of spaghetti that was overflowing with steaming sauce and chunks of ground beef. Angie busied herself washing the utensils and pans she had used for cooking.

'You're not going to tell me, are you?' she asked after Earl had finished and lit up a cigarette.

'Baker took over,' Earl said through a stream of smoke.

'I know that. I mean . . .'

'They had some grievances that the students approved. They called me 'bout seven an' tol' me they wanted me to carry the things to Old Nigger Calhoun. I went over there an' took 'im the papers and did some other stuff.'

'Other stuff relating to this?'

'I checked my own papers relating to the things in the deman's because me an' Odds and Lawman all noticed how similar they were to the things we had been workin' on.'

'Were they your papers?'

'Not exactly. Not there. I don't know how much of my stuff they have. I figure they must have copied it all or Xeroxed it, but they put it back in the same order they found it.'

'All your work is down the drain?'

'I don't know yet. It depen's on what happens.'

'How did Calhoun look when you went there?'

''Bout as happy as a man walkin' through hell wit' gasoline drawers on.'

'Oh, Earl. What did he say?'

'Jus' what I thought he would say,' Earl admitted, lighting another cigarette. 'That the list was intimidating and that he would see what he could do, but that that wouldn' be much done. Hell! They asked for a reply by noon tomorrow.'

'Noon tomorrow?'

'High noon,' Earl said shaking his head.

The phone in the living room rang and Angie got up to answer it. 'I wonder who that could be,' she said.

Earl smoked and waited, listening to Angie answer the phone, but not overhearing the muffled conversation that followed.

'It's for you, Earl,' Angie called. 'It's Odds and Lawman.'

Earl went through the open door that separated the kitchen from the living room.

'Earl the Pearl,' he said, taking the receiver from her.

'Look, Pearl,' Lawman said in his ever-serious tone. 'Do you know what's happening over at Calhoun's right now?'

'Midnight. Jus' like everywhere else in Virginia,' Earl cracked.

'Yeah. Well, midnight an' Gaines Harper and Fenton Mercer and a few other personifications just landed on our president's runway.'

'Ah so,' Earl said. 'Not to watch the Late Show, I bet.' Earl took note of the fact that he had not amused Lawman again.

'Doubtlessly not. What did you find out?'

'I'm damn sure MJUMBE got our notes,' Earl admitted.

'You gonna talk to Sheila?'

'Not if I can help it. I'm pissed off at her already. She's prob'bly hip to the fact that I'm onto her.'

'And ... ?'

'And nothing. Too late to do anything now.'

'How'd Calhoun take the paper?'

'In his hand, man. It got over like a lead balloon.'

'You swallow some funny pills?'

'No, brother,' Earl said sighing and turning serious. 'I guess I just got hung up in that ol' axiom about makin' the best of a bad situation, you know?'

'Yeah. I know. What gives in the mornin'?'

'Yo' guess is as good as mine.'

'Ummm . . . well, I guess I'll au revoir.'

'Okay.'

'I'll see you in the morning. Me and Odds tapped out. Nothin' more to report.'

'All right.'

'G'night.'

'G'night.' Earl cradled the receiver.

'Bad news?' Angie asked when he reentered the kitchen.

'No news is bad news at this stage,' Earl replied.

He lit a cigarette.

'You smoke too much,' Angie said softly.

'Thass right,' Earl admitted.

'There's goin' to be trouble, isn't there?'

'I don't know . . .'

'You're going to get in trouble, aren't you?'

'I don't know about . . .'

'You're the one who took Calhoun the papers and you know how he is about those things.'

'There's always trouble,' Earl said.

'Not like this . . .'

'Trouble is the same. When you got them they're all just big problems, and when they're gone you don' remember why you had such a hard time.'

'Calhoun is going to be your hard time.'

'Just as long as I have you for my good time,' Earl laughed gently. 'I'll just try to deal with one time at a time.'

11
Calhoun's Assessment

Gaines Harper was the last administrator to leave the Calhoun home after the president's impromptu meeting. The fat, red-faced Financial Aid Officer had dawdled, scanning stacks of periodicals in the president's bookcase until after even Miss Felch had gathered her notes and departed.

Ogden Calhoun returned to his den from seeing Miss Felch into a cab. His face was drawn and tired. He was irritated by the whole affair.

'What do you think?' Harper asked the president breathlessly. He was always breathless; grossly overweight, he was a victim of too much beer.

'Please don't ask me what I think, Harper,' Calhoun snorted as he stripped off his jacket. 'You heard everything I heard.'

'I heard it all right. And I didn't like it too much.'

'It wasn't for you to like or dislike,' Calhoun said irritatedly.

'McNeil acted as though he even wanted those things to be,' Harper continued, as though he hadn't heard. 'I wonder what Mr Ostrayer would say about that. He recommended McNeil just like he recommended me.'

'What could he say?' Calhoun asked.

'He'd have plenty to say,' Harper assured the president. 'You know how trustees think. He wouldn't like McNeil taking the students' side against you.'

'Is that what you think McNeil is doing?'

'It was plain. He told you he wasn't even angry when that student came in and disrupted his meeting!'

'Yes. But I think it's quite another thing to imply that he was in favor of these demands.'

'It's all the same to me. They'll be after him next and all

of the other white workers here. I wonder what he'll have to say then.'

'I don't see where color has anything to do with it,' Calhoun said coldly.

'Why do you think they want me fired?' Harper blazed.

'They don't say.'

'Naturally it's because I'm white. The ones in charge of that meeting today were militants. They are against everything white . . . Yeah, they'll be after McNeil soon. Mark my words. He won't be so quick to agree that the faculty shouldn't only answer to the administrators then. He wouldn't want the students looking over his shoulder, checking his books, doing things like that . . . it's only because he's on the other side of the fence now that he can afford to be so liberal.'

Calhoun shot Harper a quizzical look. 'Is that what it is?' he asked sarcastically.

'Yes. That's it,' Harper said breathlessly, hurrying on. 'You can afford to be high and mighty and in favor of student reform when you've got tenure and a Ph.D. He wouldn't be like that if it was his second year on the job like me, just trying to find his way around.'

'We'll see,' Calhoun said.

'Well . . .'

'Well what?' Calhoun asked standing up. 'Your point is that you want to know whether or not I'm going to give in to the students, isn't that it? I'd rather you have asked. But it's an indication that you've only been here for a year because then you'd know that I never respond to papers like this one. Thomas should know better too.'

'Maybe he does,' Harper said thoughtfully.

Calhoun was struck by the idea. Harper was pulling on his huge raincoat and hat.

'I'll see you at ten o'clock,' he said. 'Don't bother to see me out.'

'Good night,' Calhoun said.

Calhoun remained in the den long enough to turn off the

lights and straighten up his desk. He then made his way up the spiral stairs to the bedroom where, much to his surprise, his wife was still sitting up, reading.

'Surprised to find you up,' he said wearily.

'You're the one who needs the rest,' she said. 'I know how Norfolk tired you out. You were looking forward to coming right home from the theater and going to bed, weren't you?'

'I really was,' Calhoun said, sitting on the edge of the bed and taking off his shoes, socks, and pants. 'I'm afraid I'll have an early day tomorrow too.'

'The students are being unreasonable again?' Gloria Calhoun asked. Her husband wondered if he detected a note of sarcasm in his wife's voice.

'Damn right!' he said gruffly. 'Imagine asking me to fire Royce, Beaker, and Harper and wanting to audit all the school books and have me turn everything in the Student Union over to them plus funds so that they can invite the performers and speakers on campus. I imagine we'd have James Brown every night. Not even asking me,' Calhoun went on. 'Telling me.'

'What reason do they give?'

'None. Just a piece of paper pointing out how to do my job.' Calhoun was properly disgusted at the thought. 'And what difference does it make what reason they give? It's still an intimidating paper. They're still telling me how to do my job. I've been president here for nine years, Gloria. You know that that's not the way we get things done here.'

'Maybe the students are just trying to be dramatic,' Mrs Calhoun suggested.

'Dramatic? This is a threat!' Calhoun asserted. 'Thomas must not be any older than twenty-two. I'm damn near three times that. We're trying to teach the boys and girls at Sutton how to be men and women and cope with their lives outside. You can't take your boss a note saying do this and that by tomorrow noon or else.'

'But this is different,' Gloria said. 'You're not their b . . .'

'It's the same principles. Channels have been established!' Calhoun was raising his voice.

The last thing Gloria wanted was an argument. 'You should come to bed, dear,' she said. 'It's almost twelve thirty.'

'I know,' Calhoun grumbled. 'As soon as I wash my teeth and try to refresh myself a bit.' He got up and carried his pajamas with him into the bathroom next to their bedroom.

Gloria Calhoun listened for a second to the running water that alone disturbed the silence of the house. She was amazed at how easy it had been for her to avoid the argument that would have come and how natural it seemed for her not to challenge her husband. She remembered how, when they were courting, they had stayed up until all hours of the night arguing points about world politics or the movement or even about a movie they had seen.

The water stopped running in the bathroom and Calhoun returned to the bedroom, turning out the light from the wall switch as he came.

Thursday

12

Preparation

Ralph Baker sat brooding over an early cup of black coffee at a corner table in the Sutton cafeteria. His roommate and closest friend, Jonesy, had just left to have more copies of MJUMBE's demands mimeographed, and the big MJUMBE spokesman was alone for the first time in what seemed like days. He didn't particularly like the feeling.

Calhoun was on Baker's mind. Calhoun and Thomas and Sheila and a lot of other things, but Calhoun was a special worry. He couldn't help feeling that he had made a big mistake by not accompanying Earl Thomas to the Plantation the night before. He wanted to know what was on the university president's mind. He wondered what the reaction to the demands had been. Not necessarily what had been said, but what had flashed across the old fox's eyes. Eyes were a good sign of what was going on inside the mind. Discussing the situation earlier with Jonesy, he had spoken confidently about the bind in which MJUMBE had put the Sutton administration. Now, alone, he wasn't quite as sure. There were too many loose ends; things that he needed to know and had no way of finding out. Signs would have certainly been in Calhoun's eyes, even if he played it cagey and diplomatically. Baker felt like a blind man, lost without knowing those signs; like a blind man who would stumble, either into the light or out onto the highway with a bus ticket clenched in his huge hand.

But Calhoun was not the only problem. Just when he hadn't needed anything else to upset him, his relationship with Sheila had disintegrated. He didn't know exactly what had gone wrong. As a matter of fact he had never really intended for anything to happen between them.

He had known Sheila for almost six years. They had met

when he was an All-State candidate from their high school in Shelton Township, Virginia. Sheila was a cheerleader with a crush on him, but he had been going steady with another girl and hardly had time for the short, baby-faced freshman who followed him halfway home every day after practice. He had laughed at the thought of her and at one of the victory dances even made a joke of her crush on him. That had seemed to cool things down. During his senior year Sheila was no longer a cheerleader and Baker rarely saw her. Then he had won a scholarship to play football at Sutton.

The next time he saw Sheila was when she arrived on Sutton's campus as a freshman. He had been cordial as he would have been to any new student from his home town. But they moved in different social spheres. He was a fraternity man and a football player. She was just one of the many coeds on the predominantly female campus.

Baker had met Sheila at a party given by a mutual friend. They chatted about school and Greek organizations and football. She expressed an interest in Delta Sigma Theta, the sister organization of Omega Psi Phi, Baker's fraternity. He found himself not only interested in the conversation, but in Sheila. They began dating off and on. The young woman who had once been so much a part of Baker's life had gotten married during his freshman year and already had a child.

Upon their return to school in the fall Baker had been surprised to learn that Sheila was working as Earl Thomas's secretary. She had told him that she was going to try to get a job, but even when she landed the secretarial post Baker paid it little attention. Football had started again. The fraternity had another line of pledgees to indoctrinate. Plans for MJUMBE were only vague shadows forming in the back of his mind. The organization had been formed by Baker as a safeguard against another year of political apathy. Baker had been willing to admit that Earl Thomas was a fast talker and a man who could think politically while on his feet, but he had never felt that Earl's administration stood for radical change, which was what he felt that Sutton needed. He felt that between Earl and 'Lawman' Dean a few small problems might be alleviated, but it was a question of timing. If the students were allowed to slip into the middle of another non-productive year it would be difficult to shake them up and ignite a fire under them once they settled into a pattern or an attitude of acceptance.

But Earl had waited too long. Virginia institutions of higher education come up for their accreditation markings during the third week of October. Baker knew that the ideal time to hit the school with a list of demands would be just as the accreditation service began looking into the mechanisms of the school. This move by students would bring about more pressure on the administrators to force a quick halt to the disturbances. With these things in mind Baker moved.

He found himself seeing more and more of Sheila. Talk about her work and the SGA let Baker know what Thomas was doing and exactly what information was on hand in the SGA office. He wanted very badly to see the information that Earl and his team had gathered, but there was no way he could legitimately go into the office and ask Thomas for permission. He started an Uncle Tom campaign against Earl with Sheila.

'I shoulda known better than to think that nigga was doin' somethin',' he had said in Sheila's room one night near the end of September.

'Who you mean?' Sheila asked, looking up from her homework.

'Thomas. He said when he got elected he was gonna have somethin' goin' by October an' tomorrow's October an' ain' nobody heard hide nor hair a' him.'

'He mus' be doin' somethin',' Sheila sighed. 'Wit' all them different things he has me typin' all day.'

'I wish they'd open up them records for everybody,' Baker snorted. 'I bet I'd get something together.'

'They don't open everything up for . . .'

'No. SGA's a special thing. Thass why I was runnin'. You get a chance to look in everybody's closet. There's no tellin' jus' what Thomas knows, but we'll never find out. Lucky for Head Nigger Calhoun that some Tom always gets elected.'

'This whole political thing is very important to you, huh?'

'Damn right! Look at alla the things you have to put up with when you're here. The damn dorms are crumbling. The food tastes like warmed over garbage. The teachers don't know their asses from a hole in the ground. Somethin' oughta be done.'

'You think the records Earl has tell about how to fix these things?' Sheila wondered.

'That's what he was s'pose to be workin' on,' Baker pointed out.

'Why would he work on them if he wasn' gonna do anything?'

'Because he prob'bly knows that people like me are gonna ask him what the hell he been doin'. Then he can haul out this big pile a papers an' show us how bizzy he's been even though nuthin' came outta it.'

'But what could anybody do who's not in an office? Even if they had the papers?'

'Sheila,' Baker said seriously, 'all studen's want 'roun' here is for somebody to have guts enough to stand up to Calhoun. They don't really care who it is. It could be Thomas or me or Mickey Mouse.'

Sheila had been thoughtful and quiet for a moment. Then she got up from her desk and reached into her purse. When her hand emerged from the bag there was a short, round key in her grasp dangling from a rabbit's foot key chain.

'Take this key,' she told Baker handing him the chain. 'This is the key to the SGA office. The papers are in the filing cabinet in the back, listed under G. Everything that has been done this year is there.'

The rest had been easy. Baker had been back to the office on two other occasions to tighten up information and copy things that he thought would be needed. Aside from Sheila nobody, not even Jonesy, knew anything about Baker's access to the office. He had taken the notes and worked on them by himself, forming the list of demands from the papers he had seen and from information that he had collected before his campaign.

The entire plan had gone exceptionally smoothly. He had been very pleased with himself until the night before, when he and Sheila had argued and he had left her in tears.

He had gone into her room tense and angry. The confrontation with Thomas had been upsetting. Thomas had looked as if he wouldn't give a damn if MJUMBE took over the United States Government. He had listened to Baker and the others in the MJUMBE group talk briefly about their actions and then he had taken the list of demands and departed. That was the last that any member of MJUMBE had seen of Thomas, and no one had seen Calhoun. Baker felt as if he were somehow being manipulated instead of himself manipulating what was happening. When he got to Sheila's room in Garney Plaza, she had noticed that something was bothering him.

'You were good today,' she had remarked quietly when he sat at the desk instead of coming to sit on the edge of the bed with her as he usually did. 'I mean, your speech was good. Everybody said so.'

'Thanks.'

'Are you all right?'

'I'm okay. It's raining.'

'I was listening to it. It put me to sleep.'

'Yeah? Well, I got me some work to do, you know. I got a lotta things I got to tighten up befo' tuhmaruh.'

'Can I make you some coffee or something?' Sheila asked getting up. She slipped into her robe and lifted the arm of the record player that sat next to her bed. She lifted the stack of records that had played through and started them over again.

'Where's Bucky Beaver?' Baker asked, referring to Sheila's two-hundred-pound roommate who was a dead ringer for the animated character of the Ipana commercials in the fifties.

'She moved,' Sheila said absently.

'She moved?'

'Monday. She took her things an' changed her room down the hall.' The Temptations came on doing 'Psychedelic Shack,' and Sheila turned the record player down. She pulled a hot plate from under her bed and then went out into the hall. When she came back she had a coffee pot full of water in her hands. She filled up the top with coffee from a two-pound canister and lit the hot plate, putting the pot over one of the burners. Baker sat hunched over a pile of papers with his back to her. She started to speak and then stopped, busying herself with coffee cups and saucers from her dresser.

'She couldn' dig me, huh?' Baker asked disconnectedly.

'Huh? . . . oh, I guess not. She and I didn' really get along. She's got problems.'

'Yeah. About three or fo' hundred of 'um.'

'Ralph,' Sheila giggled, warming a bit. 'She's not that fat.'

Baker lapsed into silence. He was thinking about Victor Johnson, the skinny, bespectacled editor from *The Statesman*. He had left the MJUMBE meeting and gone directly to *The Statesman* office. Along with Johnson he had put together the issue that would greet the community when the sun rose. He had felt that he had done a good job in pointing out the things that had to be done at Sutton. He had even tempered his words to appeal to the lackeys and eggheads that he despised. He didn't particularly care for political diplomacy, but he knew that he had lost the election because there were so many soft-hearted Toms on Sutton's campus who daily sold their asses for a diploma and that he didn't dare do otherwise. Now, in Sheila's room, with copies of the paper being run off in the basement of the Trade Building, he wondered if he had done the right thing. Maybe Speedy Cotton had been right when he pointed out what kind of spot Baker's article was going to put MJUMBE in. Baker had snorted that it was time for some people to get on the spot. Now he wasn't sure if a Victor Johnson editorial and the pictures of Thomas in one corner and the MJUMBE meeting in the other wouldn't have been enough.

Sheila interrupted his thoughts by coming up behind him and wrapping her arms around his neck.

'Look! I'm bizzy. All right?' Baker snapped.

Sheila looked as if she had been kicked. She was turned off.

'Look, I didn't mean it like that . . . I'm uptight. Okay?'

'That's what I thought I was for . . . I mean, when things were bothering you and like that.'

'There ain' nothin' an' nobody who can do anything 'bout this. It'll all be taken care of tuhmaruh.'

'Will it?'

'Yeah.'

Sheila turned the flame down under the coffee and poured two steaming cups from the pot. She poured a little milk and sugar in her cup and handed Baker his black. They drank for a second in silence.

'What's going to happen?' Sheila asked suddenly.

'I wish I knew,' Baker said rubbing his bald head. 'Things went all right today except for a few things.'

'Like what?'

'Well, we called Thomas to take the things to Calhoun, but his line was busy. So we decided to carry the ball ourselves and Calhoun wasn't home. Then we got ahold of Thomas and he took the things over there.'

'That's bad?'

'Not really bad,' Baker admitted. 'Things just weren' clickin' like I thought they would. There was too much confusion. Everybody was restless. It's a whole different thing when you ain' in fronta the crowd no mo'. They come to the meetin's an' clap an' carry on, but it's just a different set when you're by yo'self.'

'You worried?'

Baker laughed. 'I been waitin' fo' this fo' three years. I'm jus' impatient to git it on.'

'You hate Calhoun?'

'Naw. I hate bullshit. Sutton could be a beautiful place fo' Black studen's to come an' get their minds together, but what happens? Fo' years a bullshit an' then ill-equipped people go back home an' ill-prepare another set to continue to merry-go-round. It's gotta stop.'

Sheila laughed a little. 'You'll never change. You always want to be the one . . .'

'Somebody has to be the one,' Baker said.

'Well, I hope it's over soon, because I'm not use to you bein' uptight.'

Baker put down his coffee cup and went to sit next to Sheila on the bed.

'I thought you were goin' to work,' Sheila smiled as he reached for her.

'I was,' Baker admitted.

'And now?'

'Well,' Baker said untying his shoes, 'I had this idea that I was gonna sit at the desk an' jot down notes an' stuff and the nex' thing I knew it would be mornin'.'

'An' now?' Sheila persisted.

Baker held her around her waist and turned her until they were both flat out on the bed facing each other. His hand was in her hair and their mouths were pressed tightly to each other, tongues sucking deeply. Baker's huge hands were fondling and squeezing, running down her side and between her heavy thighs. Sheila was gasping, scratching the small of his back with her nails and running her tongue in and out of his ear sending shivers down his spine.

He could feel her wetness, the sticky fluid of her womanhood moistening her pubic hair. He bit her on her neck and felt her jump and squeeze his hand between her legs. She tightened her hold around his neck even as he twisted her slightly to remove her robe and pajama top.

As Baker bent to kiss her breasts Sheila shivered and felt for the rising lump between his legs. She squeezed him hard and he wriggled away. She reached for his belt and unlocked it, breaking the button that secured his trousers. With impatience she unzipped the front of his trousers and lowered them so that she could gain a sure hold on his swelling manhood.

Baker groaned and teased her breast with his teeth. He could feel the pressure mounting in his loins as she stroked him up and down and sighed and moaned in his ear. Sweat was beading at his hairline and dripping onto her face. Sheila was tossing and turning under him; rising to meet him as he strained to move away from the grip of her hands. He scooted down and away from her and kissed her stomach, kicking his pants off as he moved. He pushed his tongue inside her navel and she squirmed and wiggled more frantically beneath him. Her hands left his organ for a second to grasp his testicles and tickle the hair of his lower stomach.

Baker straightened up in a kneeling position between her thighs. She was breathing heavily, eyes closed, thighs spread apart waiting for him. He teased her opening gently, allowing only a small portion of himself to lodge between her legs. She groaned and sobbed a small cry and reached for him, digging her fingernails into his buttocks, pulling him forward. With a crushing certainty he entered her. He felt a lightning flash of pain-pleasure as he eased inside her. She called his name, and wrapped her thighs around his waist; thrusting herself up to him, impaling herself totally. Baker felt a rush coming from his thighs as he moved within her. He crushed her to him and heard her groan. Their rhythm and speed increased as he strained to hold off against the surging flow of his orgasm. She screamed as she shared his liquid fire until she was left spent and exhausted.

She clung to him tightly, wanting to lie there with him and allow the heat of their bodies to smother them and shelter them. Baker withdrew slowly and pressed his head to her bosom. She squirmed closer to him, kissing his heavily muscled arm. Their heavy breathing subsided. The sweat was cooling them as it traced crooked paths down the lengths of their bodies. Sheila hooked a leg across Baker's flat stomach and fondled him between his legs, pressing it to her thigh. Baker inched away.

'Ralph,' she began tentatively.

'Yes?' he replied, sitting up on the side of the bed and looking around for his shoes.

'Ralph? Are you leaving?' Sheila asked as though frightened.

'Yeah,' the reply came hardly above a whisper.

Sheila rolled away from Baker's side of the bed. She felt hurt again. She had known what he was going to say somehow. She had known all the time that things weren't right. She had sensed it. But there was no way to stay away from him when he held her in his arms like a doll and crushed her to him.

Baker was struggling for something to say. He knew that she was hurt. He knew why. He was berating himself for feeling that he had to leave. All through the act of love he had heard the words from the Last Poets' album banging into his mind: 'All over America bitches with big 'fros and big asses were turning would-be revolutionaries into Gash men . . . Gash needs man. No experience necessary . . . Gash man. Gash man . . . Come on, daddy. And he came. Every day he came . . .' Baker shook his head. He wasn't thinking straight. That was why he was leaving. He needed some sleep. If he stayed Sheila would crawl all over him all night long and he would respond; grabbing her pillow-soft breasts, running his hand between her thighs, squeezing her firm ass. All night long. All night long. He would fuck as though he were inventing pussy and the next day he would be useless, drained, out on his feet. He knew he had to be sharp when the sun came up. That was why he was leaving. He watched Sheila out of the corner of his eye as he put his shoes on.

She was lying on her back searching the corners of the ceiling, acid tears springing from salty wells in her mind, a sick emptiness jerking at her stomach.

'Why won't you stay?' she called. 'I know I shouldn't be

raising my voice an' gettin' upset an' cryin' or anything, but I shouldn't be doing a lot of things like laying in bed with you or waitin' up all night for you. I wait an' wait sometimes Ralph and you don't come or call. I feel like Ralph Baker's private whore.'

'You're wrong, baby,' Baker said in monotone. 'You're wrong again.'

'Am I?'

'Yeah. You wrong. Tomorrow night I be by an' we'll talk about it.'

'Tomorrow night? I'm sick an' tired of waitin' for tomorrow nights that aren't comin'. You don't have to say nuthin' special. A woman can tell, Ralph. I knew all the time, but I thought I was gonna make you love me. Well, I give the hell up. You don't give a damn 'bout nothin' an' nobody but Ralph Baker. It's always been that way. You have to be the head of everything; the king of everything, the leader. When you can't get it one way, you get it the other. All I was was the key to the damn office! An' now that you have all the papers an' things I hope you're quite through with me.'

'You're wrong, Sheila,' Baker said sadly.

'Get out! Get out of here and leave me alone!'

Baker had wanted to say something special then, but the words he needed were nowhere to be found. He finished dressing quickly and left. The last sight he had of Sheila was a sad picture. She was lying in a heap on the bed, her bathrobe open exposing the glossy brown texture of her breasts, jerking as she sobbed and cried.

It hadn't done much good to go back to the room. Jonesy had been in bed fast asleep. Baker showered and fell heavily into his bed, but sleep was a stranger far into the night. He found himself turning over the day's events and the events of his life with Sheila as far back as he could remember. He had really come to like her. He had come to appreciate her and enjoy her company. He had come to love her. No. That was a lie. He didn't love her. But it wasn't the sort of plot that she thought it was. That had been a coincidence. An unhappy one at that. No. He didn't love her. But he missed her. He missed having her change the records and fix coffee.

Ben King came through the door to the cafeteria. Baker waved and King came over to the table and set his tray down.

'Git me another coffee, brother?' Baker said.

King nodded and went back to the line where the coffee was being handed out. He turned with two cups and sat down opposite the MJUMBE spokesman.

'So whuss happ'nin'?' King asked.

'Everything, man. You seen anybody?'

'Man, I'm so ready it don' even make no muthafuckin' sense. You git a look at Thomas?'

'No. Did'joo?'

'No. I seen Abul. His shit is togethuh too.'

'I figgered that.'

'He got his shit on!' King laughed.

'The gol' dashiki?'

'The brother is layin' tough.'

Both Baker and King were wearing black dashikis with gold trim.

'Hi many dudes you got lined up if we haveta boycott?' Baker asked.

'Shit! I got the whole football squad an' half the players on every othuh team near here.'

'You git any static?'

'You kiddin'?' King asked as he gulped down the scrambled eggs. 'I heard a lotta "you goin' 'bout this the wrong way" type shit, But I thought I wuz gon' hear that shit.'

'You listened?'

''Course I listened. I din' tell no punks 'bout the plan. I jus' don' wanna hear no shit when the real deal go down.'

'Right.'

King ate in silence for a moment. Baker drank his coffee

thoughtfully. The cafeteria was filling up again. A glance at his watch told Baker that it was almost eight thirty.

'I got to go,' he announced standing up.

'Fo' you do,' King said, 'tell me somethin'.'

'What?'

'What'choo rilly think gon' happen?'

Baker looked down at his big backfield mate and friend.

'I think we gonna haveta close this mutha down fo' a helluva good while.'

'Good,' King said. 'Thass jus' what I wanna do.'

13

Evaluation

'Did'joo dig whut wuz happ'nin' outside?' Odds asked, as he blasted into the SGA office on the first floor of Carver Hall.

'You mean wit' there not bein' any classes an' all?' Lawman asked.

'Yeah!'

'Somethin's cookin'. Where's Earl?'

The question was no sooner out of Odds's mouth than Earl came into the front from the file room in back with a handful of papers in one hand and a cup of coffee in the other. The SGA president took a seat at his desk while Odds hung up his raincoat in the closet.

'What'choo think's happ'nin'?' Odds asked through his nose.

'Me an' Lawman wuz gettin' ready t'take a look at the deman's again an' see what kinda changes everybody is gonna go through. They havin' a faculty meetin' at ten o'clock. I tried ta see 'bout gittin' in there, but they ain' lettin' nobody in but faculty an' administrators.'

'Where the papers at?' Odds asked sitting down.

Earl pulled a folded copy of the demands out of his desk drawer. He handed the sheet to Lawman and sat back with his coffee. He looked tired and felt the same way. He had not slept well. From the looks of things neither had Odds or Lawman.

'Numero uno,' Lawman began. 'The Pride of Virginia Food Services be dismissed.'

'Relevant, man. I had a stomach ache for fo' damn years. I'll be glad to graduate jus' to git away from this grit.'

'I had taken a long look at that,' Earl said. 'The company's workin' on the third year of a three-year contrac'. When they had the boycott at the beginnin' a las' year the SGA secretary took notes at the confrontation meetin'. They said mos'ly a whole lotta bullshit. Their real source of income comes from the canteen at night. The percentage of profit from the meals iz only 'bout two per cent ... y'know it wuz the same ol' bullshit. You cain' please everybody an' ya can only prepare certain types of food for a lot of people an' ya cain' season food to suit everybody.'

'But the question is ... what is Calhoun gonna say?' Lawman asked.

'He's gonna quote from the same damn thing I been readin' an say the same shit.'

'No new food services,' Lawman deduced and put a check mark.

'Right.'

'Number two is that Gaines Harper be dismissed,' Lawman said.

'Thass tricky,' Odds said. 'Why they wanna git rid of him? 'Cuz he's a whitey or what?'

'I guess.'

'Thass prob'bly why Calhoun will turn it down. The primary student complaint against the man is that he's a drunken devil.' Earl laughed out loud. 'They tired of goin' over there an' havin' him puff cigar smoke in their face an' treatin' what they consider a serious problem as though it didn' mean shit.'

'Whuss the real charge?'

'It can't be incompetency,' Earl admitted. 'I guess it'll have to be that the man doesn't relate to the students in terms of the job that he's doin' which is s'pose to be a personal student service.'

'No new Financial Aid Officer?' Odds asked, looking over Lawman's shoulder.

'No,' Earl said.

'Three and four are new heads of the Chemistry and Language Departments respectively.'

'Accreditation,' Earl sighed. 'Everybody knows that Beaker and Ol' Royce shoulda been gone. Calhoun iz gonna rap 'bout not bein' able t'git anybody wit' the proper credentials to take their places. You have to have a Ph.D. in those departments.'

'What 'bout Phillips in Chemistry? He's a Ph.D. Why can't he take Beaker's place?'

'Thass the student argument,' Earl said. 'An' Connoly in French has at least a leg on his Ph.D. He'll have it by the time school convenes again in September . . . I mean, the people they got in here gonna haveta finish this year anyway. They may as well be plannin' on gettin' somebody for when all these oldies fall the hell out an' die.'

'The students can get numbers three an' four?' Odds asked.

'Uh-huh. Not without Calhoun rappin' a lotta shit 'bout tenure an' alla that action, but maybe.'

'Number five. The thing about the Security Service leavin' their guns an' shit in the guardhouse.'

'Yeah. Thass in the bag,' Earl said confidently.

'I'm glad somethin's in the bag,' Odds sighed.

'You thought we wuz gonna get shut out?' Earl asked laughing.

'It wuz lookin' that way.'

'Each and every one of these things coulda been worked out in time,' was Earl's comment. 'I been over damn near alla them. If we, and I mean the formal SGA, had been given time to present workable plans in terms of alla these things . . . I mean like an alternative an' a formal plan for alla these things, everything woulda been all right. Keep readin' an' I'll show you what I mean.'

'Well, six, seven, and eight would give the SGA supervision over the Student Union Building, the book store, and the Music and Art Fund.'

'Dig it. If we had drawn up statements that documented how much better for students things would have been if we controlled these things and sent copies to the alumni an' the Board of Trustees . . .'

'An' na it's too late?' Odds asked.

'Look, brother,' Earl said. 'If you can spring a sudden thing on Calhoun an' hit him where he's weak, you can git over. But every time you go after the man an' don' make it, it gives him a chance to shore up whatever spot it was you wuz after. Then you haveta try somethin' else.'

'An' by the time we git somethin' else t'gether he will have gone through changes with the alumni an' everybody to show them how wrong we are. It's jus like I tell people when they ask who'll win if we have about a week-long nuclear war with Russia: I tell 'um ain' gon' be no war like that 'cuz whoever slides a bomb on the othuh one first is gonna win. Thass all.'

There was a minute of silence while each of the three young men became involved with himself. Lawman and Odds had been at Sutton for four years and had seen demonstrations throughout their college careers. The real difference in this one was their involvement. In past years they had been just interested students hoping that something would get accomplished. This time they sat in the SGA office trying desperately to think of something that would make the dark picture of possible success shine a little brighter. Earl Thomas was in his second year at Sutton. He was a transfer student who had turned the entire Sutton political world around when he ran for SGA office and won. He had never seen much done at any of the schools he had attended. He too was searching for a clue. But aside from all that he was searching for his own particular position. He had been thoroughly fouled up by MJUMBE and still had the power to stop the train in its tracks. He didn't know what he wanted to do.

'Number nine is about the Faculty Review Committee and Interview Committee,' Lawman snorted. 'Not a chance. The faculty wouldn' give the studen's any kinda say over their jobs.'

'Shit!' Odds exclaimed. 'All this shit is dead end!'

'Whuss number ten again?' Earl asked.

'Ten is the establishing of a Black Studies Program.'

'Maybe,' Earl hedged. 'Calhoun sent Parker from the History Department to Atlanta in August for the Black Studies

Conference that they held. I don' figger the firs' year would have alla this shit in it even if we *got* some kinda phony Black Studies thing.'

'The school would have a wider appeal if we had the program,' Lawman added. 'More students would come here and we'd get more money.'

'Yeah, that's true. But you gotta find some way to git it accredited first. You also gotta have some professors who know what the hell is goin' on. Sutton ain' got but 'bout three a them.'

'What 'bout eleven?' Odds asked impatiently. 'Thass 'bout havin' everybody open their books for an auditor.'

Earl mouthed a curse. 'Man, lemme tell you. Calhoun is gonna kill this shit dead. He's gonna rap that when they had the annual report there were only about forty students there. He's gonna say if we had been there we would know where our money went. He's gonna swear up an' down that there's nothin' wrong wit' the books (which I myself believe), an' thass gonna be all. He's gonna rap 'bout professionalism an' shit like that. Then he's gonna say that the SGA has many more things to worry about an' spen' their money on.'

'Twelve is the thing about the Medical Service,' Lawman said disconsolately.

'Thass okay,' Earl said. 'All they gotta do is move some beds an' open up those two rooms in the back. They'll do that.'

'In othuh words all they're gonna do is the shit that don' make any real difference in Sutton University whether they do it or not,' Odds managed lighting a cigarette.

'Thass the point,' Earl admitted.

'An' good ol' number thirteen says: ANSWER ME BY NOON!' Lawman said with all the theatrics he could manage.

'Thass next,' Odds breathed.

'I wishta hell I could git in the faculty meetin',' Earl said.

'I wishta hell I wuz runnin' that bastard!' Lawman said.

'I wishta hell it wuz over!' Odds contributed.

'I wishta hell I wuz dreamin',' Earl said. 'All that fuckin' work down the drain.' He laughed. 'There mus' not be no God.'

14

Ten O'Clock Meeting

It was apparent to Ogden Calhoun that every member of the Sutton faculty and administrative staff had come to the scheduled meeting early. The small auditorium where lectures and forums were held in the rear of the Paul Lawrence Dunbar Library was filled at ten minutes before ten when he entered carrying the black attaché case that held all of his papers.

There had been whispered speculation all morning as to exactly what the meeting would consider. Many of the older faculty members and administrators looked on it as perhaps the close of an era; the end of the iron hand of Ogden Calhoun. Their thoughts were centered about the fact that in their memories student protest had never detoured the regular academic duties of the institution. Therefore it was quite obvious to them that Calhoun was weakening.

Calhoun himself looked upon the meeting in quite another light. In many institutions where he had visited for various conferences and meetings he had been told by the presidents that student dissent had not only polarized the administration and students, but the administrators and faculty as well. The net result in these instances had been mergers between all three groups. The faculties on many campuses did not want to be identified with the students, but neither did they want to be considered a part of the administration. The real truth was that most college professors wanted the right to choose whatever side they wanted and make no statement at all on behalf of 'the faculty.'

Calhoun did not need another wedge driven between the administrative position and anyone else. The purpose of this meeting was to enable him to identify any members of the faculty who might be easily drawn to the students' side of the fence and make damaging remarks about whatever stand he took. He had seen the first glimmer of this sort of conflict during the outburst by Arnold McNeil at his home on the night before. In Calhoun's eyes McNeil was not a man from whom he needed any particular trouble. Not only was the man a leading American historian, but he had considerable influence among the younger members of the Sutton faculty, both Black and white.

Calhoun waved and nodded as he passed down the right-hand aisle to the small platform at the head of the meeting room. Miss Felch, looking a bit more herself, smiled as he stepped up and informed him that she had coffee coming.

Fenton Mercer walked up to the platform. His pudgy face was a mask of worry that even his thirty-two teeth could not destroy. He was perspiring freely and batting his eyes furiously as sweat seeped into the corners of his eyes beneath the thick-framed glasses. Calhoun was sitting on a cushioned seat trying to light his pipe.

'How are you?' Calhoun greeted the vice-president cheerfully.

'I'm, uh, fine,' Mercer smiled. 'Is, uh, everything in order?'

'Everything's always in order 'roun' here, isn't it, Miss Felch?'

'Yes, sir,' Miss Felch said as though she had not even heard the question.

'Is everything in order with you?' Calhoun asked, laughing perhaps a bit too loudly.

'I've, uh, just been receiving quite a few calls is all,' Mercer said. 'Y'know, mos'ly from parents here in Sutton whose sons an' daughters came to school t'day an' found out there were no classes.'

'Well, classes will resume right after our meeting,' Calhoun assured his right-hand executive. 'I would've waited until tonight to call the meeting but everyone was so insistent that their voice be heard last night ... well, I mean it wouldn't have been fair for me to come out with an administrative decision if all of the administrators weren't up-to-date on the issues.'

'There will be classes this afternoon?' Mercer asked.

'Certainly. The "*re-quests*" asked for a reply by noon. I'm sure this meeting will be over by then and I can respond to the paper ... Miss Felch, did you get copies of this form passed out?'

'They were run off first thing this morning,' Miss Felch said. 'Mr McNeil was passing them out ... oh, here's your coffee.' A student set two cups of coffee down on the desk in front of Miss Felch. Calhoun scanned the room. He saw McNeil in the rear of the auditorium smiling at Miss Anderson from the Women's Phys. Ed. department and handing her a copy of the student requests.

'Did you put those security guards in front of the door?' Mercer asked Calhoun.

'Yes. I put them there,' Calhoun said, lowering his voice as Mercer had. 'Why?'

'You know that that was a part of the student ...'

'I know,' Calhoun said with a smirk. 'But there are things that are going to be discussed in here pertaining to that question. It hasn't been decided yet what will be done about the security force. This is not an *open* faculty-administration meeting. Some of them are and this one isn't.'

'There have been students out there trying to get in,' Mercer said worriedly.

'That's why the damn guard is out there! I knew there would be some there trying to get in.'

Calhoun straightened his tie and cleared his throat. He pulled a corner of the gray kerchief in his breast pocket up a bit higher. The pipe had gone out again so he pulled out a silver lighter to set fire to the cherry tobacco. The teachers and administrators were finding their way to their seats.

'Before I begin to deal with the reason this meeting has been called,' Calhoun began, 'I'd like to apologize to the members of the faculty who were asking questions about why we were having the meeting during their class time and not tonight. The reason has been passed out to you and I speak directly now to the thirteenth point on this paper. It is very clear that some of our more impatient students sought an answer to these questions immediately and therefore a general meeting was in order. I was tempted last night when Mr Earl Thomas brought these demands to my home – and make no mistake about the fact that they are *demands* – to give an immediate answer to all of them by folding them up and tossing them in the garbage can. I am not a man who likes to be threatened. I'm sure we all feel that way. And there's a certain air of contempt involved when a student comes to you and *demands this* or *demands that* ... I put down my first impulse. I tried to talk to Mr Thomas about these issues on a man-to-man basis, but he seemed to be in quite a hurry at the time. The only thing I could do at that time was to try and call in a few of you and speak quite frankly about the issues that are raised here. During our midnight meeting last night – which might be why so many of us look like we can't open our eyes this morning – we decided that it would be best to call a meeting among all of us and discuss these things and come up with an answer on each and every one of them for the students.' Calhoun paused to sip some of the steaming coffee.

'What I would briefly like to do is go over these questions one by one and give you the administrative point of view in some sort of detail so that all of *our* cards will be on the table. If there are any questions that come up, please hold them until later after everything has been done ... just write them down and we'll have plenty of time for questions.'

Calhoun paused to finish his coffee. 'Now, under number one, if everyone will read along, they have: "the Pride of Virginia Food Services be dismissed." This is by no means the first complaint that we have had against the Food Services and each and every time we have heard a complaint we have called in Mr Morgan from the service to have certain things clarified. The last time this happened, if you will recall, was during Homecoming last year when students started throwing their trays in the cafeteria. I, uh, sent out a piece of literature on that to all the parents. It said, in effect, that for the money the students are paying here they are receiving the best, most professional food service possible. I have no further information regarding just why this issue has been raised again. When I speak with Mr Thomas at noon I will ask him if the established Student Government Food Committee would not like to have another meeting with Mr Morgan about the food.

'Numbers two, three, and four should all be handled in the same light as far as I'm concerned. There are several things that have directly to do with students, such as the food. The hiring and firing of members of the faculty and administrators is strictly *not* a student matter. If enough complaints are launched against a particular faculty member as was the case two years ago when we had to let Mr Carruthers go, then naturally the institution has to do something. But until we are given further information . . .' Calhoun paused. 'I hope you understand that the main point of irritation that I feel about *all* of these demands is that there is obviously a breakdown in communication somewhere. The students are not giving us any of the real information that we need to deal with these things. Uh, yes, so in reference to two, three, and four nothing will be done until students have given us more to work with than this statement here.'

Gaines Harper was sitting in the last row. When Calhoun stated flatly that he would not be dismissed, the Financial Aid Officer wiped his sweating face with a damp handkerchief and managed to light a cigarette.

Harper was his usual disheveled self. The dark blue suit was hanging at an angle from his neck and looked as though it had been slept in. He smelled like a brewery and was sitting in the last row in the hope that the heavy beer odor would not be noticed by any of the others present.

Professor Beaker and Professor Royce said nothing. They

had been friends of Calhoun's throughout his tenure as university president. Royce started taking notes when Calhoun had concluded points two, three, and four. He had something important that he wanted to say.

'Now, point five is another thing that has just been thrown in front of me.' Calhoun accentuated the word 'thrown' by tossing his list of demands onto the desk in front of himself. 'I wasn't really aware of all the ins and outs of the security routine if you understand me. When I received this note I made sure to set up a talk with Captain Jones this morning and we discussed things. I think that both of us had pretty much the same thing in mind. All of our guards are Black men and the students are all involved in this Blackness program. We felt that considering this it would be clear that a guard making his rounds is looking for thieves and people who are doing things to endanger university property or university people. However, it was agreed that the guards will leave their weapons inside the guardhouse from now on. It seems like splitting hairs to me,' the president added a bit sarcastically.

'Have you got everything, Miss Felch?' Calhoun asked. 'Good ... for points six, seven, and eight it should be clear that these particular problems would take a lot of legislating and reapportioning of funds. I spoke with Mr Calder, the Comptroller, this morning and we agreed that at this time it is very hard to imagine the Student Government taking on these new responsibilities which call for the proper handling of thousands of dollars when the SGA meetings are scarcely attended and the entire burden is being carried by a very few.

'Number nine is a reasonable idea,' Calhoun said as though reading it for the first time and talking to himself. He was peering a bit quizzically over the top of his glasses at his audience. The atmosphere of the room was hushed and was becoming more so with the reading and response to each point. 'Number nine is the suggestion for a Faculty Review Committee and Faculty Interview Committee. The one thing that is quite obviously in need of restating is the part that excludes Professor Beaker and Professor Royce from this committee. I would suggest that this committee consist of the heads of departments, a student representative from each class, and an administrator who could be named at a later date. I would further suggest that the committee meetings start in December so that we can have some idea of its finding by the end of the first semester.'

Calhoun stopped his monologue at that time to try and light his pipe. Miss Felch used the time to erase notes and catch up with the points that had been handled. Those attending the meeting used the time to whisper back and forth to one another. Gaines Harper got up and left, heading for the Mine, a bar that he frequently visited. He had heard enough. He was going to have a drink and go home. He felt slimy; in spite of the brisk October day his clothes were soaked with nervous perspiration.

'All of us know about the things that were covered in reference to a Black Studies Institute. True, schools are adopting a program of this nature all over the country, but we at Sutton will not be ready until we can have all of the classes accredited. I will suggest a series of lectures to start later on in this semester by visiting lecturers in this field. This can be done on a twice-a-week basis and enter our files as a course. However, it will not in any way fulfill the requirements for graduation under any heading. There will be a report in November about the progress that has been made in establishing a Black Studies Institute here next year. I mean, uh, next September.' Calhoun turned several sheets that he had placed in front of himself. He placed his pipe down in an ashtray.

'Point eleven goes back to points two, three, and four as far as I'm concerned,' he said as though he were bored. 'I would *never*, and I do mean *never*, ask any of these people to do the things requested on this page. I'm quite sure that performing their duties is job enough and that the state auditors who come in here check on things quite sufficiently.

'As far as point twelve is concerned, both Dr Maxwell and

Dr Caldwell agree that if we clear out the two back rooms and realign our stock with a couple of larger cabinets we will be equipped to treat members of the community. I would like to remind everyone that our medical staff has never refused to serve anyone in this area and that most of the community people with the exception of those people who work here at Sutton, all go to the Community General Hospital.

'Are there any questions?' Calhoun asked. He pulled a tan leather pouch from his inside pocket and started to refill his pipe.

'I'd like to know why there was a deadline on these papers,' Professor Ingram of Psychology asked. He was a small, balding man in a gray suit.

'From my talk with Mr Thomas last night I must admit that I don't have the vaguest idea what will be done when I respond ...'

Calhoun was interrupted by Gaines Harper who reentered the small auditorium practically on the run and came down the middle aisle to the platform waving his hand.

'S'cuse me,' Calhoun said quickly and got up.

'Uh, there's a reporter outside from the *Norfolk News*,' Harper whispered breathlessly. 'He was wondering what time the statement was going to be made to the press. I didn't know anything about it but he said there's reporters here from everywhere.'

Calhoun looked out through the partially open entrance to the meeting hall, but he could see nothing except the back of the uniformed security guard on duty. The faculty and others in the room were buzzing noisily.

'Are there any more questions?' Calhoun asked in a voice to discourage questions. 'If not,' he hurried on, 'I will be interested in meeting all department heads in my office in about fifteen minutes. I have something to check on.'

No one said anything, but no one made any real effort to leave.

'I want you to be in my office too, Miss Felch,' Calhoun said.

There was still no movement from the crowd in the pews. Calhoun picked up his coat and marched through them with a breathless Gaines Harper hurrying behind him.

15
Captain Cool

The young man coming down the stairs from the main lobby of the Student Union Building was in a hurry. He was dressed in black trousers, gold corduroy dashiki, and gold-framed sunglasses. His hair was bushy and natural with a part on the left side. He was almost six feet tall and weighed about one hundred seventy pounds. He had a smooth, caramel complexion and unlike his counterparts from MJUMBE wore no beard or mustache. He was called Captain Cool, but his name was Abul Menka.

When Abul Menka had first joined the Sutton University community he had gone through a great many changes. The majority of the students at Sutton were from the South and had very little to do with New Yorkers; especially New Yorkers who were so firmly aloof from the things that went on at Sutton. The majority of Abul's time had been spent drinking Mother Vineyard's Scuppernong and smoking reefers that he brought back from his frequent trips to New York.

As a freshman Abul had had absolutely no ties to anything, political or otherwise. He had a girl at Howard in Washington and a girl at Morgan State in Baltimore. On weekends he was to be found on either one of those campuses or back in New York. But as a sophomore he decided to pledge for the Omega Psi Phi fraternity. He made the move for several reasons. The first was that his uncle, who was financing his college career, was a 'Q.' The second was that on Sutton's campus and every campus Abul visited the women were 'Q crazy.'

The pledge period lasted a little over two months. During that time Abul was not allowed to use his car for anything other than errands run for his fraternity brothers. This eliminated his runs to Morgan and Howard. It also brought him into some standing within the Sutton community. He had never warmed up to anyone except for a few girls he had tried to take to bed. But after he became a member of the fraternity his coolness was attributed to being a 'cool Q' rather than a cold individual.

Six others were on the line with him when he 'went over' and became a member of the fraternity. Five of them were members of the present campus organization called MJUMBE. The other had graduated.

The reason for Abul's hurry at the moment was related to his involvement with MJUMBE. He had just finished running off fifteen hundred copies of a proclamation from MJUMBE. He was rushing to the fraternity meeting room where he had an eleven o'clock appointment with the group.

There was no doubt about the things that were happening to him because of MJUMBE's coup. People had spoken to him in the past twelve hours or so who hadn't seemed to even look in his direction before. He was thinking materialistically that the political thing he was doing would be another stepping stone for his rap.

There was nothing wrong with Abul's ability to hold a conversation with women. His major concern at the moment was the progress that had been made by the other members of the five-man committee. As he walked around the oval he saw several things that made him believe that the day before had not been wasted. One was a car that was parked in front of the Paul Lawrence Dunbar Library with the words *NORFOLK NEWS* stenciled across the left-hand door. A weasely looking whitey sat in the front seat eating a ham sandwich. There was also the sight of Ogden Calhoun and Gaines Harper turning into Sutton Hall, the administration building, damn near on the run. There was also the campus-wide news that no classes had been scheduled for the morning hours.

'Glad ta see da massuh up an' movin' 'bout so early dis mawnin',' Abul mimicked, chuckling.

A bit of nervous tension was growing at the base of his

spine. He supposed that everyone involved felt the same way now. For Abul the feeling was very new. He was a master at picking spots where he felt most comfortable and uninvolved, but the political situation intrigued him. He was a student of Black history and was fascinated by the way in which power continually shifted from one pole to another and from one party to another, Democratic or Republican, and yet people who were the victims of one administration managed to gain absolutely nothing from the installation of a new regime. The same sort of political showdown which could be viewed nationally at election time was emerging at Sutton. Nothing had ever been gained from the use of student power because the wishes of the students were rarely followed. The requests were an indication that the student form of protest was about to take another road just as the protests of minority and disadvantaged groups were taking a different form everywhere. On some campuses, such as Berkeley, Abul could understand a comparison with New York City where there always seemed to be a strike or some kind of disorder. Students on these campuses had damn near over-demonstrated and the real reason for attending a college in the first place was lost. That was not the feeling on Sutton's campus. Everyone felt the mounting tension. Abul and the members of MJUMBE felt it more so, Abul decided, because they knew what the next step would be if Calhoun and his bunch of black and white flunkies didn't have their stuff together by noon. Most of the students were uneasy because they didn't know what to expect either from MJUMBE or Calhoun, but many had the feeling that Baker and his group were headed for the highway.

'We'll see who's headed where,' Abul muttered.

Under his arm the tall MJUMBE chieftain was carrying mimeographed sheets. He only hoped that the ink had dried sufficiently so as not to blur or stain the printed words. Abul was particularly proud of this paper because he had written it himself before Baker showed up. All Ralph had done was take a look at it and okay it.

As he neared the fraternity house he thought about Earl Thomas and MJUMBE's move to take over the functions of the SGA. He had been waiting to see what Earl Thomas was going to do the night before in the meeting room. Earl had done and said nothing. Maybe they had had Earl in more of a bind than was apparent. Abul knew that anything Earl might have said to discredit him, Abul, could have been denied, but the point was that he hadn't had to deny anything.

His thoughts returned to the paper he had under his arm:

TO ALL FACULTY MEMBERS AND ADMINISTRATORS

The thirteen demands that were submitted to President Calhoun by the Sutton student body were pleas for necessities long overdue. Sutton University, once a leading Black institution, has fallen far behind in every respect. The reason has been the administration's unbending, inflexible position in terms of the needs of the students who must, for nine months out of each year, call Sutton University their *home*. It has been the understanding of the students that college was a place where one learned to deal with life as a man or a woman must upon leaving the institution for the last time. Sutton students are now prepared when they leave to accomplish the same things their parents were able to do – or less. The reason is the fast pace that one is forced to live with inside this rapidly changing society.

For years Sutton students have been good niggers, waiting and hoping that the bare essentials they have requested would be granted them by the administrative powers that be. They have, for the betterment of the community, chosen all except disruptive patterns of revealing their needs by working through the system. All of this has been to no avail. Sutton University continues to sink 'grain by grain.'

110 | The Nigger Factory

The demands that have been submitted may appear at first glance to be dramatic and hasty, thoughtless proposals. On second glance and a look at the Sutton history of students' requests, however, one will realize that these are the same types of things that students have been after for twelve years here.

Students on Sutton's campus have been asking for three years that the Pride of Virginia Food Services, Inc. use a meal ticket system that will give students an option over whether or not they pay for the slop that is served each and every day. The Food Service has refused because they know that a majority of students would not touch that poison a majority of the time.

Gaines Harper is a man whose professional qualifications are questionable. We feel him to be absolutely incapable of sharing the personal confidences finance-wise of the Black students on these premises.

Professors Beaker and Royce are both past retirement age. They are fine individuals for whom students have high respect. The problem is that their methods of conveying the subject matter are archaic and in this modern world students cannot plunge into society ill-equipped to face the challenge of competition that awaits them.

The Security Service guards have been known to drink while on duty and there is a student committee investigating the relevance of their role at Sutton. In the interim period we cannot allow a man without all of his wits about him to walk among us with a gun on his hip.

The Student Union Building, book store, and Music and Art Fund all need to be under the auspices of the SGA. The monies from these departments go now into the pockets of Pride of Virginia (for the canteen), Educational Assistance (books), and the Music and Art Fund, which seems to be tossing its student monies down into a bottomless pit for the amount of pleasure students receive from the artists they hire. The need within the student body for more jobs which could be supplied in the canteen and book store, and for better entertainment due to our geographic location, is obvious. The need is also immediate.

The Faculty Review Committee and Faculty Interview Committee were originally proposed by Mr McNeil of the history department. They were not intended to frighten members of the faculty. The saying goes, 'The guilty fleeth when no man pursueth,' and it is true here. The question was raised often about student academic apathy. The answer can only be discovered in more and better communication between students and faculty members. Too often faculty members get the guided tour of Sutton, seeing only what the administration wants them to see, and then sign a contract that becomes an unpleasant situation for both faculty member and student. The Faculty Interview Committee would attempt to avoid this and the Review Committee would keep those who become sluggish and lackadaisical about their duties on their toes. The ideal situation in both cases would liven Sutton professionally and academically.

A Black Studies Institute is essential. This is a time in this country where a Black man or woman cannot afford to bypass the quantities of information that are suddenly available about themselves. Too long now Black people have been forced to carve an image out of rock in order to survive and lead a successful life. Too often also Black people have been forced to copy the white man's life style and this both frustrates and kills the Blackness and beauty within him. Black Studies would teach us about ourselves and give us a direction that we have never had before.

Seniors have been graduating for years from Sutton having spent over ten thousand dollars during their college careers with very little idea of what happened to the money. The administration has been playing too many word games when asked serious questions about the whereabouts of X amount of dollars. The word games consist of things like 'general fund' and 'student activity fund' and 'community fund.' People have not asked for a cent of their money back. They have asked to see where in hell it went. This should entail a dollar-by-dollar description if necessary because it is *their* money. Once again we say: 'The guilty fleeth when no man pursueth.' There are state *legislators* and *Congressmen* who are required to give detailed accounts of their monies. This is what we want. Proof that our money is being put toward the best possible end.

The community surrounding Sutton's campus is Black. The people there are poor people who need medical services that at times they cannot afford. We ask that our services be available to them and that this point be publicized so that the Black people will never be in doubt as to whether or not medicine and aid are available to them.

Abul had to curb a smile of pleasure when he thought about the diplomatic job he had done in the statement. There was very little fault to be found. Even the last lines had been written in good taste:

We are not here to protest or demonstrate or discontinue the academic routine of the university, but there comes a time when men must be men and women must be women. We feel that if we cannot receive the respect that we believe men and women deserve, then we must take this respect 'by any means necessary.'

* * *

Abul took the fraternity steps two at a time. MJUMBE had a scheduled meeting at eleven. He did not intend to be late.

16
Executive Conference

Ogden Calhoun was raging into the receiver. 'Well, why in hell didn't you call me, Miller, if you were so goddamn hard up for something t'print in that rag sheet? Why didn't you call me an' ask for a story? . . . huh? I don't care if you weren't there last night. The man didn't leave 'til this morning an' you were there then!'

The harried president of Sutton had never gotten as far as taking off his coat before he was on the phone speaking to the editor of the Norfolk newspaper. Gaines Harper sat in the chair across from Calhoun with sweat pouring off his face and his breath shouting up from his lungs in fiery gasps. The fat Financial Aid Officer was in no shape to chase Calhoun around.

'Well, when he calls in you be sure that he gets up here to get my side of the story before you print. You hear me? . . . all right! Yeah. Well . . . I wasn't having any trouble until somebody saw your man. I still don't have much. I just don't want or need any of my people panicking an' shooting off their mouths. I'd have trustees down here going through their bullshit . . . well, I'll talk to you!' Calhoun slammed the phone down.

'He said he was going to call me, but the night editor sent a man down here last night because everybody else was sending somebody down here. You know them newspaper guys. Nobody wants to do any real work, but nobody wants to get scooped either.'

'You mean there's more down here?' Harper asked in a gasp.

'He said AP an' UPI and some more . . .' Calhoun pressed his intercom button down. 'Miss Felch?' There was no answer.

'She probably didn't get over here yet,' Harper choked.

'Right.' Calhoun dialed a three-digit number. 'Miss Charles?' he said in a syrupy voice. 'Miss Felch hasn't come in yet and I am in desperate need of a cup of coffee and the morning paper. Do you ... Thank you.'

Calhoun took off his coat and gloves. He hung the coat in the corner closet and sat down again in the leather high-back chair leaning against a large window overlooking the oval.

'I don't have any idea what Thomas is doing,' he admitted. 'I know he'll be in trouble once I find out.'

'This doesn't change anything, does it?' Harper asked.

'Not for me,' Calhoun grunted. 'Not until I get some more information about exactly what's going on.'

Miss Charles, a young honey-blonde from Fenton Mercer's office, came in with a copy of the morning paper. She gave both Calhoun and Harper a dazzling smile.

'The coffee'll be ready in a moment,' she said in a soft Southern drawl.

'Good!'

'Here's the paper. How're you Mr Harpuh? I so seldom get to see you.'

'I'm fine,' Harper lied.

'Back in a minute,' she said, starting to leave.

Fenton Mercer almost ran her down coming in as she was exiting.

'Excuse me, Miss Charles,' Mercer said. 'I was just looking for you.'

'I was gettin' coffee for Mr Calhoun.'

'Good. Would you get me a cup too? Good and strong,' he grinned his business grin.

Miss Charles managed to get out at last.

'I see ...'

'We saw,' Calhoun muttered drily. 'I s'pose each an' every one here has seen by now.'

'Well, everybody saw them parked there when they came out of the meeting,' Mercer supplied.

'Where's Miss Felch?'

'She's comin',' Mercer said. 'There's some more information coming from the meeting you left. I think it would be best if I let the department heads tell you.'

'All right. Where are they?'

'Coming.' Mercer began thumbing his way through the morning paper.

'We'll need some more chairs,' Calhoun observed. 'Gaines . . .'

'I'll get them.'

'They're in the closet out front.'

The various department heads came in at that moment. Beaker agreed to help Harper get the chairs while the others stood around. Calhoun was nervous about what he might hear from the faculty, but he said nothing.

Before everyone was seated Miss Felch came in with her pad and pen. Miss Charles also returned with two cups of black, steaming coffee.

When everyone was seated Calhoun cleared his throat to begin. He stopped himself:

'Where's McNeil?' he asked.

'He's not coming,' Marcus from Political Science said quietly.

'Not coming! I asked all department heads to be here!'

'We took a sort of quorum in the auditorium,' Nash from the Music Department said finally. 'I suggested that since we all knew the issues that we make things simpler by not really having a meeting here. I suggested that we simply give you our approval.'

'That was when McNeil said he was leaving,' Marcus said, barely above a whisper.

'I'll be damn!' Calhoun muttered. The meeting was over.

17

High Noon

Isaac Spurryman of the *Norfolk News* was the first reporter in the crowd to see Ogden Calhoun appear at the front door of Sutton Hall. He broke away from the small huddle of reporters who were comparing notes near the steps and tried to enter the building. He was cut off by the president's secretary, Irene Felch, who opened the door and squeezed her narrow frame through.

With the secretary's appearance the group of photographers and reporters scrambled closer and the buzzing from the group of gathering students subsided.

'The president will be out momentarily,' Miss Felch said as loudly as she could. 'We're waiting for a microphone to be brought over from the Music Department.'

'May be waitin' all day,' a student snorted.

'Will the president be holding a question-and-answer session?' reporter Spurryman asked.

'I have no idea,' Miss Felch said. 'I don't really know what he'll be saying . . . I would imagine that if he held one it wouldn't be here.' She tossed an expression of disdain toward the milling students.

Spurryman nodded and walked away with his head buried in his note pad. There were students at the base of the walk carrying three wooden platforms that they sat on top of each other. A small, sturdy-looking podium sat in the middle of the make-shift platform. The students nodded at each other and then moved off.

'Ike?' Spurryman heard his name called and looked up to see Arnold McNeil wading through the crowd toward him.

'How are you, Neil?' Spurryman asked as they shook hands. 'You look like you've had it.'

'Hot,' McNeil said, consulting his watch and attempting a smile. 'How have you been?'

'Fine. Everybody's fine,' the reporter said. 'How's Millie?'

'Good. She's expecting!'

'I'll be goddamned!' Spurryman said. He looked around for a second before continuing. 'You old sonuvabitch! I'll tell ya. Drinks on me after I knock this off.' He nodded toward the still-closed door.

'Nothin' said so far?'

'Naw. Calhoun's secretary came out an' said he'll make a statement when a mike gets here.'

'What're *you* doin' out here?' McNeil asked. 'You're a front-page man most of the time.'

'Well, I'll tell ya. We had a policy of either ignorin' these student things or sendin' cubs out to cover them. I guess we went through that for nearly three years. We got burnt a couple of times though. We got burnt bad at Virginia Union. They had tipped us off about a thing an' we didn't check it. When the damn place had to close we weren't even informed enough to do anything for ten hours.'

'So now you check everything?' McNeil asked smiling tightly.

'Well, the desk got a call las' night. Emple called UPI and AP an' they said they were sending people ... what's it all about?'

'The students supplied a list of demands an' turned them over to Calhoun ...'

'What were the demands?' Spurryman asked poising his pen.

'Haven't any students been over to talk to you all?'

'Not a soul. Well, maybe I jus' didn't see them. They here?'

'I don't see ... Wait! You see the tall one next to the tree over there?' McNeil pointed through a cluster of students to a six-footer with a thick head of hair who was talking confidentially to two companions.

'Uh-huh.'

'His name is Earl Thomas,' McNeil confided. 'He's the head of the SGA. You could ask him. He's the one who gave the demands to Calhoun.'

'O.K.' the reporter agreed. 'Where will you be? I'm serious about that drink.'

'Good, I'll need it. I'll be right here afterward.'

Spurryman waved and drifted away through the crowd. He found himself approaching Earl at the same time as a number of others. Two of them were reporters. The others were students.

'Mr Thomas,' he began, 'I'm Ike Spurryman of the *Norfolk News*. I was wondering if I could ask a few questions.'

Earl looked up curiously. 'I don' really have anything t'say right now.'

'I'd just like to ask you about what your demands were an' what you are expecting from President Calhoun.'

'There are thirteen deman's an' we are expecting Mr Calhoun to comply.'

'What are the thirteen demands?' a reporter asked.

'I don't have a copy with me,' Earl said. 'I hadn't planned to deal with the press. I'm sure Mr Calhoun will give everyone a copy.'

'Do you have any idea who called the press if it wasn't a representative from your office?' Spurryman asked still writing.

'The student body was informed of the deman's yesterday afternoon so it could've been any student or faculty member.' Earl knew who had notified the press.

'What time yesterday?'

'About four thirty.'

'And when were the demands served on the president?'

'About ten last night.'

'Did the demands call for a statement today?'

'It called for a statement today at noon.'

'Any particular reason?' someone quizzed.

'I suppose noon is the best time because mosta the studen's are not in class as you can see. We knew everyone would be anxious to hear for themselves.'

'Testing. Testing. One-two-three-four-five. Testing,' a voice cut through. A white youngster with long, dirty hair was speaking into a round, mesh microphone that had been set up next to the podium.

The microphone testing attracted the attention of the crowd. It also brought Ogden Calhoun into view. The president strode purposefully through the reporters and students who stood between the administration door and the makeshift platform. His glasses were in place and he held several sheaves of notes in his hands. Several reporters attempted to stop him for comment, but he only shook his head 'no' and kept right on going. Flash-bulbs were fired at him. Miss Felch and Fenton Mercer walked right alongside him.

The crowd continued its murmuring even after the president stepped up onto the stand. The reporters who had been clustered around Earl edged closer to the hastily prepared stage. Students who had been laughing and talking among themselves from the sidewalk across the street ignored the possibility that they might be hit by cars driving around the oval. They left the opposite sidewalk that circled the huge Sutton flower bed and walked into the road blocking off traffic.

Calhoun had imagined that there would be quite a few students present, but the gathering before him seemed to simply go on and on. He wondered for a second if he shouldn't have called the meeting in the large auditorium. Clearly every member of the student body and faculty was there.

'Members of the community,' Calhoun began, 'I was asked by what I shall refer to as a list of "intimidating *requests*" to respond to these *requests* by noon today and here I am. I want to speak directly to the issues, but before I do I want to say a few words to the students in the community and particularly to those students who find themselves in leadership positions.

There are certain channels of communication established on Sutton's campus through which problems that bother students can be handily dealt with. I refer now to the committees on which both students and faculty are members. I refer now to the Board of Trustees and members of the administrative staff. These channels are present because everyone realizes that within all institutions there are needs that must be met. They are there because we all realize that neither students nor faculty members nor administrators have all the answers. May I also add here that none of these groups has all of the problems. A problem of one member of the community is a problem of all. If one is to deal with a problem one must be made aware of its existence. There are certain ways to make others aware of an existing problem. This particular way *can* be used but at times it serves to cause another problem if not considered carefully. I refer now to the fact that these particular *demands* (not requests) were given me last evening at ten o'clock. The last point on the page was that I respond by noon.

'This can be construed as little other than a threat. My first reaction was to throw the entire list into the garbage can. Let it suffice to say that there are proper channels that are available to us all. Let us use them ...' Calhoun paused and looked around. There could be little doubt that the atmosphere had changed during the president's opening remarks. An unmistakable tension was becoming evident.

For the first time Earl noticed the gold-trimmed black dashikis circulating through the crowd. Fred Jones walked directly in front of him and handed a card to reporter Isaac Spurryman. Other members of the press were being handed these cards by Speedy Cotton and Ben King.

'Somethin's up,' Odds whispered.

'Git a look at one a' those cards,' Earl said.

'Better let me,' Lawman said. He moved over until he was directly behind the Norfolk reporter.

Calhoun's voice could be heard as he continued discussing the students' demands.

'Point number one relates to having the Pride of Virginia Food Services dismissed. We are directing Mr Morgan of the Food Services to make himself available for another meeting with the established Student Government Association Food Services Committee.

'Number two is a demand that Gaines Harper, present Financial Aid Officer, be dismissed. The administration is responsible for the hiring and firing of its staff. That includes administrative personnel and faculty members. When evidence is presented that indicates a necessary change, we make it. No such evidence has been placed at our disposal. Mr Harper will not be dismissed.

'Numbers three and four require that the heads of our Chemistry and Language Departments be dismissed. I, uh, will remind everyone present of an organization called the Southeast Accreditation Association which is in charge of accrediting all colleges so that degrees received from these institutions will be valid. This in itself is enough to make it impossible for us to dismiss Dr Beaker and Dr Royce. In addition, the issue about a lack of formal complaints holds true here also.

'Number five demands that the Security Service be forced to leave all weapons – clubs, guns, and so forth – inside the guardhouse while making their rounds. We consider it regrettable that our own community members do not realize the importance of our guards, who carry arms to protect our people and property, but we have talked to Captain Jones and he agrees to have his men leave their arms in the guardhouse.'

'Did'joo git a look at the card?' Earl asked Lawman.

'Yeah. I tol' this cat I was a member of *The Statesman*'s staff who had obviously been overlooked. The card sez that there's gonna be a student meeting in the large auditorium right after this one.'

'Izzat all it sez?'

'What else?'

'Does it say why or anything?'

'No. It doesn't.' Lawman turned away toward the droning Calhoun who continued to read from his notes. He was turning down the suggestions that the various Sutton departments – Student Union Building, book store, and Art Fund – be placed under student control.

'Whatta y' think?' Lawman mumbled.

'Can't say,' Earl admitted, looking around. 'I haven't seen Baker or Abul.'

'Thass a dangerous bastard,' Odds said. 'Abul Menka, I mean . . . Baker too, but . . .'

'I feel the same way,' Lawman said, reaching across Earl to shake Odds's hand in agreement.

'Number nine,' Calhoun was saying, 'indicates that we should establish a Faculty Review Committee and a Faculty Interview Committee. I have suggested that these committees be established and that they consist of the heads of the departments, or a faculty member from each department, a student representative from each class, and an administrator. The specific people can be named when we hold our next faculty meeting.'

There was a murmur rippling through the crowd at this announcement. Even Earl and Odds had to exchange pleasantly surprised glances that turned into weak smiles.

'That wudn't the whole deal,' Lawman reminded them.

'It's more'n I expected,' Odds said.

Calhoun completed his speech by mentioning the series of lectures he was establishing in order to supplement the curriculum until a meaningful Black Studies program could be instituted. He raised his voice in dismay when commenting on the request that certain administrators' books be audited by students, and he concluded the session by reporting that he had conferred with the Sutton medical staff and that the suggested changes would be instituted.

'As for this morning's missed classes,' Calhoun said, handing Miss Felch his notes, 'there was nothing that could be done to avoid it. This afternoon's classes will be held . . . I would stop at this time for questions and answers, but since it is almost time for classes to resume I will schedule a university assembly for later in the week when I can handle these questions and answers from the community. I will meet the press in my office directly after this for their questions. They will be given duplicate copies of the demands.'

There were a few raised hands, but Calhoun turned quickly from his audience and followed closely by Miss Felch and Fenton Mercer he strode back down the walkway and into Sutton Hall.

The whitey with the long, dirty hair started to take the microphone down. As he did the students who had assembled the makeshift platform gathered to take it down.

It was then that Ben King stepped onto the impromptu stage and facing the far corner of the oval raised both fists. The next instant brought the echoing ring of the auditorium bell. This was the traditional signal for a university assembly. Before Earl and his two comrades were able to comment on Calhoun's hasty departure, King, Cotton, and Jonesy were double-timing across the path that split the oval.

'MJUMBE is at least a *little* organized,' Odds said drily.

'They run good,' Lawman said laughing.

The auditorium bell continued to hammer away. The student body was drifting toward the meeting. Faculty members could be seen gathering in small apprehensive clusters. Reporters were comparing notes and asking one another which way they should go. Earl Thomas was asking himself that same question.

18

MJUMBE Mandate

It was a typical early autumn day for southern Virginia. The temperature was in the mid-fifties. A breeze kicked the colored leaves closer to the curb and across the oval. The residents were dressed in sweaters and light jackets. The sun watched from a sky decorated with whipped-cream clouds that floated south with the wind.

The weather was not the reason Earl Thomas was fastening the top button on his light safari jacket. He was chilled with the prospect of being put on the spot at the meeting ahead of him. Each thump of the hollow bell in the auditorium chapel seemed to bang equally hard at the pit of his stomach.

He paused at the auditorium entrance and lit a cigarette. Ben King handed him a copy of a statement from MJUMBE and a copy of *The Sutton Statesman* which this afternoon was a one-page special that carried a picture of the five MJUMBE chieftains as they had appeared the day before. There was a larger picture of Earl himself. The two articles on the page were both editorials of a sort. One had been written by Ralph Baker. The other was signed by Victor Johnson.

The three entrances to the auditorium were being manned by King, Jonesy, and Cotton. As students or faculty entered they were handed the MJUMBE statement and *The Statesman* special edition.

'Let's skip to the john,' Earl said, nudging Odds.

The three men entered the lobby and cut right, crossing in front of congregating students until they reached the southern corner where they turned downstairs to the lounge area and rest rooms.

'Bone up,' Earl muttered once inside the lavatory. He banged the pages across the palm of his hand.

'Gittin' tighter,' Odds noted, making a choking gesture. 'Ya know what this indicates, don'choo? This sez right here, this picture, that you are down wit' MJUMBE.'

'Iss almos' too hip to be anywhere near Ben King,' Lawman said. 'I have dug the whole damn thing an' there's not one word about you. The whole implication stems from the picture.'

'I wasn't even thinkin' las' night when I saw Johnson. I wuz damn sure the paper wuz gonna knock me an' give me a free opportunity to say anything that I wanted.'

'You still can,' Odds snapped. 'Shit! You didn' call this meetin' or the one yesterday. This ain' rilly got nuthin' to do wit' you or your office.'

'I know ...'

'But nuthin'. All you gotta do is say what you feel, man. You won the election. You still in a helluva good position.'

'Say what I feel where? Here? I didn' call this meetin', you say? Then what gives me a right to speak?'

'You the Man! You the Head Man! If you see the studen's headed in the wrong direction you haveta speak up!'

'What direction do you think they're goin' in?'

'No direction yet.'

'Right. But Baker's gonna play on emotions. If he directs them through this emotion they will not be ready to hear from me.'

There was a loud feedback screech from the level directly above the three men. Another man entered the washroom. Lawman signaled his companions to exit. Out in the hall at the bottom of the stairs Earl's former campaign manager grabbed the back of his safari jacket.

'Play it by ear,' he advised. 'Whatever goes down you gotta be cool. Right?'

'Right.'

On the upper level the three men took seats along the side near the middle of the student body. Ralph Baker and Abul Menka were onstage huddling. Meanwhile, two microphones were being set up and hooked into the public address system.

Victor Johnson was seated behind the two MJUMBE leaders scribbling away at a pad on his lap.

When at last the microphones were set up and the MJUMBE men were ready, Baker approached the podium with his papers. The three MJUMBE members who had been passing out the MJUMBE statement and *The Statesman* climbed the steps to the stage and took seats.

'We are trying to give everyone time to read the paper we issued and *The Statesman* before we begin ... Uh, for those of you just coming in there are copies of the MJUMBE paper on the tables to your right. Take one and a copy of *The Sutton Statesman*. The essence of these two pieces will be our text.' Baker moved back into another huddle with his associates. The audience buzzed again. Earl lit a cigarette.

'First of all I'd like to thank everyone for comin',' Baker said after a moment. 'I had thought we'd lose some people to the lunch line an' some to the dispensary who were sick to their stomachs after the things they had just heard.' There was a muffled laughter.

'We would like to come right to the point this afternoon. We did not like the answers that we heard from President Ogden Calhoun. His reply to our requests displayed a portion of the same tired, bullshit replies that Sutton students have been receiving from administrators for as long as there has been a Sutton. Some of these buildings that we're in lead us to believe that there has always been a Sutton.' More laughter.

'The question becomes, however, what we plan to do about it. Do we plan to merely laugh at our situation an' go on pretendin' that it doesn' exist? Do we plan to go back through the same clogged channels of communication an' watch our hard-earned money go down the drain? ... These are questions that I want answers for. Will we allow Ogden Calhoun and his band of legal pirates to continue to rob us? I'm asking you?'

'No!' came a voice from about the fourth row. Then a chorus of 'no's' rang out.

'Will we continue to sit around daily wondering what

happened to our money when the only thing that keeps us from findin' out is Ogden Calhoun?'

'NO!'

'Will we continue to eat the slop dished out in the cafeteria like garbage piled into a pig's trough?'

'NO!'

'Will we continue to cooperate with Sutton under the present conditions with only token response from Sutton Hall's shirt an' tie renegades?'

'NO!'

'The members of MJUMBE are proposing a students' strike against Sutton University until such time as all of these basic needs that we have requested receive a positive response.'

There was an initial smattering of applause that grew and grew until it seemed to Earl that the building's foundations had been loosened. Students were whistling, clapping, and stomping their feet.

'This student strike,' Baker continued, 'will call for the boycott of all classes, all conferences, lectures, coed-visitation rules, and all other university functions.

'The end of this strike can only be caused by an administrative 'yes' to each an' every demand that we submitted ...' There was more applause. 'The student strike will go into effect as of now.'

One of the sisters in the first row was raising her hand. Baker nodded to her.

'How will the students be kept informed of what happens?'

'A Strike Communication Center will be established in the MJUMBE office on the third floor of the fraternity house. All information will be available there. We will also have brothers going from dorm to dorm distributing information at night.'

A male student asked a second question. 'It was my impression that student body had a SGA president who was in charge of all of these types of activities. I'd like to know why he's not on the stage an' how he feels.'

Baker flashed a quick look at Abul Menka and then scanned

the thousand people in the auditorium. 'Earl? You wanna say somethin'?'

Earl got up stiffly, feeling the weight of the two thousand eyes that were on him. Lawman flashed him a grimace. He found himself still questioning exactly what he would say when he fully faced the audience, so he trotted down the side aisle to the stage. Baker moved away from the microphone hesitantly.

'Salaam,' Earl said greeting the students. 'Brother, you are absolutely right when you refer to the SGA. I think you might be overlooking one fact however. It was pointed out yesterday, I understand, that *I* would be giving the petition to President Calhoun. *I* was the one who served the, pardon me, proposals, on the president. I was aware of the possibilities when I served the papers. Calhoun has made his move. It is now time for us to make ours ... it's not so much a question of who leads. No one can lead without a following. Do we all agree that something is necessary?'

'Yes!'

'Do we all agree that a student strike is necessary?'

'Yes!'

Earl nodded to Baker and trotted back down the stairs and walked quickly back through the audience to his seat, sweat forming at the edge of his face, itchy patches seeming to appear all over his body.

Just as Earl found his seat the audience erupted. Focusing on the stage Earl saw Vice-President Fenton Mercer waddling toward the microphone. The sweating, obviously upset vice-president said something to Baker who spoke into the mike.

'Brothers and sisters, I have been asked if our vice-president, who came over since the president couldn't make it, uh, I've been asked if Mr Mercer could say a few words ... I'm gonna leave it up to you, but I say now that the man is not here wit' anything new to say. He is here to rationalize and philosophize, an' bullshit. MJUMBE IS LEAVING!'

For one breathtaking instant the entire auditorium was

silent. The silence lasted long enough for Baker and the MJUMBE leaders to take two steps toward the stairs. Then, as though on signal, the huge meeting hall was turned into an echo chamber of screaming, applauding students and chairs being pulled back. The noise was so loud that no one could hear Fenton Mercer's plea for attention. The entire aggregation turned toward the exits, leaving the disturbed administrator on stage.

19

A Three-pronged Spear

'Iz everybody in place?' Baker asked Ben King, when the largest MJUMBE member entered the new Strike Communications Center.

'Everythin's good,' King said dramatically. 'All of our enforcers is on their posts makin' sure don' nobody go to class. I sent a few men ovuh to the women's dorm to break the coedvisitation rule . . .'

'I'm sure they were disappointed at their jobs,' Baker laughed.

'Ha! Yeh. They wuz real disappointed . . .'

'What the faculty doin?' Speedy Cotton asked.

'Ain' nobody messin' wit' them. It seem like they went on ovuh to their posts an' waited fo' alla the knowledge seekers to show up.'

'Do they know who the enforcers are and exactly what they're there for?'

'Hell, yeah! Wuzn't no real way to keep them from knowin' that. We gittin' bettuh cooperation from the studen's than I thought though.'

'Because of the enforcers or because of the studen's?' Baker asked.

'A little bit a both,' King admitted.

'Today means nuthin',' Abul Menka said suddenly. The entire group turned to him where he sat in his favorite corner looking out over the campus. 'Today people have a small dose a strike fever. They're all anxious t'be activists an' radicals. Niggers always go in for fads like this to show everybody how goddamn militant they are. Tuhmaruh iz gonna be a better indication a whuss happ'nin'.'

'I'm onna try it one day at a time,' King laughed. 'The point iz we got the thing offa the groun'!' King reached over with a huge grin on his coal-black face and Baker and he exchanged the African handshake.

'An',' Speedy Cotton mused, 'wit' Thomas's help.'

That was a point that Abul Menka had been mulling over in his mind but had not brought up. There were some very puzzling things going on with Earl Thomas. Abul had agreed that a picture of Thomas in the issue of *The Statesman* might serve as an intimidating factor and keep the deposed SGA leader quiet. The indication in the meeting had not been one of intimidation. But neither had Earl appeared anxious to jump on the emotional MJUMBE bandwagon and share any of the credit for the campus political mobility.

Abul had been watching Earl all through the meeting. He had not liked what he had seen. The reason for his distaste was the lack of responses coming from a man who had been, all through his campaign for SGA office, decisively emotional, never giving an indication that in the thick of a political confrontation he would sit like the proverbial Iceman and do nothing. Abul hated niggers he couldn't figure out.

'Abul? . . . Abul?' Baker was calling. 'Where you at, brother?'

'Right here.'

'Yeah. In the flesh you there. Where you at in the head?'

'Right here.'

'You got them notes ready to be typed?'

'Guard notes?'

'Yeah. We cleared the office down the hall an' imported a typewriter you can use 'til we rustle up a secretary for you.'

'What happened to . . .' Abul's question was cut off.

'She said she couldn' make it,' Baker remarked.

Abul picked up his folder and left the meeting room. He was followed closely by Ben King.

The room adjacent to the regular MJUMBE headquarters was being prepared for business by Fred Jones who was standing with a broom in his hand in the middle of the floor when the other two associates entered. Jonesy waved at them and continued his clean-up job.

'What were we using this room fo' anyway?' King asked.

'Lamps,' Abul mumbled, referring to the Omega Psi Phi pledges.

'Huh? Oh . . . Look, here's my list. We gotta have at least eight copies. One for each of us an' one to be posted in group commander rooms. We forgot that shit 'bout postin' anything on the bulletin boards cause some ass would take them . . . or some administrator would.'

'Some ass,' Abul agreed. The MJUMBE man in the black and gold dashiki sat down at the large portable typewriter and rolled in a sheet of typing paper. King lounged in a near corner watching Jonesy sweep.

'I wanna ask you somethin',' he admitted finally to Abul. 'What'choo think come over that bastard Thomas?'

'When?'

'T'day. I wuz jus' linin' him in my sights for a good right han' when he up an' agreed wit' us.' King shook his head in wonder.

'Y'know,' Abul confided, 'that might jus' be the reason he agreed.'

King thought that over for a moment. He looked down for some sort of sign that Abul had been pulling his leg. But the man in the sunglasses continued his typing and said nothing.

The office door was locked and the shades were drawn on the first floor of Carver Hall. There were three men inside the SGA office, but none of them made any move toward answering either knocks on the door or the constantly ringing telephone.

'Y'know in all likelihood that phone has been ringin' fo' good reason,' Lawman pointed out.

'Reason bein' that someone somewhere was callin' here,' Odds quipped drily.

'I'm talkin' 'bout important calls,' Lawman said.

'That may be why I ain' answerin',' Earl sighed, running long fingers through his bushy head.

'Ha long we gonna stay here?' Odds asked. ''Til the coast iz clear? I think the coast is gittin' more an' more unclear wit' each passin' minnit.'

'Point,' Lawman agreed looking quizzically at Earl.

The harried SGA president got up from the swivel chair behind his desk and poured himself a cup of the mud he had made as the result of an inexperienced attempt at instant coffee.

'Yeah, I know. I'm s'pose to be makin' all sortsa brilliant political moves, but everything I think of is a trap of some sort. Dig all this. If I call Calhoun an' try to establish some sort of communication, I'm trapped. Either I confess that things are outta my hands an' tell him who's runnin' shit . . . that's one. Or I reenforce the deman's an' bring an open confrontation that I can't afford. Or . . .'

'Stop!' Lawman ordered. 'How can't you afford a confrontation? Personally or politically?'

'Neither way! Politically he has the power. I mean, you can rap all you want 'bout student power an' alla that shit, but until the Board gits organized an' places a clamp on that automatic boot of his . . . Wait! The Board! The Trustees!'

'What about 'um?'

'They can do jus' what I wuz talkin' about – put a clamp on that automatic boot!' Earl reached for the telephone.

'Wait a minute!' Lawman said. 'Let's have everything together in our heads befo' we make any moves. We been in here damn near twenny minnits. I think we agree that however much time it takes, our first move had bes' be a good one.' Odds nodded. 'Now. What you gonna say to the Board? I mean, let's face it. They ain' jus' sittin' 'roun' waitin' for a call from you. They got specific times when they meet. Somethin' like two big meetin's a year an' small cluster meetin's the resta the time. What action can you get from a phone call? The Trustees are spaced all over the U.S. map . . . first, who you callin'?'

'I'll call Miz Stoneman.'

'Okay. Where is she?'

'She's in D.C.'

'All right. How long you think it'll take her to get anything together?'

'I see yo' point,' Earl said a bit crestfallen. 'It'll take hours. But it won' take hours for her to call Calhoun!'

'Thass exactly what you don't want her doin'! If she calls Calhoun he's gonna minimize this shit to a speck an' try an' keep her from doin' anything national. The ol' man don' want no publicity!'

'How long do you think it'll take Calhoun to move?' Earl asked.

'I can't say. For all we know he's already gettin' walkin papers formed for a lot of us.'

'Doubtlessly,' Odds added.

'Then I gotta call Miz Stoneman,' Earl said picking up the receiver. 'I have ta impress upon her the need for her to get in touch wit' some people an' have them *all* call Calhoun unless they're comin' out here in person. Then they can call each other back an' get a conclusion together.'

Earl dialed the operator. Lawman agreed by his silence, but he was shaking his head from side to side as though he believed it to be the wrong move.

'I'd like an outside line,' Earl said. 'This is Earl Thomas.'

'I've been ringin' an' ringin' you,' the switchboard operator said in a whining tone.

'I jus' got in,' Earl lied. There was a momentary pause before he started dialing a number from an address book he located in the top drawer of his desk. There was a long period of silence.

'Hello,' Earl said when the phone was finally answered. There was a clear expression of relief on his face. 'Mrs Stoneman? This is Earl Thomas of the Student Government at Sutton. Yes, ma'am. Well, I have quite a few things to tell you too ...'

*   *   *

Ogden Calhoun was facing what was doubtlessly his most trying day as president of Sutton University. Not only had the past sixteen hours produced a group of demands that he had seen coming for over six months, but it had also produced a militant student faction called MJUMBE of which he had been totally unaware, a series of conferences that he had detested, and a student strike in the midst of a press conference that had seen him lose almost every ounce of restraint with a Norfolk newspaperman.

The last of the reporters had just left his office and he was leaning back in his upholstered swivel chair when the intercom buzzed.

'Yes?' he replied dimly.

'Still no reply from the Student Government office,' Miss Felch reported. 'No response from the business office either.'

'Keep trying the SGA office,' Calhoun said. 'And please bring me a cup of coffee and send out for a sandwich and some tea when you get a chance.'

'Yes, sir,' came the reply. 'There's a student here to see you from the Inter-Dormitory Assistants. She says it's rather important.'

'Send her in.'

The oaken door to the president's inner office swung noiselessly open and a young coed came in with books under her arm. She was about twenty and dressed in a short plaid skirt and white blouse, red sweater, and knee socks. Her hair was fixed in a pony-tail and wide round sunglasses were propped on her nose. Calhoun rose to greet her.

'How are you?' he asked with extra charm. He grasped her hand lightly and directed her to a seat.

'I'm all right ... I'm Allison Grimes. Do you remember me?'

'From the Inter-Dorm meetings,' Calhoun asserted. 'What can I do for you, Miss Grimes. So much going on.'

'Yes, sir. I know.'

'Seems like everything happens at once,' Calhoun pointed

out, waving his arms in a general gesture. He smiled and reached for his pipe and cherry blend.

'I jus' wanted to ask about how we, as dorm assistants, should be conducting ourselves in terms of the things that are happening,' Miss Grimes asked nervously. She removed her sunglasses and wiped them on a handkerchief. 'I mean, it's understood as how we take care of things under ordinary circumstances, but there are men all over my dorm an' these aren't visiting hours an' all of the girls are upset about their jobs and everything.'

'I understand exactly what you mean, Miss Grimes. It's unfortunate that the students are so insistent on their points that they place other students in jeopardy. I haven't gotten all of the facts, but in military terms this would be referred to as "smoke-screen" tactics or "distracting" tactics. I think that the whole point is to place every student in some sort of trouble with the administration so that no students can be punished for their actions.'

'But the other girl assistants and I . . .'

'Have a job to do. But under the circumstances it would be unreasonable of me or anyone else to expect the assistants to keep up with every male and female involved in these types of activities. All I can really ask is that you try and maintain as much order as you can and wait for other instructions from Mr Bass or Miss Freeman. Is that all right? . . . just understand that we know how hard everyone is trying to do their jobs. That might also be considered on the other side of the fence in relation to administrators trying to do their jobs too.' Calhoun finished with his best political smile.

'All right,' Miss Grimes said for lack of anything better to say.

'How're the grades and schoolwork coming?' Calhoun asked.

'Oh fine,' the student replied rising. 'I'm on the list.'

'Good!' the president boomed. 'I have a lot of room on that list! Ha! Ha!'

Calhoun showed the student to the door. He was no sooner seated than the intercom was buzzing again.

'Yes?'

'There are just an awful lot of things going on!' Miss Felch said, irritated past any previous standards. 'The Student Government line was busy, but now I can't get an answer. Mr Mercer wants to talk to you in private. Mr Harper wants to talk to you. Your wife has called. She'd like to have you call back. Victor Johnson wants a statement for *The Statesman*. He says he's running another special . . .'

'Did you tell him what I . . .'

'Yes. He said this issue would be getting your side of everything. He said he had to go to press and you weren't here for comment. All he could print was the student side.'

'Where is Mercer?' Calhoun asked.

'He's in his office,' Miss Felch replied.

'Tell him to come up. When the food arrives please don't hesitate to bring it in.'

'Fine.'

Calhoun was left alone then for a moment. He had been on the go constantly since sunup and he was just beginning to realize how little food and rest he had had. At the same time he thought to himself also of how quickly and authoritatively he would once have dealt with this current crisis. He had ruled the school with an iron hand. But in more ways than one the heat was being applied by the Sutton students, and the question was whether or not Ogden Calhoun's iron hand would melt.

The thought that he had already exhibited too much concern for student opinion shot the silver-haired president straight up in his chair. He was jotting down the outline for an ultimatum that he would issue when Fenton Mercer scurried breathlessly into the office.

20
Self-help Programs

'Mrs Stoneman sez she'll do what she can,' Earl spat out mockingly. He pushed the telephone to the far corner of the scarred desk.

'How hip!' Odds offered. 'I could tell from yo' expression an' the things you were sayin' that you wudn' gettin' too far.'

'Jus' what did she say?' Lawman asked.

'Shit! Yo' guess is as good as mine,' Earl admitted, lighting a cigarette. 'She wuz a pure politician. "We'll have ta investigate this thoroughly," an "Why wudn' it be wize fo' me to call *Brother* Calhoun if I'm to get to the heart of the matter?" ... *Brother* Calhoun! Can you dig that shit? I'd sooner call Lester Maddox a damn brother.'

'Jus' shows that it don' take much to qualify in some circles,' Odds sighed.

'Well, *Sister* Stoneman got a long way to go,' Earl confided.

The wheels were turning inside Lawman's head. He had not thought it to be a good idea to call the present Head Trustee, but he hadn't been able to suggest anything better. Now, with time slipping through their fingers and one trump card already nullified, it was apparent that another course of action had to be taken.

'You gonna have ta see Calhoun one a these days,' Earl was reminded.

'I think I'm gonna have ta do mo' 'bout seein' that it ain't today,' the SGA leader laughed.

'What can he do to you?' Odds asked. 'Crucify you?'

'It's not a matter of that,' Earl said. 'I just would rather have him make a move now. The lines are drawn.'

'But you ain' entirely satisfied wit' the lines that have been drawn,' Odds supplied. 'You think that by lettin' that phone ring and ring you turnin' the fire up under Calhoun?'

'Not necessarily. But if I go to see him an' try to bail out, all I can do iz cause further division among the student body. The question wuz put to them in the auditorium an' they made their decisions.'

'An' you got up there an' agreed,' Lawman said wearily.

'That wuz the right move!' Earl exclaimed. 'It's time to do *something*! Shit! You know that as well as I do. Sutton people have sat an' waited an' sat an' waited until every drop of blood in their bodies has gathered in the asses. Jus' like Black people everywhere. We waited long enough.'

'But whenever you decide to move agains' the man you gotta be prepared.'

'I can't say how prepared MJUMBE wuz. All I've been doin' for the past month is gettin' ready to try an' organize somethin' along the same lines. Che said nobody would be ready when the revolution came. I wasn't ready, but I wasn't gonna try an' stop people from standin' on their feet jus' because Earl Thomas wasn't at the head a the damn thing ... thass the problem! Too many chiefs an' no fuckin' Indians!'

'So now Calhoun's on the spot?' Odds asked.

'I din' say that. I said it was his move.'

'An' what if he moves on you an' MJUMBE an' goes through his "My way or the highway" routine?'

'Then we'll find out jus' how committed people were to all that shoutin' they were doin' over in the auditorium. If people are committed there won' be no leavin' campus for one group without the others. What I don' need to do is show any signs of weakness. That's what I would be doin' if I got into any extended dialogue with the man. He knows what we want. He knows how to stop the strike.'

'He knows several ways to stop it,' Lawman interjected.

'I wonder how I can rationalize my sudden arrival at home,' Odds said to no one in particular.

'The eternal optimist,' Lawman commented drily.

'Look for the silver lining, my mama said.'

Earl wasn't particularly concerned about the reactions that his mother and grandmother would have. There was no question about how disappointed they would be. They had been disappointed when he decided not to go back to Southern University in Baton Rouge. They had known that he would lose credit and spend more money to attend the Virginia university, but they had said very little. They took pride in watching the man of the Thomas family making his own decisions and doing what he thought was best. And if he was sent home from school, after the inevitable questions, they would still be proud of him.

Earl was berating himself for being so thoroughly unprepared. To him the politics of the university were as complicated as national and international politics. In order to organize a campus one first had to organize the organizations: the fraternities, sororities, clubs, classes, and foreign students. One had to appeal to the best interests of all cliques and still apply himself to the whole picture of campus improvement. Money was a problem. Most of the things that were needed simply could not be handled by a small, predominantly black school's endowment. Funds were not available to attract the best professors. The rush was on for Black professors with the proper qualifications and the great cry for Black instructors was falling on deaf ears because Black teachers were being lured away from their communities by the smell of fresh greenbacks. As for equipment, it was the same story. Sutton was capable of doing but so much. You had to spend the money for the purposes it was donated. The money was being donated so that you would name a building after your great (white) benefactor. It was not there to purchase a 16 millimeter camera or film for photographic experimentation. It was not for badly needed instruments or uniforms for the marching band. It was not meant for buying a new bus for the teams to travel in. It was not for a new burner in the cafeteria. It was for a new gymnasium or dormitory which gave Sutton the capacity to expand in one direction, but not the ability to facilitate the present enrollment in other areas.

The job of distributing the student activities and organization funds fell to the Student Government. Organizations submitted a budget for the following year in May. It was the first order of business for the new SGA president. Earl arrived in office just in time to discover that a congressional filibuster was holding up appropriations of institutional funds and that at best he would have to make appropriations in September. Enter September and less funds for student activities than in the previous eight years when the institution was three-quarters its present size. There was a great deal of grumbling: 'How do you expect us to present a program on this much money?' The noises came from everywhere. The Homecoming Committee was up in arms. The Greek organizations were furious. The object of their anger was not the U.S. Congress, however, but Earl Thomas. The women were outraged. Proportionately the women on Sutton's campus outnumbered the men almost two-to-one, but the Women's Association budget only allowed them half the money they requested after Earl's budget cut. The president of the Women's Association had vowed even after Earl's explanation that though he was eligible for another year as SGA leader, he would not receive the support of her organization as he had during his first campaign.

Earl was recalling the campaign and all of the preparation he had gone through to get elected. He wondered now why winning the election had been so important to him. All he had gained from his victory was a series of migraine headaches. He didn't know now if he had been unprepared for the true responsibility his position required, or if he had never really stopped to consider how many moves it would be necessary for him to make once he had gotten background and prepared his statement for Calhoun.

The paper that he had given the university president was a list of essentially the same things he himself had listed as priorities, plus a few points that he had not deemed as important. Thus, he was politically clear on the issues. The issues were vital. Somehow at that moment he was feeling naïve because he had no plan. Had he expected Ogden Calhoun to drop dead at the sight of the demands? Of course not. Had he expected the president to agree with him if he also submitted a supplementary document to prove that he had done his political homework? Another no. Then why was he totally unprepared to do anything at this moment while his political followers sat around their dorms waiting for words of wisdom?

He decided that the answer lay in his political idealism. He had long ago silently decided that when the people in charge of the system were given proof positive of the negative effects that the system was having, they would move for change. The U.S. Government had wrecked his national ideal, but he had never thought of Ogden Calhoun in terms of analogies with the U.S.A. Maybe that was another oversight. What did they always say in political science? 'It doesn't boil down to a question of race. It boils down to *haves* and *have nots*.' Earl was a have not and Calhoun was a have. All of the recommendations meant extra work and extra effort on Calhoun's part. Therefore the students weren't getting anything for the asking. They were placed in a position where they had to take what they wanted. But how long could they enforce any position like that? There would definitely be a confrontation in Calhoun's back yard, so to speak. Using the proper channels was just another way of trying to beat a man at his own game.

'I blew this one,' Earl muttered aloud.

'Not yet,' Lawman hedged. He took a quick glance out of the side window. 'We were not truly prepared, I admit. I don' know how many times we'd have to say that before I'd figure I realized it. But we're still in a better position than we could be.'

'Howzat?' Odds asked.

'We could be by ourselves,' Lawman pointed out. 'If we had

waited until Earl got alla them surveys together an' all that other information, we could've gone to Calhoun an' been flat on our asses. Doubtlessly, since the students knew what we were workin' on, there would have been no need to approach them before we made our first appeal. Then when we received a flat no and went back to get the students, Calhoun would've been over-ready for us.'

'An' we would've gotten another no,' Odds said solemnly.

'But at least this is not an indefensible position,' Lawman went on. 'We've made an offensive move so we can afford to retreat. There could be no retreat if our backs were up against the wall.'

'Exploratory surgery,' Odds said.

'What?'

'Takin' a look to see how sick somebody is. You cut into the patient and peep aroun'. If there's anything wrong you try to isolate it.'

'Isolate it?' Earl asked. 'Isolate it!' The second time he repeated the phrase it was as though he had come across a new meaning for the two words. 'Odds, my man. I think yo' pointless conversation might've had a point anyway.'

Odds put his index finger to his temple and pulled the trigger, indicating to Lawman that he thought Earl was insane.

'Suppose we call a faculty meeting without Calhoun,' Earl suggested, barely concealing his excitement. 'And try an' put a wedge between our Head Nigger and his hirelings?'

'What can we base the meeting on?' Lawman asked. He too thought that Earl might have a point.

'We can say that we're ready to publicize our position nationally an' wouldn' want to say that we were striking against the faculty an' administration if we were only striking against the administration. We can say that all we want to know is where they stand.'

'I know right away we can pull a few faculty members,' Odds said. 'We can get McNeil an' Coach Mallory an' . . .'

'It's not important how many we get,' Earl said. 'All we want the faculty members to say is that they don't share Calhoun's viewpoint. Once they say that we ask them to strike with us or hand us an alternative position.'

'Naturally they'll give us an alternative that has something to do wit' formin' committees an' shit like that.'

'Fine!' Earl said. 'That then will become our safety valve. We wait until Calhoun goes through his thing about acting to keep from being intimidated or threatened an' we call this meetin' to his attention.'

'An' then what?' Odds asked, still not fully understanding.

'An' then *we* decide who'll be on the committees. Don't you see? The faculty pulls away from Calhoun. Calhoun can't dictate who goes on our committees. The committees are split evenly between the students an' faculty an' all we need is one faculty member who agrees with us to throw every decision our way ... Then if this committee finds the student view to be correct, Calhoun has no alternative but to abide by it.'

'When do we start?' Lawman asked, catching Earl's enthusiasm.

'Right now,' Earl said. 'We put notices in the faculty boxes and wait.'

21
Reactor

While the three men in the Student Government office prepared notification of the *Faculty Only* meeting for the next
morning, Ogden Calhoun was not inactive. He had eaten
a sandwich for lunch in his office, assured his bumbling
second-in-command that no sudden moves would be made
without him, talked briefly over the phone to a seemingly
inebriated Gaines Harper, and now faced a neurotic Victor
Johnson, editor-in-chief of *The Sutton Statesman*.

'You got my message, sir?' Johnson asked without looking
up.

'I got it,' Calhoun agreed noncommittally. 'I don't necessarily swallow it, but I got it.'

'You were unavailable for . . .'

'I know what you said,' Calhoun said, trying to light his
pipe. 'But you place yourself in a very dangerous position
when you do things like this issue.' Calhoun raised a copy
of the day's *Statesman*. 'All right. You have the position, and
I gave you the authority to print specials, but you have to do
this sort of thing with a discriminating eye. Especially when
you're playing politics . . . from the role of pure objectivism
you become a participant by reporting a slanted story.'

'Yes, sir,' Johnson swallowed.

'What can be done is this,' Calhoun suggested. 'Take a copy
of the demands, a copy of my reply, which you can get from
Miss Felch, and a copy of this interview. Go to press again
tonight. I want the usual number available for the student
body and copies sent to the alumni an' trustees. Plus all the
major newspapers. Is that clear?'

'Yes, sir.'

'I assume that as in the past you did not send a copy

of today's special to alumni and trustees.' Johnson nodded. 'Right. Now along with the issue you send to the newspapers send the public relations photograph. Not that picture you took today. The one upstairs.'

'Right. Well, when I asked for this interview I had no idea 'bout a studen' strike. I guess that this will change the whole slant of the story.' Johnson had known full well about the strike.

'Not necessarily. You can print the story and say that there had been rumors of a coming demonstration to protest my decision.'

'But once again, sir,' Johnson said, 'I would be leaving my role as objective reporter and giving a slanted account.'

Calhoun turned away from the chore of lighting his pipe and faced Victor Johnson squarely. The small reporter nervously took his glasses off and wiped them with a handkerchief that dangled from the breast pocket of his suit.

'I think that you should know I hold you partially responsible for the things that happened today,' Calhoun said acidly.

'Me?' the editor squeaked.

'From my reports this paper of yours was an ingredient in the emotional concoction that served to bring a strike here.'

'I'm sorry, but I still have my job to do.'

'Print what you want to about the strike,' Calhoun warned, 'but choose your *objective* terms carefully. There are certain things about government I suppose I should tell you. The first is that any government is subject to criticism. You can see every day in the papers and on television examples of this sort of criticism. But a government does not pay to support this criticism. . . . Now hear me out. I'm not saying that because I allocated money for the newspaper that it should be slanted in my direction, but I do say that I would be foolish to allocate money to an organization that is directly responsible for a certain amount of my administrative trouble. Are you clear?'

'I believe so,' Johnson replied. He was bristling from the threat implied in Calhoun's speech.

'About the demands I have this to say. They called for a total realigning of a great deal of the Sutton financial system. At this time it is inconceivable that the students maturely handle the sort of responsibility *demanded* in this document. Many of the matters brought up in the paper had never come to our attention in this manner before. I have referred certain issues to the Student-Faculty Alliance and I will look into others myself. Under no circumstances do I intend to crawl on my belly before the students, however. I think that my record indicates an intense concern for Sutton University and a proficiency in my position as president. I will do my best in the future as I have in the past. I am willing to work with students, but I will not be dictated to by them.' Calhoun finally succeeded in lighting his pipe.

Victor Johnson, head down, made a few final notations on his crowded note pad and then looked up.

'Is that all?' he asked.

'That's all unless you have questions,' Calhoun said, looking out of the window. The president's concern about the activities outside his window kept him from seeing the middle finger on Victor Johnson's right hand being raised in his direction, indicating the editor's heartfelt opinion of the whole thing.

The intercom came on.

'Yes?' Calhoun waved unconvincingly at the editor's retreating back.

'Coach Mallory is on the line,' Miss Felch reported.

'Good.' Calhoun switched lines. 'Lo, Coach ... right ...'

'They didn' come in,' Coach Mallory reported. He had read the note from the president's office instructing him to send in the four members of MJUMBE who played football.

'None of them?'

'Baker, Jones, Cotton, and King. Those right?'

'Those are the four. I wanted to talk to them because they seem to have as much to do with this whole mess as Thomas does. I can't locate Thomas either.'

'Oh.' The coach wasn't paying a great deal of attention.

Thirty of his men were on the field doing calisthenics. He thought he would be able to deal with the missing four when he found them.

'Tell me, coach,' Calhoun was saying, 'are those four boys on some sort of athletic scholarship?'

'Yes,' Mallory said guardedly. 'They are.'

'I see,' was Calhoun's comment. The way the two words were said raised the hair on the back of the young Black coach's neck. 'Well, have a nice practice. I'll be at the game on Saturday looking for a victory.'

The phone was returned to its cradle. Mallory stood behind his desk for minutes staring down at the instrument. He was dressed in a sweat suit and baseball cap. He had yet to trot out onto the baked Virginia soil and take the three laps with which he generally started his practices, but there was a line of perspiration reaching his thick eyebrows and sweat stains stood out against his armpits and crotch. In the dead silence of the empty locker room, Mallory decided to break his long-standing rule about practice. He stepped quickly into the corridor and trotted out to the door that led to the practice field. He immediately caught the eye of his assistant coach and beckoned him.

'Run them through everything, Bob,' Mallory said hurriedly. 'Double on the running an' the calisthenics. I've got an emergency.'

The Sutton senior physical education major who served as assistant coach frowned and was tempted to ask what was happening, but he knew better. He nodded, walked toward the players, and the last thing Mallory heard before the wooden door slammed shut was the shrill whistle splitting the early autumn calm.

Edmund C. Mallory was a Sutton graduate. He was a short, stocky man with a fierce, driving determination that he instilled in his athletes. It was not uncommon for Sutton to walk onto a football field as heavy underdogs and walk away as winners. For even though the university did not give out as many scholarships as they needed to compete athletically, Mallory teams were well trained physically, psychologically, and strategically. Mallory loved to tell his team: 'There are no underdogs as far as we're concerned. When you go on the field the score is zero-zero. Your action from that point on decides who the underdog is.'

The sort of relationship that Mallory sought with his athletes went beyond the coach-player relationship. Most of the time Mallory got to know the men who played under him rather well. Mallory thought he knew Ralph Baker, Ben King, Speedy Cotton, and Fred Jones very well. The four seniors had all advanced from the freshman team together. Cotton, King, and Baker were at starting positions for their third consecutive year, and though they had never gone into any great amount of detail about their campus-political involvement, the coach was reasonably sure that their college careers were now on the line because of their political commitments.

The thought of Ogden Calhoun's sly but pointed inquiry into the financial situation of the four men made Mallory positive that the political move dictated by MJUMBE was pushing Ogden Calhoun in the direction of repression.

As he showered it occurred to Mallory that he had not yet decided exactly where he was going and what he was going to do. Then he thought of Arnold McNeil and vowed that some preventative moves would be made. Standing there under the steaming water, he could not resolve completely what direction he would take, but he knew something had to be done to stop Calhoun.

22

Counterthreat

The members of MJUMBE had been busy. The members of their 'enforcer' program had met and been informed of what to do in practically all possible situations. These were the men, primarily athletes and members of Greek fraternities, who guarded the entrances to class buildings and informed students who were thinking of going to class that Sutton was on strike. There had been no physical restraint used during the first two hours of the strike. None had been necessary.

Baker had written another newsletter. His article referred to Ogden Calhoun's noon declaration and called it 'extremely unsatisfactory' and vowed that Sutton students should be prepared for a long wait. It stressed the fact that under no circumstances should the members of the student body be willing to accept less than the requests called for since the list had only mentioned 'the bare essentials.'

Abul Menka had typed up lists of needed equipment for the Music Department student who had asked if any microphones or sound machines would be needed. MJUMBE proposed to invite in a series of lecturers for a seminar program if the strike stretched into the next week. A second list was sent to the Fine Arts Building requesting majors to contact MJUMBE for possible lecture assignments. There was a great apprehension about the students moving to break the strike out of sheer boredom.

'We'll be all right this weekend,' Baker asserted. 'The Alphas are havin' some kinda dance. As long as the niggers can dance they'll be all right.'

'If we wuz to knock the dance they'd turn on us,' Cotton quipped.

'In a minnit.'

'If we get to the weekend,' Abul said, coming into the main meeting room. 'I expect Calhoun to move on us before then.'

'He'd be movin' on the whole community,' Cotton said.

'Idealistically,' Abul admitted, 'but if we had that much faith in any type of ideal unity we wouldn'a needed to have the brothers on the doors blockin' classes.'

'But . . .'

'But nothin',' Abul stepped in. 'That meetin' in the auditorium means zero. If Calhoun moves before we get the necessary power nobody leaves here but MJUMBE an' Thomas.'

'What necessary power?' Cotton asked. 'What mo' can we git?'

'Thass the problem. We gotta make Calhoun think we got more goin' for us than we do.'

It was at that instant that Fred Jones came through the door with a tray of sandwiches and plastic cups filled with Coke.

'We're bein' paged in the student union,' he said quietly.

'We who?'

'We all of us,' Jonesy replied. 'Ben King, Ralph Baker, Everett Cotton, Fred Jones, and Jonathan Wise.'

Baker laughed. 'I had forgot yawl's names,' he said, turning to Speedy Cotton and Abul Menka. No one on campus could have pointed out Everett Cotton or Jonathan Wise. 'Jonathan, my boy,' Baker said to Abul, 'we gotta educate people 'bout you.'

'What were we bein' paged for?' Abul asked Jonesy.

'We're wanted in the Administration Building.'

The sandwiches and Cokes were distributed and the men ate in silence. When the phone rang Jonesy answered and told the person on the other end to call back later.

'Maybe we should go,' Abul said suddenly.

'Where?'

'To see old Assbucket,' came the reply.

'What good would it do?' Ben King asked. 'He knows where we stand.'

'Does he?' Abul quizzed. 'He knows one thing. He got a

buncha deman's an' a strike. There's two ways of lookin' at a meetin' wit' him. One way is the way you lookin', Ben. A sign of weakness. The other way of seen' it is as a chance to find out what the ol' bastard's into.'

'Is he gonna tell us?'

'Sure. He'll tell us by the type of questions that he asks. He'll tell us by the way he approaches the whole set. If we don' go he can look at that as a sign of fear. If we show up an' freeze him, he won't know what to do.'

'Freeze 'im how?'

'Freeze, baby, freeze! You can dig that! He's gonna throw out a lotta stimulators aimed at makin' us blow our cool an' goin' through an' emotional thing. You're right when you say he knows what we want, but he doesn't know what our limits are; what we're willin' to do to get what we're after.'

'He don' care,' King said.

'Maybe not,' Abul admitted, 'but you gotta remember he ain' never really been put to the test. No one student movement on this campus ever had total support. Las' year Peabody had the frats an' the sororities. The year before Coombs had the block-heads. This is a thing that has everybody pullin' an' Calhoun may be walkin' on eggs.'

Baker made the decision. 'Let's go! If he had everything under control he wouldn'a been pagin' us. Maybe if we show a little more unity he'll be even more shook up . . . Lemme do the talkin'.'

Jonesy was about to suggest that they let Abul do the talking. He had never heard Abul say as many things as he had heard today. The strange thing was that he found himself agreeing with all of the things that he heard. He said nothing.

23

Choosing Sides

Edmund C. Mallory, Sutton football coach, found out from Mrs Millie McNeil that her husband had telephoned from a Sutton bar called the Mine where he was having drinks with an old reporter friend. She admitted that the call had been placed at one thirty and though it was already three she assumed that her mate was still there.

Her assumption turned out to be a valid one because Mallory spotted McNeil and a man he did not recognize sitting in a booth just inside the air-conditioned bar and grill.

'Ed Mallory,' McNeil said, doing the introductions. 'This is Ike Spurryman, an old college friend of mine. Ike, this is Ed Mallory, our highly productive football coach.'

They were approached by a waitress who appeared startled when the coach ordered a 7-Up. She quickly regained her composure however and departed.

'Knowing that you're not a drinking man,' McNeil began, 'I suppose I must have something to do with your visit to this little hideaway.'

It appeared to Coach Mallory that his proposed ally was a little drunk.

'You have everything to do with it,' Mallory admitted, getting right to the point. 'I'm quite sure that you and I didn't agree with all of the methods that Calhoun or the student group have been using.'

'Indeed,' McNeil smiled. 'Both parties are wrong. Stop! You're both wrong! ... Pardon me, but I'm a product of the television age.'

'The question is what we propose to do ... can I talk in front of you without fear of jeopardy, Mr Spurryman?'

'Of course. And call me Ike,' the reporter replied.

'Well, I don't like the idea of the student strike,' the coach admitted. 'But I don't like the way Calhoun is going about dealing with the student leaders either.'

'How's he dealing with them?' McNeil asked, sobering up a bit.

'Intimidation as far as I can see. He called me a little while ago and asked me if the MJUMBE members were on scholarship.'

'Whew! Trouble. What can I say? The people knocked me last night for admitting that I was a member of the Bullshit Squad.' The history professor chuckled again.

'We can't just sit around. Who else is with us?'

'Mrs Pruitt. Most of the younger people, I suppose.'

'Why can't we set ourselves up as sort of mediators?'

'The main reason is because the people who suggest this, namely you and I, are known student sympathizers. If we could talk Royce and Mercer and people like them into taking some kind of stand, we'd be all right.'

'Why them?'

'Because most of the young faculty members who are on our side are white. That's giving the students a way out. They are naturally suspicious of the white faculty members, or they overreact to them to show their militancy. It would just be better to have some solid Black figures for them to ally themselves with.'

'And any mediation tactics we tried to implement would be put off by whom?' Mallory asked.

'Initially by both sides,' McNeil asserted. 'We'd be more clearly in the middle than ever before.'

'Then at least this would give us an opportunity to break away from being constantly identified with Calhoun. I'm tired of political discussions with students about what needs to be done at Sutton starting off with, 'You people.' The students clearly mean the administrators but they don't see the faculty as other than the administration.'

'How can they?' McNeil asked. 'You have to look at political things on a college campus as a conflict on many levels. It is youth against the Establishment. It's youth against age. It's freedom against repression. It's both real and symbolic. We are not of their generation.'

'I can't talk that generation gap theme. I think it's fairly well played out.'

'You don't have to talk it, man. You're living it! You have kids, don't you? What do you think they're going to throw at you when they're old enough to start wanting special privileges? They'll say: "You don't understand. You don't realize what I mean." Mark my words. It will take a lot of serious time and energy for you to even begin to remember when you were in the same situation aside from vague generalities. I mean, aside from major events. Feelings. That's what you won't be able to remember.'

The 7-Up came along with another draft beer for the reporter who sat in the corner of the booth smoking a cigarette and saying nothing. The arrival of the waitress took on the appearance of a signaled time-out. Mallory sipped from the glass, watching the bubbles and clinking the two small ice cubes together. McNeil pulled on his drink and tamped his cigar against the side of an overloaded ashtray.

'Then what do we do?' Mallory asked, 'if we can't set ourselves up as mediaries or a liaison sort of body. Do I sit by and watch four of my men railroaded onto the highway?'

'I'm not saying we can't set ourselves up that way, but if we did we would be doing it for the students, right?'

Mallory nodded.

'Who says they want us?' McNeil asked. 'They won't completely trust us. They might reject us publicly and alienate all but a very few of us ... I propose that we find out first of all whether or not they believe we can do anything positive. Then if they do, we can move. I don't think we should try to do anything at all before that.'

'And how do we find out if we can do any good?'

'Contact them,' McNeil said, finishing his drink in a gulp.

'Where would we find Thomas at this hour. It's nearly three thirty.'

'I suggest we try and find your football players,' McNeil said. 'They are the ones who seem to be most directly under the gun. And the young man who has allied himself with them was very impressive.'

'Who?'

'This one.' McNeil proffered a copy of *The Statesman* and poked a yellow finger at the only MJUMBE man who was not a football player. 'Captain Cool?' McNeil asked.

'Abul Menka,' Mallory said. 'Where could we ... wait! I know. They'd probably be at the fraternity house. We can go there.'

'I don't know how wise that would be,' McNeil balked. 'That could be misconstrued in several directions.'

'Man, I ain' got time fo' no who construed what!' Mallory said, raising his voice for the first time. 'If we gonna be concerned about what we might construe, we can stop now. Somebody's always gonna get the wrong idea from what's done.'

'All I'm suggesting is that we call and let them know we're coming,' McNeil said. 'That way they'll know why we're coming and that might break down a little of the suspicion that would lead them to believe that we're administrative spies or some such nonsense.'

'Call if you want to.'

McNeil left the table. It was then that Spurryman voiced his personal opinion.

'Just my luck,' he said finishing his beer. 'Seems like damn near every *real* story I get I'm bound by some kind of personal thing not to print.'

'If you weren't a friend of McNeil's you wouldn't have been in any position to hear what you just heard,' Mallory pointed out.

'Yeah. But nevertheless ...'

'May just turn out to be talk,' the coach said, slowly turning back to his glass of soda.

'A damn chess game!' Spurryman exclaimed. 'If there had been no student strike I could've been back in Norfolk with my wife. Tomorrow's her birthday.'

'I could've been gettin' ready for my Saturday game.'

'You play A & T on Saturday, don't you?'

'Right here.'

'At least I'll get to see a good football game if the damn thing's still on an' they tell me to stay.'

McNeil came back to the booth and slid in opposite the reporter and the coach.

'The entire MJUMBE team has left the fraternity house. The information center could not inform me as to where they were. I told the man on the phone that I would call back.'

'I guess that's all you could do,' Mallory admitted nervously.

McNeil reached for his drink and realized that it was empty. Anyone who knew the history teacher would have easily been able to tell that he, too, was more nervous than he was letting on. They would point out the fact that he rarely drank as proof positive that something was troubling him. They might have been able to narrow it down to the student strike if they had the background. No one could safely say any more than that, however. Arnold McNeil himself couldn't safely talk about more than that. There was something eating away at the corners of his consciousness, something he could not put his finger on for the life of him. It caused him to raise his hand and order another drink.

24
On the Spot

Miss Felch's ironclad composure was so severely punctured when the five young Black men entered her office that she almost poured the steaming coffee from the pot in her hand down the front of her suit.

'MJUMBE here to see Mr Calhoun.' Baker spoke as if he had not noticed the nervous juggling act.

Miss Felch pushed down the far button on her telephone and spoke into the receiver. 'MJUMBE here to see you, sir,' she reported.

'Send them in!' was Calhoun's audible reply. Miss Felch gestured toward the door to the inner office.

Calhoun was on his feet when the five men entered. The four football players all wore black center-pocketed dashikis. Their heads were shaved and hardened muscles were revealed below the short sleeves of the shirts. Abul Menka wore a gold dashiki with black trim. He had a thick head of bushy hair with a part on the left side; sunglasses concealed his eyes.

'Sit down, please,' Calhoun said, gesturing to a sofa and chairs in the corner of the room closest to the outer office. The men sat down. Abul produced a package of cigarettes and lit one. He looked around for an ashtray and found one on the desk behind him. He had never been in the president's office before and to him its most apparent aspect was a sickly odor of cherry tobacco.

'I understand from this copy of *The Statesman* that your organization is known as MJUMBE,' Calhoun said, holding a copy of the paper. 'You have to excuse me, but the only organizations that I'm aware of on campus are the organizations that have university charters.'

'We're a newly formed organization,' Baker said. 'I don't

necessarily see the need of political organizations to form any kind of communications with the charter anyway. We don't need money from the Student Government or the university proper either.'

'That's not the purpose of the SGA charter entirely. There are quite a few groups listed who don't come under any university funds. I suppose the primary purpose is in a social vein. If your organization wanted to hold a function on campus and needed permission you would need to be included in the charter. Especially if you wanted to charge an admission fee.'

'It would allow the administrators to keep tabs on us,' Ben King suggested.

Calhoun smiled thinly. 'You can look at it that way if you choose to,' the president admitted. 'I'm sure that Mr Baker, having been a candidate for Student Government office can give other reasons. It seems particularly appropriate if you intend to organize yourselves as another political party or even as political spokesmen since I had no knowledge of your group or of how to get in touch with you.'

'We heard that you were pagin' us,' Baker said. 'We'll be glad to leave our number with your secretary.'

'Frankly,' Calhoun said, looking away momentarily, 'I had an idea of talking to you men along with Earl Thomas of the SGA. I wouldn't want to give one side of the issue any information that was not available to the other team. Maybe I should have Miss Felch try the SGA number again.' Calhoun left his guests where they sat and talked to his secretary on the intercom.

'Mr Thomas was seen in the building not long ago,' Miss Felch said. 'I sent a messenger over to his office.'

'What was he doing in the building?' Calhoun asked.

'He was in the lobby when the messenger saw him.'

'Thank you.'

Baker had taken Calhoun's absence as an opportunity to make sure that Ben King muzzled all side remarks such as the one about administrative tabs being kept on organizations.

'I'd really like to have Thomas here,' Calhoun said regretfully, 'since he brought the demands to my house last evening.'

'We don't represent diff'rent points of view,' Baker said.

'I have to feel that there is some sort of dichotomy,' Calhoun said diplomatically. 'Otherwise there would be no real need for two representative bodies.'

'We are a group of concerned students who were not appointed to any Student Government posts through election. We didn't feel that that was any reason for us to abandon our political feelings. We work with the SGA and Brother Thomas has been workin' with us.'

Ogden Calhoun's eyes hardened considerably. 'Then I will say this to you with the assurance that it will get back to Thomas,' he said. 'I have not appreciated the tactics used; the attempt to *force* me to make decisions contrary to my belief and my experience as president of this university. I have prepared a statement for the press when they reconvene at four thirty. Here are copies for all of you.

'Follow along please: The call for a student strike against Sutton University by the members of a political organization (unchartered and unrecognized) along with the Student Government Association is an obvious attempt to continue the intimidating and provocative means that were initiated by the set of demands placed before me last evening. I remind the community that these demands were issued with an ultimatum included, namely that I reply by noon of the following day. The SGA leader who visited my home gave no indication that the SGA would be available for the type of constructive dialogue that has always marked progress at Sutton. Neither did he indicate as much as one reason why any of the demands should be agreed to. The idea of a student strike was never mentioned. The number of demands that I should answer positively was not set as a condition for averting a student strike. Therefore, with a clear conscience, I state that if the student leaders responsible for the student action do not reconsider their immature decisions and offer other more democratic channels for administrative consideration, I will be forced to take action to restore order to the university. This includes probable action against the student leaders and against all students who participate in the student strike.'

Calhoun looked up upon concluding his press statement. The faces that he saw aside from the face of Ben King were absolutely emotionless. The expression on Ben King's face read: Danger.

Baker tapped his copy of the statement against his nose. 'I hope you are as prepared to deal with the situation as this statement indicates,' Baker said, getting to his feet.

'I prepared this statement when it appeared that all of the "student leaders" had gone on vacation,' Calhoun said, trying hard for a smile that he could not get. 'You must understand, gentlemen, that it is now three thirty and I haven't been able to contact a soul about negotiating these demands.'

'That's because the demands are not for negotiating,' Baker said. 'I feel obligated to tell you that *those* demands are only a few of the students' most pressin' needs. There are a hundred other things that will need negotiating that we didn't include because they are things that can be dealt with later.'

'Such as?'

'I just said that those other things shouldn't be approached now . . . You have to remember, Mr Calhoun, that for you Sutton may only be a job as it is to a number of administrators, but for the students it is home. The workers *go home* after a day's work. We are here all day every day for nine months. We can't take our home situation too lightly.'

'But the things on this paper can be worked on,' Calhoun said.

'That's where you're wrong. These things *must* be done. They must be done, instituted, before *we* have anything to do with calling off the student strike.'

'Then it is very clear that we both have things to do,' Calhoun said with incalculable coldness. 'I must prepare for the press conference. I am glad, however, that your group is forewarned.'

'We are happy to have had the opportunity to forewarn you,' Baker said with a sour smile touching the corners of his mouth. 'We'll see you.'

Within seconds all five members of MJUMBE had left Calhoun to the solitude of his office. His first thoughts were that he had to see Earl Thomas and find out if there was any division in the student point of view, but the assurance with which Baker had confronted him and the fact that Thomas had been unavailable for almost four hours made him realize that if there was to be a power showdown it was now his time to show.

The intercom buzzed.

'A Mr Isaac Spurryman from the *Norfolk News* here to see you,' Miss Felch informed Calhoun.

'I can't have any private interviews,' Calhoun snapped. 'Tell him that I will make a blanket statement here in half an hour as I had planned. Did you get Thomas?'

'Nothing, sir,' Miss Felch said, contemplating overtime. 'Nothing.'

'Call Mercer and Hague from Admissions,' Calhoun sighed. 'Tell them I said I need them here immediately ... you may have to stall the press because I'm preparing an alternate statement.'

No sooner had Calhoun put the phone down than the intercom was signaling him once again.

'Yes?'

'Mrs Calhoun wants to talk to you,' Miss Felch reported.

'Put her on ... Hello, hon.'

'I've heard so many things about what was going on,' Mrs Calhoun said in her small worried voice. 'What has happened and how are you?'

'I'm fine,' Calhoun said gruffly. 'I just talked with some of our responsible student leaders. They are unreachable.'

'How do you mean?'

'I was trying to impress upon them the need for some sort of negotiating proposals. They as much as laughed in my face.'

'Oh, Ogden.'

'I think I'm going to have to be forced to close school down and go through a readmission program.'

'Oh, Ogden!'

'I'm waiting for Hague and Fenton right now.'

As Calhoun spoke Charles Hague and Fenton Mercer entered his office. With very little formality Calhoun cut his wife off. She was still protesting his decision when he hung up.

25

Calhoun Moves

At five o'clock the auditorium bell had summoned virtually all sixteen hundred members of the Sutton community. The dorms had been cleared of their thirteen hundred occupants, eight hundred female residents and five hundred males. The commuting students had been sitting in the lounge area of the Student Union Building waiting for word from Earl or Baker as to what they should do. The administrative staff had been completing a day's work at their posts in Sutton Hall. In the entire community only a few faculty members had already left campus for the day. They would learn of Calhoun's statement at six o'clock when the news was broadcast statewide.

The MJUMBE members sat in the first row talking softly to one another. Baker had already prepared a statement in reply to Calhoun's expected ultimatum. Earl, Odds, and Lawman, caught totally by surprise in the canteen, stood near the rear door with a group of MJUMBE enforcers who planned to hold students inside long enough for them to hear Baker's counter-statement.

The SGA representatives had been working intensely on a statement that they had planned to read at the Friday faculty meeting. The last thing they had wanted was a political reprisal from the president so soon.

When Calhoun stepped up to the microphone conversation and chair scraping ceased. The enforcers blocked the paths of all who were not inside to that point. Flashbulbs popped from directly under the podium.

'There is much about the job of president that one likes,' Calhoun began, 'and then there are those aspects one is not so fond of. I have been at Sutton for nine years and I suppose I have had it easier than most men who have held my position. Nevertheless I am always hurt when situations of today's nature come about. I am hurt because it indicates a lack of communication. It indicates a breakdown between my office and the students who make up Sutton University. It indicates a lack of understanding on both parts.

'Sutton has had a Student Government Association for over seventy years. It has had responsible leadership from members of the student community for over seventy years. It is of the utmost importance that this leadership be chosen with the most critical eye possible. It is important because it indicates a political understanding of the nature of campus government.

'When I received the demands last evening I went to work immediately to do as much as I could on so short a notice. I looked into every demand with thoroughness. I replied to each of the demands as I saw fit. I did, in short, as much as I could. But it seems as though my best was not enough for your student leadership. I offered to sit down and negotiate the demands with them. This too was insufficient.

'Based on this, I have decided to close Sutton University until such time as the university can institute a readmission program to make sure that the community is able to function at one hundred per cent efficiency.

'We will begin to take new admission requests next Tuesday, October fifteenth, and will reopen on November first. Our school year will last until June ninth instead of May twenty-second.' There was a dramatic pause. 'Are there any questions?'

His audience was stunned. More flashbulbs popped. The roar from the assembly erupted as though provoked by electric shock. The members of MJUMBE were on their feet screaming at the president, but no one was able to hear above the noise. It was then that people realized there were armed security guards at almost every exit and standing at both stairways leading to the stage.

Calhoun shouted into the microphone, 'I can't possibly handle the questions that I am sure are on everybody's mind unless there is silence. Mr Baker, you'll get your chance!'

There was a question from a female student: 'As of what time is the university officially closed?'

'As of right now, Miss,' Calhoun replied. 'We are giving students until six o'clock tomorrow evening to leave the dorms.'

'What'll happen then?' Baker shouted.

The security guards looked to Calhoun for instructions, but the president said nothing. The newsmen were scampering for the exits to get their stories in. They turned in shock when the audience screamed and the five MJUMBE men were leaping directly onto the stage. Baker squeezed in front of Calhoun and grabbed the microphone. The crowd was on its feet in a veritable frenzy. The guards were blocked by Ben King and Cotton from one side and Abul Menka and Fred Jones at the other. The guards were shouting to Captain Jones, stationed at the rear of the building, asking what they should do.

'Don't leave!' Baker screamed. 'Whatever you do, don't go home! If we allow him to run us away we'll never git anything for as long as Sutton University stands. We must stand our ground.'

Captain Jones broke through the crowd that was swarming around his men. He led the charge, billy stick in hand, that carried him into the waiting arms of huge Ben King who pinioned the older man's flailing arms until he saw Baker leap back to the floor from the platform.

Calhoun was trying hard to maintain some semblance of order from the stage when Abul Menka ripped the microphone from the wall sockets and wrenched the instrument itself from Calhoun's hands and dropped it roughly to the floor.

Baker had started a chant of 'Hell no! We won't go!' that swept through the entire audience until it was as though one thunderous voice was shouting the words in unison and pointing at the retreating figure of the president. Reporters at the front exit were pushed to the ground and cameras purposefully torn from their shoulders and smashed to the floor.

The security force formed a wall to protect Calhoun's way

through the back exit. The crowd of a thousand students pushed its way out of the auditorium and continued the chant on the sidewalks, in the street, and across the oval.

The three SGA representatives became separated briefly during the surge out of the building, but found themselves staring dumbly at the procession led by Ralph Baker that cut a trail directly across campus to the door of Sutton Hall where the chanting continued.

'The wimmin hangin' tight wit' that SNCC shit, ain' they?' Odds asked. 'Out here leadin' the damn revolution. Need to have they asses kicked so they go the hell inside!'

'They've got to leave. We have to protect them from the cops.' Earl breathed heavily. 'Le's git the car an' put the speaker on it. We can direct dudes to stay if they wanna but we need to git the wimmin outta here.'

'Calhoun gonna call the man?' Odds asked.

'You bet'cho balls he is,' Earl asserted. 'Le's go!'

The three men started off at a trot angling away from the crowd forming at Sutton Hall. They were going to get a small, portable public address system that Earl had used during his campaign to solicit votes. It had been taken from Earl's car and stored over the summer months in a back closet in the Student Government office.

'You think they gonna leave?' Odds asked, wiping a handkerchief across his nose.

'We gotta do a convincin' job,' Earl said. 'Remind people of Jackson State an' Kent State, things like that.'

'I ain' anxious to stay an' get shot either,' Odds admitted.

'Better leave with everybody else, then,' Earl said, pulling up in front of Carver Hall and fishing for his office keys.

'This is gonna be the split,' Lawman said, glancing back over his shoulder.

'What split?'

'MJUMBE tellin' everybody to stay. You tellin' people to go.'

'I'm jus' tellin' wimmin to go,' Earl snorted irritably. 'I ain' askin' none a the nigguhs to leave.'

'If you think you can ride aroun' here loudspeakin' about Kent State an' Jackson State an' Orangeburg without niggers flyin' you must be crazy.'

'Malcolm said it wuz a new Negro,' Odds laughed.

'There's some new ones,' Lawman agreed, 'but it's a whole lotta ol' ones too . . . Earl, if you tell people to leave you gonna be cuttin' off yo' own nose,' Lawman pleaded. 'Who in hell you think Calhoun is after? You an' MJUMBE, thass who. If the students leave you as good as finished here.'

Earl managed to get the door open. 'I know,' he said softly, continuing into the back of the office. 'But I gotta do what I think is right. Don't I? How can I ask people to follow me if I'm leadin' 'um to Bull Run jus' to save my own ass?'

'This may not be Bull Run,' Lawman argued.

'But it might be Jackson State revisited,' the SGA president offered.

Odds picked up the connecting wires from the public address system. He took a long look at Lawman and shrugged. Then the two men followed Earl out of the door.

The green Oldsmobile was in the Carver Hall parking lot directly next to the old science hall. Odds scooted in under the wheel and started connecting the sound equipment. Lawman and Earl watched what resembled a congregation of ants standing in front of the Administration Building on the opposite side of the oval. They could still hear many of the students shouting. Others stood in smaller groups watching the windows of Sutton Hall and talking among themselves. Security guards blocked the entrance to the building itself.

'Somebody gon' shoot them fuckin' F Troopers,' Lawman reasoned.

'I wouldn' be surprised,' Earl admitted.

'Ready,' Odds said.

The three men rolled away from the lot, Odds behind the wheel and Lawman in the back seat. When the car made its first turn around the oval in front of the con-gregated demonstrators Earl began: 'This is Earl Thomas, president of the Student Government Association. We are asking that all female students leave Sutton University as has been proposed by the administration. We are making money available from our emergency fund for transportation and for phone calls and telegrams. We ask nothing of the male students, but we ask that all women co-operate. This is not a question of politics. This is a question of safety and I feel that my office has no way to offer protection to the women of the community. Need I remind Black people of what happened at Jackson State when devil policemen fired into a women's dormitory? Need I remind Black people of the slaughter of the four students at Orangeburg? Need I remind Black people of the treatment we have always received from the devil law officers in America? Brothers, our first responsibility is to the women on campus and we must not ask them to risk their lives ... Sisters, please go home.'

The chanting had subsided as students watched the green auto cruise around the oval.

'This is Earl Thomas ...'

MJUMBE continued chanting at the door of Sutton Hall hoping to overcome the damper that Earl had put on its demonstration. As if on cue a police siren was heard wailing in the background. Many of the men stayed to save face with their friends, but women slipped quietly away. Earl continued his broadcast and was not only heard, but listened to. Teachers and administrators nodded silently.

'But baby, there ain' rilly nuthin' like that goin' on, is there?' a tall male student wearing a Sigma sweat shirt was asking a coed.

'Not now,' she admitted, speeding up her exit toward the dorm.

'Thomas is jus' a jive-ass Uncle Tom,' the fraternity man continued. 'I been tellin' you that for the longes' time.'

'Maybe,' the girl admitted walking faster. 'I don' know.'

And so it went all over campus. Men talked freely and loudly about the stands that they would make and complained about their 'Uncle Tom' Student Government president who was chasing their women away. But still coeds made hasty plans to leave Sutton University, Sutton, Va.

26
Lying in Wait

Angela Rodgers sat nervously in front of her television set waiting for the six o'clock news. She had received only enough information from a girlfriend who attended Sutton to set her nerves on end.

When she called Earl's home and got nothing but more questions from Mrs Gilliam, who had not seen Earl since seven thirty that morning, a call to the Student Government office put her in touch with Earl's secretary. Sheila Gibson explained that Odds had gotten her away from her luggage to man the SGA telephones. Earl, she said, had been last seen driving around the oval asking women to go home. That had been an hour ago.

The assurance that Earl had been all right up until five o'clock set Angie's nerves at ease for a moment. Then a radio report informing her that police were conferring with the university president put her on tenterhooks again.

'Good evening. In tonight's WSVA headlines Sutton University is closed until November first. We'll have the details on this and other stories making today's Big Six news in just a moment.' The minute seemed to stretch over a week before the deadpan face of the newscaster reappeared on the small screen.

'At Sutton University this afternoon university president, Ogden Calhoun, stated that he has decided to close the school until a readmission program is instituted on October fifteenth. Calhoun stated that the reason for closing the school was based on thirteen non-negotiable demands placed before him at ten o'clock last evening. He says that it was demanded that he reply by noon today and that his answers brought on a student strike called for by the Student Government Association and an unauthorized campus political organization known as MJUMBE. Earl Thomas, the Student Government president, was unavailable for comment, but Big Six reporter Larry Herman was on hand for Calhoun's five o'clock announcement which brought on a near-riot at the eighty-seven-year-old institution. For that report we switch you to Larry Herman at Sutton University.'

The scene changed to a younger reporter standing in the middle of the oval path with perhaps one hundred or more male students in the background standing in front of Sutton Hall.

'Behind us you see the remaining demonstrators after almost one thousand students congregated to protest the closing of Sutton University by university president Ogden Calhoun who said and I quote: "I have decided to close Sutton University until such time as the university can institute a readmission program to make sure that the community is able to function at one hundred per cent efficiency." The demonstration here at Sutton Hall came after five students in dashikis took over the stage and microphone following Calhoun's announcement. The leader of this group called MJUMBE, Ralph Baker, a senior football player, urged students not to leave the campus saying that students at Sutton would never achieve their goals if they allowed Calhoun to close the school. The students then shouted: "Hell no! We won't go!" and marched on this site you now see in the background. The demonstration continued until a car driven by members of the Student Government Association toured the campus with a public address system urging female students to go home. We are waiting now for a statement from Ogden Calhoun and Police Chief Michael Connors who have been conferring somewhere on campus for over half an hour now. Larry Herman. Big Six News.'

'On other campuses nationally . . .'

Angela turned off the television and sank back into the sofa. She ran long, slim fingers through her short natural hair and started to remove her earrings. She suddenly realized that she hadn't changed her clothes since she had arrived home from the office or even thought of Bobby's dinner. Her thoughts were interrupted by the sound of the four year old's running down the stairs from his bedroom.

'Mommy? When we gonna eat?' the youngster asked.

Angie reached out and pulled his cowboy hat over his eyes.

'Soon. Mommy's had a lot of things on her mind. Why don't you go out an' play with Peanut?'

''Cause Peanut's eatin' his dinner,' Bobby replied. 'Is Uhl comin' to eat dinner?'

'I haven't seen *Uhl* today,' Angie said, starting to slip out of her dress.

'Mommy? You gonna marry Uhl, Mama?'

'I know a certain little cowboy who's gonna get scalped,' Angie said smiling at her son. Bobby ran behind the sofa and laughed heartily. Angie made a gesture as though she would chase him and he scampered to safety up the stairs.

Angie thought seriously about her son's question all through the preparation of dinner. She rarely liked to think about the implications of her relationship with Earl although she was sure that she loved him and that he loved her. She was more than a little bit nervous and afraid to give herself totally. She wondered sometimes if it wasn't an unbreakable wall of suspicion that she had built up around herself. It always seemed as though, real or unreal, someone was taking from her and she wasn't getting anything back. Often she felt empty after she quarreled with Earl. Even when she felt that she had been right during an argument she felt that he walked away with a piece of her inside of him.

She heard the shrill toot of the toy train that Earl had bought Bobby for his birthday. Bobby was a blessing. For a while he had been all that had kept her going. She couldn't imagine facing the house without him; without the echo of his laughter in the yard as he ran and ripped with the young boy from next door; without the big grin on his face when he had been doing something that he had no business doing. He was the spitting image of his father. Round head with curly hair, dark brown eyes planted carefully in a caramel face like the pieces of coal on a snowman, large grin and even teeth. Bobby indeed was a blessing.

Earl was a blessing too. He had completely changed her life. In his own way he had given new shape and strength to her life. She had taken pains to explain her family situation to him over dinner on their first date. She suspected that he wouldn't be interested in her any more and considered that unfortunate because she had such a wonderful, natural time with him, laughing and talking as though they were long-time friends. He had surprised her by approaching her during lunch the following day and asking for a second date, which she had happily arranged.

They met in midtown on the following Saturday. Saturday was always her shopping day and Bobby usually spent the afternoon with Peanut, the youngster next door. Angie picked up the few articles that she had in mind for Bobby before meeting Earl and taking in a movie. After the show he had driven her to the shopping mall and helped her select the groceries and then had taken her home.

Earl and Bobby hit it off like old friends. Earl was up-to-date on Batman, Gunslinger and Mighty Mouse, to name only a few of Bobby's favorites. Angie had commented that apparently Earl spent as much of his Saturday morning in front of a television as the four-year-old.

Earl and Angie began to see each other regularly. She began to feel he was what had been missing in her life during her self-imposed isolation after Bobby's father had left her. She began to realize that all the frustration she had felt during that time was a result of her need for a strong, mature man. Earl Thomas was that type of man.

She also felt that Earl was good for Bobby. She had approached the situation of rearing Bobby with anxiety. As far as she was concerned all boys needed male figures to identify with and the only question in her mind was how much Bobby would be hurt by the absence of a man in the house.

It had seemed as though the summer lasted only a few days because before Angie knew it Earl was back in school. She had been happy that he seemed so pleased with his summer earnings. He told her that he had never made as much before during a summer. He had also been offered a permanent opportunity at the factory, but he had turned it down to concentrate on his schoolwork and his duties as president of the Sutton Student Government Association.

Their lives had slid into a nice groove as far as Angie was concerned. No less than two or three nights a week, many times more often, Earl was at the house when she got home from work. She would cook for him and he would talk to her about the things that he was doing. That was more than important for Angie. It was necessary. Earl had opened her eyes to the fact that she was lost without a man and he had turned out to be the kind of man that she needed. She had come to depend on him to be there when she looked for him. And now there was trouble on Sutton's campus and Earl was neck-high in it. She felt helpless and frightened. She felt alone.

27

The House on Pine Street

In the kitchen of Mrs Gilliam's boarding house on Pine Street two other interested observers had watched the six o'clock news on WSVA, the local channel. Mrs Gilliam and her favorite tenant, Zeke Dempsey, were discussing the news report when Earl Thomas barged directly into the kitchen through the back door from the driveway.

'Well, if it ain't the star of the show,' Zeke said lightly. 'How you doin' stranger? You know Miz Gilliam, I believe.'

'Yeah. Right. How're you, ma'am? Whuss the put-on?' Earl asked, sitting down opposite Zeke at the kitchen table. Mrs Gilliam, as usual, was stirring up a concoction at the stove.

'Well, we see ya so rarely 'roun' here,' Zeke began laughing. 'Thought it might be a good idea to reintraduce ourselves an' start all over.'

'I guess I know what you mean,' Earl apologized. 'I'v been rather brief. I came in late last night an' when I got up Miz Gilliam had already had her breakfast an' gone to the market. I don' know if you was at work or what.'

'I went to rake leaves at the Coles's this mornin',' Zeke admitted. 'I guess that was 'bout eight.'

'I was later than that,' Earl said.

'I'm usually here, but I went out in the country this mornin' to get some fresh veg'tables. Me an Old Hunt,' Mrs Gilliam replied.

'That car runnin'?' Zeke asked laughing. The talk in the boarding house generally was that Old Man Hunt's Dodge wouldn't run downhill.

'Didn't go too fast,' Mrs Gilliam laughed, waddling back over to the table. 'Every time we did above forty or so it start coughin' like a tubercular, but did all right.'

'Fresh veg'tables?' Earl asked picking up the lost thread.

'Had to, child,' Mrs Gilliam mocked. 'Sto' bought veg'tables start to tas' like wax after while. I hate to go to the country 'cause it generally take so long after you talk to them 'bout everything thass happened since you las' saw them, but I had bought this oxtail for some oxtail soup an' I couldn' see the point in havin' it without havin' some good veg'tables.' She took the top off the large pot with a potholder. The warm, tantalizing fragrance of oxtail escaped from what Earl referred to as 'the cauldron.'

'Heard school been closed down,' Zeke said offhand.

'Yeah,' Earl said quietly. 'I was out there all day tryin' to get different things together. We called the head of the Board of Trustees in D.C., but she was so busy talkin about how great "Brother" Calhoun was that I knew I wouldn' get anywhere. Then we printed notices an' put 'um in faculty boxes callin' a Faculty Only meetin' for in the mornin', but I don't know what I'll say if we have it. The things that we had in mind aren't really relevant any more.'

'Calhoun took care of that,' Zeke said.

'I s'pose it was my fault,' Earl said. 'I'm sure that most of the overall picture is my fault, but it seems that I should know better than to think Calhoun will take a long time to move by now. I should've been expectin' him to close school down when I handed him the paper las' night.'

'I don' think you're right this time at all, Earl,' Zeke said quietly. 'Now I know I'm not a college man like yo'self an' I have always regretted that I wasn't, even if I hadn't had any particular use fo' a degree in the kinda work I'm doin' now,' the handyman smiled. 'But many's the person has tol' me that I'm blessed with what I call common sense, good ol' horse sense. I believe that along with the bookin' that you have done God gave you some horse sense also. None of the other school presidents have reacted so quickly to their protests like Calhoun. I don't think there was any way for any person to predict that he would do that ... I think sometimes you try to carry more than your share ...'

'Amen,' said Mrs Gilliam.

Earl was sitting opposite Zeke and looking out of the window. He hadn't looked at his friend and fellow-boarder once, but it was obvious that the words were having their effect.

'You know it's not but so much that one man can do,' Zeke continued. 'It's not but so much that one man should do ... you know I heard you talkin' las' week 'bout how you had to hurry to get them papers together because the students were expectin' them an' would be on yo' back.'

'That was about keepin' my word,' Earl said, interrupting and lighting a cigarette. 'I was ...' the young man cut himself off. He began to feel as if he were becoming defensive though he didn't feel a need to be defensive with Mrs Gilliam and/or Zeke.

'You remember what I'm talkin' about?' Zeke asked, lighting a smoke of his own. 'Na mebbe this thing today an' las' night has got somethin' to do with yo' not havin' yo' papers done, but how many a them was helpin' do the work? I mean aside from the two friends who come by here?'

'Nobody really,' Earl admitted.

'An' yet they wuz the ones you *knew* wuz gonna be on yo' back,' the handyman said laughing. 'The firs' complainers an' the las' workers. Thass been a problem wit' Negroes forever an' a day in the United States. The firs' complainers an' the las' workers.'

'I had things I was s'pose to do,' Earl said, refusing to see the point.

'Right!' Zeke agreed. 'But the whole thing is that you would have done yo' work an' been in the same situation. You'd be still the only one doin' any. Martin Luther King did his work. Malcolm X did his work. But when they died the movements that they started died.'

'Oh, man,' Earl exclaimed.

'All I'm sayin' really is that you were workin' for a buncha ingrates who wouldn' appreciate you if this was yo' thing by yourself. That with a li'l help you mighta made it ... what I mean is that you always blamin' yo'self somehow no matter what happens. You ain' never gonna make it through life that way. It's all right to take yo' responsibilities seriously. It's the bes' thing in the world for a man if he's gonna be a man, but you gonna fin' that yo' responsibilities are gonna be enough without you takin' on what people should be volunteerin' to share since it's for everybody's own good.'

'I agree,' Mrs Gilliam said. 'How're your grades? I bet you don't have a point in none of 'um. When was the las' time you wrote yo' mother? I bet she don't know nothin' 'bout this foolishness. You still ain' been to see Dr Bennett about that tooth I gave you that stuff for . . . you see what I mean? Neglectin' yo' own good for a bunch that won't even help you. I know that Sutton crowd. They always have upper-class students who're too lazy to work.'

'Middle-class niggers,' Zeke said. 'The Deltas an' A.K.A.'s an' Alpha niggers who wouldn' know a job if it bit 'um. Thass the kind you wastin' yo' time on.'

'I don't agree,' Earl said. He lit another cigarette as he got up. 'You know when you get a job what it entails. You know that a great many students don' know anything about the campus politics an' that most of the res' don' care. You take on the job 'cause you have a certain set of ideas that you'd like to implement for the good of the community.'

'An' what if the community won' help you?'

'Thass not the point. They do somethin' when they elect you.'

'Write a X nex' to yo' name on a piece a paper. I think . . .'

'I don't agree,' Earl said cutting in brusquely. He was standing with his back turned to Zeke and Mrs Gilliam watching more of the red and brown leaves being added to a small fire in the middle of the back yard. He always felt he was watching something beautiful when he saw Old Man Hunt putter around in the yard. At that moment the warm glow of the fire illuminating the old man's face seemed to disclose some secret pleasure that was causing a smile to creep across the burnished wrinkles. 'I know that this talk was staged to make me feel better or somethin', but I don't feel the same way.'

'It wasn't meant that way at all,' Zeke said. He met Mrs Gilliam's questioning glance with a quieting gesture indicating that he would handle it. 'I'm quite sure that Miz Gilliam an' I would need a whole lot mo' facts befo' we started to tell you what to do, but we've been watchin' you go through these months of work an' school an' we'd been talkin' about how wrapped up you get in the things you feel need to be done.'

'The people at Sutton elected me to do a job,' Earl reminded them. 'Anything else is a cop-out.'

'It's good to be committed to yo' race,' Zeke said. 'Miz Gilliam will tell you that as ol' as I am I wuz right out there wit 'um in Selma in sixty-four. I was doin' all I could with the NAACP right here . . . an' one a the things that held me back in terms of maybe leadin' in the community was the fact that I didn' have much education. Both of us feel that you can be a great man in terms of helpin' our people an' that the thing you really need is yo' diploma.'

Earl turned around very quickly. Somehow he had been missing the point all through his conversation with the handyman. He was amazed to see why Zeke had been so persistent and had not let the subject drop. Zeke had seen the news. He had heard about the closing and the readmission program. He and Mrs Gilliam would easily see that if this were carried out that he would not be admitted. Zeke was asking him to back down.

'You can't think I'd go to Calhoun,' Earl said.

'No,' Zeke said, taking up the cup of coffee that Mrs Gilliam placed before him. 'I didn't think you would. But you should. I believe you should.'

'Earl's response to that was cut off by the jingling of the phone in the hallway. He waved Mrs Gilliam away and moved through the hall to answer it, discarding his sweater as he went.

'Mrs Gilliam's,' he said. 'Earl Thomas speaking.'

'Earl, this is Sheila,' the SGA secretary announced into the receiver. 'I've got a problem. We've gone into the limit for emergency funds. I've given out almost two hundred and twenty dollars. I'm sure there are more people coming in too. Especially after dinner.'

'Cut into some of those dance allowance funds then. It doesn't matter because all the money has to be paid back. It's jus' for gettin' students home in bad situations. Keep a good record.'

'Okay,' Sheila said. That should have been the end of the conversation but Sheila stayed on the line.

Earl felt embarrassed. He told himself that his conversation with Zeke and his experiences over the past twenty-four hours had made him hypersensitive.

'It doesn't matter now,' he said into the receiver. 'I know what's gone on, but it doesn't matter now.'

'I feel like an ass,' Sheila said. 'I feel like I ruined everything. I could sort've see it when you got up at the meetin' in the auditorium at twelve o'clock when the strike was called.'

'It's all over now,' Earl said.

'Not really. I wanted to tell you something when you came in and asked for me to distribute this emergency money, but I didn't know what to say. I was embarrassed.' There was a long pause. 'Did you know all the time?'

'No.'

'Did you know that that key was probably the only reason he went out with me?'

'No.'

'Earl, what's gonna happen tuhmaruh?'

'You've got me,' Earl breathed heavily. 'You have got me.' The SGA president laughed. 'Who knows? Ask Head Nigger ... Hey! How long you gonna be on campus?'

''Til tomorrow afternoon,' the secretary replied.

'Well, man the station 'til I get there. It's about six thirty? I'll be out there by quarter-to-eight. That letter that I left out on my desk needn't be touched 'cause it's already useless since Calhoun closed school. I'm comin' out to do another one that I'll run off myself. Me an' Odds or somebody'll be out there tuhmaruh also, so leave the checkbook where I can find it.'

'Okay ... what's the new letter gonna say an' to who?'

'It'll be to the faculty at this meetin' if we have it. I have no idea what it's gonna say. Prob'bly: Help!' Earl laughed feebly. 'Later on,' he said.

'Good luck,' she said.

'You eatin'?' Mrs Gilliam asked when she heard the phone being returned to its hook.

'Yes, ma'am,' he called. 'Do I have time to get a shower?'

'I make time fo' musty men to get showers befo' they set at my table,' Mrs Gilliam assured him loudly. 'You go 'head.'

Earl hurried into the shower and lathered himself under the hot spray. He felt the tension being soaked away and realized for the first time all day that he was bone-weary. For Earl, being bone-weary was quite different from being tired. It was a state in which he found himself after having to do a great deal of work in a short period of time. After stretches like this when the work was completed his bones turned to lead and his muscles to rubber. He needed to sit down. He found when he stood he was sure that his bones and organs would slip into fatty pouches and vacuum caves within his frame and be dragged into a bed and allowed to redistribute themselves. He was sorry that there would be no bed waiting for him within the next few hours.

The shower completed, Earl stepped from behind the dripping curtain and dried himself with the rough-grained towel. He then slipped into his house robe and brushed his teeth, gargled, and flip-flopped back out into the hall. The downstairs cuckoo was chiming. Earl counted. Seven bells.

Before he could get to his room Zeke poked his head out of his doorway.

'There's two professors here to see you,' he said seriously. 'The coach and another man.'

'Where are they?' Earl asked.

'Downstairs. You know Miz Gilliam wuzn' gonna let 'um up here 'til you said it was okay.'

Earl nodded and walked to the banister that overlooked the first-floor alcove and sitting room. Below, Coach Edmund Mallory and the head of the History Department sat discussing something between themselves.

'Hello . . . how are you?' Earl said, attracting their attention. 'Come on up. I was in the shower . . . Mrs Gilliam never lets people into anyone's room.'

The two men smiled uneasily. They picked up their coats and walked up the thirteen spiraling stairs to the second floor.

'Won't you come in?' Earl asked, showing the faculty members into his room. 'I'm not really prepared to handle a great deal of company, but I do have a couple of chairs.'

'That's fine,' Coach Mallory said warming a bit. 'We don't want to take up a great deal of your time, but we received the notes that you put in the faculty boxes this afternoon, and we have been tryin' to get in touch with you or MJUMBE all day . . .'

'I was a little hard to catch up to,' Earl admitted.

'Well, we were curious about this meeting,' Mallory continued. 'Because we don't think that the proper thing's bein' done. The truth is, we wanted to do somethin' constructive befo' we even learned that Calhoun was closin' school. What can we do?'

Earl smiled as he thought the question over and lit up a cigarette. There was a bit of comedy to be felt in the scene. The ever-serious football Simon Legree posing a sensitive question; the quiet, studious history professor sitting bolt-upright in a disheveled brown suit, sporting a red nose that indicated a taste of too much whisky. Mrs Gilliam had probably smelled it too. That meant a night of phone calls to inform all of the neighbors that McNeil had visited Earl drunk. He would have to ask her not to mention to anyone the fact that McNeil and Mallory had come to see him. Because of their jobs, he would say.

'I don't suppose you could do anythin',' Earl finally said, sucking on the cigarette. 'I had planted those notices before Calhoun announced that school was closin'.'

'But the meetin' was called . . .' McNeil began.

'To find out if the faculty as a separate entity thought our demands were unfair,' Earl supplied.

'Some of us don't,' McNeil said. 'A few of us are in positions where to agree or disagree means little because we are the head of a department,' he tapped his own chest, 'or a coach with a winning record for eight straight years an' a Sutton alumni.' Mallory was indicated. 'There are others, mostly the young white members, who also agree, but I'm afraid it's really not enough of the cross-section that you would need to make a big impression.'

'Yes,' Mallory grunted. 'Your agreers are all either political radicals or Phys Ed teachers who aren't supposed to have a brain in their heads.' He laughed without humor at the thought.

'Then there'll be no meeting,' Earl said with finality.

McNeil set fire to a cigar. 'We'll go 'round an' get some signatures in the mornin',' he said, puffing to make sure he was lit. 'If there is anythin' to say, come to the meetin'. Otherwise, we'll just know that nothin' positive has happened.'

'What will the signatures be for?' Earl asked.

'MJUMBE has issued a statement referring to slanted reports being made to distort the facts to parents. They insist that the parents could help the student cause if the students were not being type-cast as hoodlums an' thugs. Our letter will back up their earlier notes and statements, and perhaps some literature of yours, and be sent to the parents. This might include a plea that school not be reopened without a community hearing to discuss what punishment, if any, your group and MJUMBE should receive.'

'What punishment, hell,' Earl snorted pulling on a T-shirt. 'We won't be allowed back fo' a hearin'.'

'What I'm sayin' is that it should be petitioned or added to the list of demands. Something like: "No punitive measures shall be taken against the students who participate in this strike."'

'Calhoun would laugh at somethin' like that if he laughs at the things we have down there now,' Earl said without enthusiasm. 'But there's a long way to go befo' we get to that.'

'Howzat?' McNeil asked.

'Befo' Calhoun can *keep* us off of Sutton's campus,' the SGA president said, 'he's got to get us off.'

28

Destruction

The Strike Communications Center on the third floor of the fraternity house issued a six-thirty plea to all female students. It read as follows:

Dear Sisters,
    The members of MJUMBE, Ralph Baker, 'Speedy' Cotton, Fred Jones, Ben King, and Abul Menka are not certain at this time what measures of force will be used to make members of this community leave before the six o'clock deadline for tomorrow. We understand the concern exhibited by both our sisters and our brothers over this issue and we too are concerned. We ask that all sisters who are asking their parents to pick them up notify their parents of a proposed three o'clock meeting in the auditorium where we can explain the student side of the issue. As usual the administration has bottled up the media so that students appear to be nothing more than trouble-making hoodlums. We hope you will convey this message and we ask that you all be present.

                                        ASANTE,
                                Brothers of MJUMBE

This particular statement was used by Ogden Calhoun to bolster his position when shortly after eight p.m. violence erupted on the campus of Sutton University.

There had been meetings within all fraternal organizations, both male and female, to draw up statements pledging varied degrees of support to the student leaders. On the way back to the dormitories both men and women said that they were harassed by members of the Sutton police force who were patroling the campus area. The reply to this harassment was unleashed fury in the halls of the dormitories where windows were smashed, lounge furniture was thrown through doors and windows, and public address equipment and telephones were ripped from the walls.

Calhoun received a phone call at his home where he was relaxing, dressed for bed.

'Excuse me, sir,' the speaker began, 'but they've gone crazy out here on the campus. They're tearin' up everything.'

'Who? Who has done what?' Calhoun asked sitting bolt upright.

'This is Captain Jones. I don't really know what brought any of this on. My men were on foot patrol an' the police from town were cruisin' in their cars. I was near Sutton Hall an' I heard all this glass breakin' an' people shoutin' an' yellin'. I run down to Washington Hall in time to see a lounge chair gittin' pitched outta the winda.'

'What have the police done?'

'Nothin' but locked they cars, sir, but they scared.'

'Tell them . . .'

'This is Earl Thomas,' a second voice cut in. 'We're in the guardhouse in the parking lot. Call off the damn cops!'

'Thomas? What's goin' on?'

'The police are goin' on. They provoked everything. You're gonna have a real riot if you keep them here.'

'Where is Chief Connors?'

'He's not here, I don't think,' Earl said.

Calhoun muttered a curse. 'I'll be there. See what can be done. Put Jones back on the line . . . Jones! Do somethin'.'

'Yes, sir. You comin'?'

'I'll be right there!'

Before Captain Jones had thoroughly replaced the receiver Earl was already galloping across the campus to his car where the P.A. system remained intact.

Sounds of crashing glass were still echoing across the oval

and lights in the dormitories were being flashed off and on. Earl thought that the flashing lights might be signaling an S.O.S. His car almost backed into the school ambulance being driven by one of the security guards toward Sutton Hall. He paced himself and entered the back half of the oval directly behind a cruising patrol car. He turned the P.A. system up as loud as he could.

'Brothers and sisters. This is Earl Thomas. I have notified the president of the university about the harassing tactics used by members of the Sutton police force and he is on his way to the campus. I am askin' all of you to cease the destruction of our own property.' Earl's drive was interrupted by the opening of his car door on the passenger side. For a moment his heart seemed to stop. He felt sure that it was a member of the Sutton police. It was Abul Menka, carrying a .22 caliber rifle with a box of bullets in his hand.

'Keep drivin' an' talkin',' Abul breathed.

'Brothers and sisters. This is Earl Thomas. I am askin' for peace. Please stop tearin' up our homes. Please do not respond to the police by destruction an' vandalism. We can hurt no one but ourselves that way. I am askin' too that the Sutton police drive over to the Administration Building and wait for further orders from their superior. I am askin' for peace.'

'You layin' to get a piece a lead from one a these devils,' Abul said lighting a cigarette. 'Man, who you think you are? Martin Luther King? Talkin' all this peace shit . . . these devils baitin' the brothers an' sisters, jus' doin' they damndest fo' an excuse to shoot yo' people down!'

'Our people,' Earl reminded Abul.

'Yours if they crawl on their bellies!' Menka snapped. 'I'm down here to defend.'

'Hi many can you defend wit' one .22?'

'Hi many guns did we have at Jackson State? If we'da had one .22 Black people might not a been the only ones that died.'

'Or mo' Black people mighta died,' Earl said. 'Brothers and

sisters.' The SGA president turned his attention back to the P.A. Abul was silent.

'At leas' turn yo' light out so you won' be such an easy target,' Menka said.

Earl doused the lights. They watched two patrol cars pull up in the driveway next to Sutton Hall. There were still two more somewhere.

On their third turn around the oval the sound of breaking glass and screaming had subsided. Outlines of people were stretched across the screens in the windows of the dormitories.

'Please turn off yo' lights an' stay away from the windows,' Earl said, continuing to drive slowly with his lights off. 'Stay away from yo' windows an' keep yo' lights off.'

All four patrol cars were accounted for. The only people seen walking out in the open were the security guards. Earl's car was caught in a blaze of headlights as he started his fourth cycle. Both Earl and Abul recognized the car as the Lincoln belonging to Ogden Calhoun who sat stiffly behind the wheel. Calhoun passed by them as though he had not seen the Oldsmobile. Earl sighed his relief.

'Misser Big Nigger,' Abul sneered. 'A plague on his people. A fuckin' star-gazin' parasite! A curse on the race!'

Earl cut the engine off and sat quietly for a minute in front of the path leading to the fraternity house.

'We all got a long way to go,' the SGA president breathed.

'You can' git but so far runnin' off at the mouth while you on yo' han's an' knees.'

'You cain' git nowhere dead.'

'Better dead than a slave,' Abul spat, lighting another cigarette.

'Is that the way you felt last May when I saw you an' yo' guest at that bar on 211?' Earl asked lighting his own cigarette.

'I wuz waitin' fo' you to bring that up las' night,' Abul said, his anger and sneering tones dying.

'I asked you a question,' Earl said.

'Do you wanna know if a white bitch turned my head around?'

'I wanna know what turned you around.'

'Knowledge, man. I learned where I wuz wrong. Thass all.'

'An' you aren't wearin' dashikis because the fay broad blew yo' program away?'

'She had nuthin' to do with it. I was sick! I was wrong.' Abul was getting angry again.

'Then learn somethin' else,' Earl said softly. 'You don't face a bazooka with a water pistol. You don't fight a tank with a slingshot. You don't risk the lives of future Black mothers jus' because you have an emotional commitment to a .22.'

'All dead bodies that leave this world undefended tonight will be placed on yo' doorstep,' Abul said.

'All brave Black fools who fight when it is not time to fight will be brought to you.'

'We'll see. The pigs will show us,' Abul said as he got out of the car.

While the pig police occupied the minds of the two young Black student leaders, Ogden Calhoun was dismissing them from any further duty on campus, and making another call.

'Yes, I know it's inconvenient. It is an emergency,' the Sutton president was saying. There was a long pause while the man to whom he wanted to talk was summoned to the phone.

'Yes? ... yes, Governor. How are you? Yes, sir. That's the point. I am havin' trouble an' I'll prob'ly get a whole lot more tomorrow ... I asked that the campus be cleared by six ... good ... if they won't leave at six I'll call your men ... They'll be right outside of Sutton? Wait, let me take that number ... yes, I'll call back tomorrow ... right.'

Calhoun reclined in his high-back chair and let the exhaustion that had followed him all through a tense and tiring day take over. He had been assured that a National Guard unit would be available if he needed it for the next night. He felt a fearful certainty that it would be needed.

29

Plans Abandoned

Arnold McNeil was sitting in his living room reading a book when the phone rang. It was answered by his wife, Millie.

'It's Edmund,' she said, referring to the head football coach.

'Good,' McNeil said, coming to take the receiver. He had not been expecting a call from the coach. 'Lo, Ed,' he began. 'What's up?'

'Arnold? There's been some more trouble down here this evening,' Mallory said quickly.

'What's happened?'

'The students tore up some furniture an' things in the dorms 'bout fifteen minutes ago,' the coach breathed. He was standing in the pay phone booth in the lobby of Sutton Hall.

'Where's Calhoun? How did these things get started?'

'Calhoun is in his office,' Mallory said. 'He came runnin' in a few minutes ago with Jones an' one a the men from the Sutton police force.'

'Did he say anything?'

'Not to me, but he seems more resolute than ever about closing the place down.'

'How do you know?'

'He sent the local force home, but Nancy, the girl on the night switchboard, said he made a call to the governor.'

'For what?'

'For the National Guard, I suppose,' Mallory fumed.

'Oh, my God,' McNeil shouted.

'What is it, honey?' Millie McNeil asked.

'I'll tell you in a minute,' McNeil waved to her. 'So what are you sayin', Ed?'

'That I don' know what good any alliance we've formed at this stage will do. I know that Calhoun wants the school closed.'

'We all know that. What can we do?'

'Talk to Admissions the first thing in the mornin'. Try an' see if we can't form an ad hoc faculty committee to investigate the new admissions program.'

'Do you think Thomas added that demand we suggested?'

'I don' have any idea. I wonder seriously if he'll come to that meetin' in the mornin' too. I think the boy's fed up with the whole thing.'

'I didn' feel that way,' McNeil said. 'He's got to do something.'

'Well, whether he comes or not I suggest we go out an' get the signatures of the faculty members who are willin' to serve on the new Admissions Committee to see what happens to Thomas an' MJUMBE.'

'We know what'll happen,' McNeil said. His tone expressed frustration at the prospect of the bureaucratic whirlpool. 'They won't be allowed back. Calhoun will say that they're keepin' the school from operatin' at one hundred per cent efficiency. That was the "catch phrase" in Calhoun's pronouncement . . . and all of the ol' guard will fall in behind him waggin' their tails.'

'Especially after what happened today an' tonight,' Mallory admitted. 'What can we do?'

'Get the signatures from people at that meetin' in the morning,' McNeil suggested. 'That's about all.'

'In other words we really can' do anything,' Mallory said.

'That's right,' McNeil confessed. 'That's exactly right.'

Earl Thomas was not having an easy time explaining the activities of the day to his girl, Angie. He had left the campus minutes after the four Sutton patrol cars were dismissed and had flopped exhausted on Angie's living room sofa.

'I jus' don' want to see your whole college career ruined,' she said, stroking the back of his neck. 'I'm sorry, but you know as well as I do what will happen tomorrow.'

'I'm not leavin' tuhmaruh,' Earl said. 'I'm stayin'. I tol' the women to leave.'

'The women want to stay. You said so yourself. They mus' feel as deeply about the whole thing as you do . . . an' besides, there are more women than men on Sutton's campus.'

'Not the point. The point is that they have to go.'

'An' what if they don't go?'

'Then I'll leave 'cause I won't want to see them gettin' their heads kicked in.'

'You really think that's goin' to happen? Then I don' want you there either. I don' want to see . . .'

'You sound like Zeke an' Mrs. Gilliam earlier this evenin'!' Earl exclaimed. 'What is this? A conspiracy? Get Earl to chump out on his commitment day?' He sat up and lit a cigarette, saying, 'I don' tell you about things I want to do to start a damn debate! I tell you so you'll know where I stand!'

'Or where you lay,' Angie said, walking to the easy chair and reclining in it. Earl could barely make out her features in the darkness. He could see that her head was back and that her eyes were closed. She was rocking a bit and her bare feet were rubbing across the carpet. He got up and walked over to her, standing her up before him and kissing her forehead.

'Nothin' will happen to me,' he said. 'I promise.'

'How can you promise that?' Angie asked. He could see for the first time that her eyes were brimming with tears.

'Nothin' will happen to me that's bad,' Earl said. 'I mean that the worst thing I could do would be to stay away from where I belong. If I'm not there I couldn't do you any good or myself any good. No matter how healthy I looked, I'd be dead inside.'

'Earl! I know something will happen to you. Something always happens . . . Earl! Make love to me, Earl. Please?'

There were mixed emotions in the man's eyes. More than anything else in the world he wanted to slap his woman; feel his palm smack with all the conviction he could muster across her tear-stained face. He wanted to grab her and squeeze her until she begged him to release her. He wanted to turn and walk away from her, leaving her there in torment wondering what she had said to anger him.

'Self-pity?' he asked. 'Selfishness an' self-pity? Something always happens to the things that you love? Make love to you one last time before I die? I should knock hell out of you! Doesn't how I live mean more than whether I live? I'm ashamed of myself, you know? I'm damn ashamed because when I met you I thought you were so stuck up and now I see that it was an ice wall of self-pity; a walking martyr. Angie Rodgers. Her old man is dead. Her boyfriend screwed her and left her with a baby in her belly. She's twenty-two years old and walks around with a foot in her ass that was placed there when she was born. I swear and be damned!'

Angie was stunned. She tried to force Earl to meet her eyes and see the tears that ran more freely now, across her nose, salt water stinging her lips and tongue.

'Is that what it is, Earl? Is that what you think? My desire to make a good home and be a good mother was an "ice wall of self-pity"? My putting aside the things that twenty-two year old women do because I had no man to help me was self-pity? Was it? What can a woman be but cold when she's got to make it by herself? . . . Earl, I love you. I'm a woman . . . Maybe I was wrong to ask you, beg you to make love to me, but I couldn't think of any other way to let you know how much I really love you.' Angie could find no more words to say. She hadn't even looked up during the last part of her monologue to see the pain burned across Earl's face. She hadn't even noticed that Earl was an open book of confusion and agony because of the things he had said that suddenly became obscene and too incredibly wrong to tolerate any balance or consolation. She walked slowly from the room and up the carpeted stairs.

Earl sat under the lamp smoking a cigarette, asking himself where all of the understanding he had thought he possessed was now, when he was faced with a crisis that called for understanding. Halfway through the cigarette he stubbed it out and turned off the lamp. He had made up his mind to go and talk to his woman. He wanted to find out if he could be forgiven for being a man.

Friday

30
Final Word

Mrs Gloria Calhoun, the former Gloria Vernon of Saginaw, Michigan, sat quietly in the upstairs bedroom waiting for the ten o'clock news report. The door had slammed downstairs only minutes before and she had been expecting her husband to come into the bedroom, but now supposed that he was watching the news on the television set in the den.

She felt rather foolish watching television for information about her husband when he sat just one floor beneath her, but she was somewhat afraid of what the news would be. She hadn't been able to help overhearing the tense phone call that had come from Captain Jones at just past eight o'clock. She hadn't been able to ignore the fact that for some reason Earl Thomas, the Student Government president, had cut into the phone call. As a matter of fact it had seemed as though the usually soft-spoken young Thomas was screaming, his words audible from her seat across the room. A disturbance had taken place and had doubtlessly involved the Sutton police. She hadn't wanted her husband to ask them for any assistance. The Sutton students hadn't demonstrated any need to be contained by armed bullies. She crossed her fingers and prayed that none of the students had been hurt. She hoped that a student's injury had not been the reason that her husband had not come up the stairs to face her.

When Ogden Calhoun completed his doctorate in 1946 he went straight to Saginaw to marry the woman he had met during his undergraduate studies at Howard University. Calhoun had been one of the youngest black Ph.D.'s in psychology in America. There had been times when neither of the two thought that he would make it. The war, the money, the pressure on Blacks in the higher realms of the educational system had all been against the young couple, but somehow Calhoun's determination had paid off and brought a ray of hope to friends and relatives who saw an almost fairy-tale ending placed on the Calhoun story when the couple married in the Vernon family church.

Unfortunately that was *not* the end of the story, but rather the beginning of a new phase. The second phase included Calhoun's appointment as the head of the Psychology Department at Small's College in West Virginia, radical contributions on the causes of Black psychological problems to national psychology journals that lost him his appointment, the loss of their only child, Margaret, from polio at the age of two, and a subsequent wall of frustration built between them by Calhoun's long, exhausting work schedule and his wife's boredom.

The appointment of Calhoun as president of Sutton had been a second beginning of the second phase. Neither of them had really expected the appointment because in the fifties there was an open fear of Blacks who spoke out so openly against racism and Black oppression. It had been felt that Calhoun's articles of the fifties would be held against him even ten years later by the white corporations that supplied much of the financing for private Black institutions.

The first year at Sutton had been like a breath of fresh air for the couple. Each became involved with new duties. Mrs Calhoun was a frequent speaker for Women's Day programs at churches in the Black community. Her picture often appeared in the local paper when she was endorsing another one of her many charities.

As a still-life photo of Ogden Calhoun appeared on the television screen, Mrs Calhoun began to regret the very involvement that she had once been so happy to discover. Her community responsibilities had practically severed her ties with her husband. The two of them had lost touch with one another. Their ability to communicate had faded. Their interest in one another had become impersonal. Their sex life had disappeared.

'Sutton University in Sutton, Virginia, was closed today by University President Ogden Calhoun who reacted to a student strike due to nonimplementation of twelve demands with these words: "I have decided to close Sutton University until such time as the university can undergo a readmission program that will insure the community an ability to function at one hundred per cent efficiency." Sources have intimated that the Admissions Office will not be considering new applications received from Student Government officials or members of a new radical student faction call MJUMBE. These student leaders touched off two near-riots today when first they seized the stage at a meeting where Calhoun announced plans to close the school, and tonight when students destroyed an estimated eight thousand dollars' worth of furniture and dormitory equipment. During the interruption of this afternoon's meeting the Sutton students were urged by a MJUMBE leader named Ralph Baker to defy Calhoun and remain on campus. The Sutton police were called in to patrol the grounds, but were asked to leave by Calhoun after the vandalism began. The eighty-seven-year-old institution has been ordered cleared by six o'clock tomorrow evening, but many students have vowed to stay.'

Mrs Calhoun used the remote control to turn off the television when the announcer turned his attention to other news-making events. She was relieved that no one had been hurt, but there was clear frustration and tension etched into the corners of her mouth and around her eyes, frowns penciling crooked furrows across her forehead. She reached for her coffee cup, but finding it empty returned it to the night table beside her bed. She was tempted to switch off the light and avoid the confrontation that would occur when her husband came up for bed, but she did nothing of the sort. Instead, she allowed her mind to wander, floating across the days, weeks, months, and years of which her marriage consisted. She was so lost in thought that her husband startled her when he opened the door.

'How are you?' she tried tentatively.

'Tired,' Calhoun spat out, puffing his pipe.

'Is everything all right on campus?'

'For now,' Calhoun shrugged, sitting on the edge of the bed. 'I went over and did what I could.'

'Was anyone hurt?'

'Of course not. I don't think there was any real reason for the entire incident. Probably started by MJUMBE.'

'You think so?'

'Glo, if you had seen them this afternoon you would have no doubt at all. Savage! Ripped the microphone right out of my hands this afternoon. Tore the wires out of the control panel and threw it on the floor ... student leaders ...'

'You couldn't talk to them at all?'

'That's why I'm closing,' Calhoun snapped. 'I had them in my office and tried to talk them into negotiating the demands. Damn if they'd have anything to do with anything I suggested.'

'What did they say?' Mrs Calhoun asked, sitting up.

'Said they'd bring me some things we could bargain with after I'd done what *had* to be done. Ain't that rich?' Calhoun stood and removed his coat, shirt, and tie. He dropped all three articles into a plastic laundry bag that hung from the closet door. 'Tell Arnie that I'll need these things Saturday at the latest when he comes by ... do I have any shirts down at the laundry?'

'Yes. He said he'd bring them by when he picked up tomorrow. In the meantime you have plenty of shirts in the bottom drawer.'

'Good,' Calhoun replied. He took a fresh pair of pajamas out of the middle dresser drawer and proceeded into the bathroom.

Mrs Calhoun stared blankly at her husband and in her mind's eye she could see the years of her life turning to water and swirling down an hourglass-shaped drain. What had happened to them and to their lives? she wondered.

Where had *her* Ogden Calhoun gone? How long had he been gone? Where was Gloria Calhoun, the woman who had saved herself for this one man?

Her musing was interrupted by a clap of thunder followed quickly by a jagged snake of lightning that blazed across the darkened sky, as drops of silver-paint rain appeared on her windows. She got up and closed the huge windows that looked out over the back of the yards, her carefully tended gardens, and down perhaps a quarter of a mile where a thousand lights still shone bright inside the dormitories on Sutton's campus.

The lightning flashed again causing the lights in the Calhoun bedroom to blink. The wind was picking up. Once again the vision of the young Calhoun, the young Black radical, the advancer of new psychological theories based on the experiences of Black people, danced through Gloria Calhoun's mind.

'It's so sad,' she was thinking, 'to think of what has become of my knight in shining armor . . . my knight in rusty armor.'

31
Faculty Only

Ogden Calhoun enjoyed the luxury of an extra hour's sleep on Friday morning. He had ignored the seven-thirty alarm that generally started his day and informed his wife to wake him at eight thirty instead. He was expecting a long and trying day on the campus once he got there, a day crammed with meetings, conferences, phone calls, and unexpected problems. Upon arriving on campus shortly before ten o'clock, however, he was happy that he hadn't elected to report to work any later. Fenton Mercer, the portly second-in-command at Sutton, was sitting in his office fidgeting with a damp handkerchief.

'Mercer!' Calhoun exclaimed with his best everything-is-roses greeting. 'So early in the day and you're here already. What's up?'

'There's a meeting I think you should know about,' Mercer said nervously. 'I recalled when I heard about it what you had said about my not informing you about the last impromptu meeting that was called and . . .'

'My God, man!' Calhoun snapped, placing his attaché case down on the desk. 'What in hell is it?'

'There's been a Faculty Only meeting called in the Dunbar Library,' Mercer managed. 'I went over there, but they didn't admit me.'

'Who?' Calhoun asked. He had greeted his vice-president with a bit of sarcastic comradery, but now he was all business. 'Who wouldn't admit you?'

'Well, they didn't exactly bar me,' Mercer admitted, 'but they told me that I wasn't welcome.'

'They who?'

'Arnold McNeil . . . I heard about the meeting when I first got here this morning, but when I tried to call you your line was busy and Miss Felch had told me that you weren't expected to be late so I waited. I called again 'bout ten minutes ago, but the line was still busy.'

'Gloria was probably talking to somebody,' Calhoun muttered. 'What time was the meeting scheduled for?'

'Ten.'

'It's a little after,' Calhoun said checking his watch.

'I went over at ten, but they hadn't started.'

'Who called the meeting?' the president asked.

'I didn't find that out,' Mercer admitted. 'Nancy said there were notes placed in all faculty members' mail boxes.'

'Probably Thomas or MJUMBE,' Calhoun said, placing his case on the floor and searching through the papers on his desk until he came up with a pipe cleaner. 'Let's go.'

The meeting hadn't started on time because the assembled faculty members were waiting for Earl Thomas, the man who had called the meeting. Arnold McNeil and Edmund Mallory stood at the entrance to the library talking quietly. Both were hoping that Earl would appear, and neither of the men felt that the Student Government leader would come late.

They were wrong. Just as McNeil was about to take matters into his own hands Earl came through the library door with Lawman and Odds at his side. He smiled vaguely at the two tense faculty members and then slid inside where the rest of the professors sat talking among themselves and smoking.

Earl wasted little time. He went directly to the small table that was in front of the audience and put his notes and papers down. Odds and Lawman sat in the seats where the secretary and presiding officer of a meeting generally sat. Earl never sat down when he was speaking, and did not do so now. The SGA chief waited until everyone present had been seated. McNeil and Mallory were in the last row waiting. Earl lit a cigarette.

'Good morning,' Earl began. 'I had given serious thought to not attendin' this meetin' at all even though I called for it. When the thought of a meetin' with the faculty first occurred to me several things had not taken place that have become overwhelming factors in the student stance during the current crisis. First of all, when the meetin' was called school was still open. That has a great deal to do with our stance.' Earl smiled a bit, realizing that he had stated an over-obvious fact. 'But more important, when I called for this meetin' I wasn' aware of the lengths that our president would go to, to make sure that Sutton University stands still.

'Granted that perhaps President Calhoun considered himself under attack when presented with our "proposals", I still deny emphatically the fact that these issues had never been broached by students at Sutton. I will remind you all of the proposal last year presented by then SGA president Peabody that Sutton go on the meal-ticket system to cope with the inadequacies of the food served up by the Pride of Virginia Food Services. In brief, this was a system where students would buy a monthly meal ticket with a certain amount of holes that could be punched out when a student attended a meal. At the end of the month the tickets would be turned over to the central SGA office and another ticket would be issued. At the end of the semester all holes not punched would be refunded from the initial fee paid by boarding students.

'This is an example of the type of thoughtful proposal that President Ogden Calhoun says he is in favor of. Yet this proposal was rejected and the students were never informed in detail as to why. The only explanation given was that it might be difficult to keep track of food tickets; that some might be lost or stolen and that other students who were not paying might be eating on a friend's meal ticket. I agree that in case of a lost or stolen ticket the university might suffer, but only if the lost tickets were unnumbered and the hole puncher in the cafeteria was not given a list of tickets that had been reported lost and were no longer valid. In other words, all of the objections to the tickets were things that could've been easily worked out. The real reason that the idea was rejected, I suggest, is that the Pride of Virginia Food Services is aware of the quality of their meals and knew that no one would eat in the cafeteria if they had an option.'

Earl paused to light a cigarette. 'Perhaps that's enough about the food. Issues two, three, and four called for the resignation of Gaines Harper, Professors Royce, and Beaker. I suppose that everyone here has read the newsletter published yesterday by members of MJUMBE, but for those of you who haven't, it simply states that Gaines Harper is not presentin' the image that students need to see in order to confide very personal information. I'm sure that some of you will remember your college careers an' a lack of finances that made some of the goin' extremely rough. I'm sure that you didn' relish the idea of discussin' your family circumstances with *anyone*, but I assure you that you would find it doubly difficult to discuss these matters with Gaines Harper . . . As for the two professors referred to, I will take this opportunity to assure them that it is not a personal condemnation. What the students seek is a way to be better prepared for what awaits them after graduation . . . I have here a petition signed by ninety per cent of the majoring students in both the Language Department and the Chemistry Department who feel that new department heads are needed for progress.'

'He's a diplomatic bastard, ain't he?' Odds asked Lawman.

'He has to be,' Lawman said. 'But he's sincere.'

Odds nodded and lit up a cigarette of his own. He was beginning to relax a bit. Earl's diplomacy and ability to articulate had surprised even him, and he had sworn that nothing Earl would do could surprise him after the upset SGA election victory. He took a drag on the cigarette and leaned back. The issues of the demanded resignations from Beaker and Royce had been the matters that had troubled him all night. He had wondered how Earl would enlist the faculty support while asking for the dismissal of two of their most respected colleagues. The whole meeting would be a snap from here.

The next snap Odds heard, however, was the snap the entire

assembly heard as the door to the auditorium had its lock sprung and Captain Eli Jones of the security guards ushered Ogden Calhoun and Fenton Mercer into the meeting. The only man in the room who responded was Arnold McNeil, who was instantly on his feet.

'You were not invited to participate in this meeting,' Calhoun was told by McNeil.

'I'm well aware of that,' Calhoun remarked openly. 'But as the president of the university I am also the chairman of the faculty until such time as a replacement is found for me. Any meeting of this sort should definitely be of interest to the chair . . .'

'Then I so move,' McNeil said fuming.

'Motion denied, I bet,' Odds quipped behind his hand.

'The purpose of this meetin' was to inform faculty members of some things that the students consider important,' Earl said, facing Calhoun at the top step of the elevated platform.

'Let me tell you somethin', Thomas,' Calhoun said pointing a finger at the younger man's chest. 'I hold you and Baker personally responsible for damages to this university that may yet total more than ten thousand dollars. Did he talk about that?' Calhoun asked, turning to the assembly. 'Did he bother to go into the actions taken against Sutton yesterday at our meeting?'

'That's not the point!' Arnold McNeil said, rising from the seat he had slumped into and coming toward the stage. 'I, for one, am tired of being forced to see every issue from your point of view. I think that faculty members have as much stock in this community and in the particular situation that has come up as anyone else, and that our feelings and opinions to this point have been based primarily on hearsay and biased reports. I think,' he said, turning to his colleagues, 'that we need to hear the other side of the story.'

'Could I ask a question?' Mrs Pruitt singsonged above the hubbub of the gathering.

'Please do,' Calhoun said as though he were chairing the meeting.

'Just what do you hope to accomplish, Mr Thomas, or should I say did you hope to accomplish by calling this meeting?'

Earl paused. Lawman nodded to him. All eyes were on him.

'We had hoped to enlist the aid of the faculty,' Thomas said.

'I mean,' Mrs Pruitt interrupted, 'there had to be more to this than simply informing us about things . . .'

'We wanted to suggest two possible alternatives,' Earl said. 'I will be glad to go into them if this meeting is returned to its former state. I mean faculty only.'

'What have you got to say that I can't hear?' Calhoun asked defiantly.

'This is not a debate!' Earl said facing Calhoun squarely. 'The purpose was not for you an' I to argue points here. You know my perspective an' I know yours. You called a meetin' yesterday morning an' Captain Jones had his men on the door. That was not an open meeting! This is not an open meeting!'

'I think we should hear Thomas out,' McNeil suggested. 'Doesn't anyone want to hear the students' side of this?'

'I do!' Coach Mallory said speaking out for the first time.

Unfortunately the coach was the only faculty member who chose to speak out. Earl couldn't decide whether the others were speechless because of Calhoun's presence or because they simply had nothing to say.

'I was goin' to ask members of the faculty to go on strike with us,' Earl said through the icy silence with a weak grin on his face, 'or suggest that certain faculty members safeguard the readmission program in order to establish a buffer for the repression. But I don't suppose the questions I wanted to raise are relevant any more . . . how can you seek protection from a fellow victim?'

32

Exodus

Friday on the campus of Sutton University was generally a day of preparation for weekend activities that almost always included a mixer of some description that night and post-mixer parties in the dorms that lasted far into the morning. The student body would open its collective eyes by noon on Saturday, eat a hurried sandwich in the cafeteria or canteen, and get a good seat from which to cheer the football team (in the fall), the basketball team (in the winter), or the track team (in the spring). If the events were on other campuses, there would be cars loading on Friday night or Saturday morning to take students to the contests.

The cars and buses were leaving on Friday afternoon this week. The Saturday game had been cancelled. The students were milling about in front of the dormitories and the Student Union Building discussing the campus developments and waiting for a break in the depressing atmosphere.

The clouds hovered gray and forlorn over southern Virginia, reminders of the showers that had fallen the previous night and threatened to return.

Aside from the emptying resident facilities there were three centers of action on the campus early that afternoon. Sutton Hall, the administration building, was one. Carver Hall, where the student government was housed, was another. The third was the Sutton fraternity house's third-floor Strike Communications Center.

The five members of MJUMBE were closeted in a closed meeting at one o'clock in the back room of the Strike Center. They were planning what had become for them the most important phase of their strike program: a meeting with the parents of female students who were coming to deliver their daughters from the campus. It was now the most important phase because it would be their last opportunity to gain a measure of protection against the force that Ogden Calhoun was bound to use to clear the university buildings.

'Is it clear to everybody why we're usin' the same papers that we passed out yesterday?' Abul Menka asked.

'I still think it's gonna be a little tight on the oldies, man,' Cotton grumbled. 'Especially dudes an' chicks who graduated from here because they come off like a buncha Toms . . . when you be rappin' 'bout how ain' nothin' gone on here since they opened this crypt, man . . . whew! I don' know . . .'

'Some of the things we said won't be very acceptable,' Abul admitted. 'But you heard 'bout what happened to Earl when he tried to hol' a closed meetin' this mornin'. Ol' Assbucket broke in on the set an there wasn' nothin' nobody could do.'

'We could use the enforcers,' Ben King griped.

'No good,' Abul said stiffly. 'That would never get over wit' Calhoun-type people. We gotta face some facts, man. The folks who comin' to the meetin' is only comin' because their daughters is tellin' 'um to. They basically don' wanna come, think it's a waste a time, an' ain' gonna like the looks of us from jump street.'

'What you sayin' is that we really ain' gonna do no good to have the meetin',' Baker said.

'I s'pose thass the truth,' Abul said, sitting back down to the table. 'But we can't possibly give out new statements. One a them administratin' flunkies is boun' to point out the diff'rence. So there can't be none.'

'We definitely be sunk if Calhoun come over an' rap all the bullshit that the parents wanna hear,' Cotton said with a sigh.

'He won't be there,' Abul said. 'That may be a point in our favor. The bastard's confidence may be gettin' the best a him. All we really need is a handful a chicks. Then everybody in the community would be poised to leap on his shit if he sent big guns after us.'

'How you know he ain' comin'?' Cotton asked.

Abul fished around in his dashiki's breast pocket. He brought out a package of cigarettes, a book of matches, and a piece of folded paper. He lit a cigarette and unfolded the paper. 'It sez here,' he began, 'if you wanna know why school is closed an' you wanna talk wit' us, schedule an appointmen' wit' the secretary for nex' week.' Abul took care to slow his speech into a drawling slur to mock the president.

'Man, these folks ain' comin' back out here nex' week. Thass a lotta bullshit an' Calhoun knows it. I think we should move on all these bastards!' Ben King got up and paced the floor for a minute pounding a huge fist into his palm. He seemed on the brink of an explosion. Even more so than usual.

'Jobs,' Cotton mumbled to no one in particular. 'People got jobs to go to. They prob'bly think comin' out here *today* is a pain in the ass. An' anybody who ain' got no job an' can afford to live nowadays ain' sendin' his daughter to Grade D Sutton University.'

'Thass the point,' Abul said. 'All they gonna know is what we tell them. Unless they run inta one a them flunkies like Mercer.'

'No-Check Mercer,' Baker laughed. 'Thass a worthless muthafuckuh.'

There was a period of silence while members of the group pulled their thoughts together.

'We have ta do a heavy sympathy thing,' Baker commented. 'Otherwise we get our asses kicked t'night.'

'We need to wipe out all a them pigs from Sutton,' King urged.

'We can deal with t'night when it gets here,' Abul said. 'Let's list a few things that we want Baker to rap about when the party starts. After we do that Ralph can move off to the side an' organize the stuff in whatever order he wants to present it.'

'I don't buy it,' King said. 'I don' buy all a this crawlin' aroun' an' sayin' this instead a that an' doin' this instead a that like we in the wrong. Man, this iz some bullshit!'

'You gotta face the truth some day Ben,' Abul said as though to calm the fuming giant. 'Everything that we after you can't take. Everything you wan' ain' available jus' 'cause you're bigger than the nex' cat or you got some "enforcers" to back you up. Some things depend on yo' ability to convince people with words that you're right. When you bang somebody in the head they may go along wit' you, but they always layin' for a chance to go up 'side yo' head too. Thass why people who take things by force can' never sleep.'

'No lectures,' Ben King snarled. 'I don' know whuss goin' on wit' *you* anyway. It's only since the deal got under way that you started openin' yo goddamn mouth! An' it's only the las' couple days that all a the ideas we had have started fuckin' up.'

Abul Menka got to his feet. 'I'm gonna forget that you said that the way you did,' he said slowly, tossing his cigarette away and freeing his hands. 'I'm gonna attribute that remark to pressure, because my balls are out there on the line jus' like yours. I started speakin' up because I knew I had jus' as much to lose as anybody else an' I wuzn' gonna let some big mouth bluffin' get my ass kicked outta school. I was determined that if I left, it would be because we planned things out an' jus' didn' make it . . . you dig?'

'Fuck you!' King said turning his back. 'You guys can doodle an' dally an' meet an' pray like a buncha en-double-ay-cee-pee niggers if you want to, but I'm gettin' my guns together fo' t'night . . . I'll see yawl at three.'

'Without the gun,' Baker said to King's retreating back.

King said nothing. The only sound from him was the echo of his footfalls as he thudded heavily down the stairs.

Sheila Reed was writing a check for twenty dollars for an impatient coed who stood in front of the secretary's desk with a hat box in her hand. Sheila had been working since nine o'clock that morning with no break to speak of. Earl had asked a couple of times if she wanted Odds to take over while she prepared to leave, but she had assured him that the few belongings she was taking were packed and ready. Her parents had been informed by phone that she would be at her job in the SGA office when they arrived.

'When will the last bus leave?' the coed asked when Sheila gave her the check.

'There's a special bus scheduled to leave at four forty-five,' the secretary replied. 'That gives you plenty of time.'

'What time do you have?'

'Two minutes past two.'

'Good. Thank you.'

The phone rang, but before Sheila had a chance to answer it the extension light at the base of the phone went off, signifying that Earl had answered it in the inner office.

'Thomas,' he announced, leaning back in the swivel chair with a cigarette clamped in his mouth.

'Earl? This is Lawman. I'm in Garvey Plaza. We got 'bout fifty dudes left over here. Mosta the people either leavin' soon or on the border line between stayin' an' goin'.'

'What 'bout the women?' Earl asked.

'Pretty good. I haven' heard a woman yet say that she definitely wasn' goin' home. Mosta them whose parents are comin' said that they goin' to that MJUMBE meetin'. You gonna speak?'

'No.'

'Why not?'

'Because it's MJUMBE's meetin'.'

'I think you coppin' out,' Lawman said.

'What? Coppin' out? How?'

'If you're makin' a split wit' MJUMBE you gotta speak up. You can't tell the women to leave an' then have their parents show up an' have a buncha so-called studen' leaders who're bein' identified wit' you tell them the opposite.'

'The women know how I feel. They heard me yesterday,' Earl retorted.

'The parents didn' hear nothin'.'

'MJUMBE knew how I felt before they called the meetin'.'

'You made them call it when you wen' aroun' las' night,' Lawman persisted.

'I didn' call . . .'

'You the president, man!' Lawman exclaimed. 'I'm trippin' out behind all these moral games you play wit' yo'self that seem to relate to some unknown group a sacred principles. Too much goddamn thinkin' is bein' done when there ain' none necessary. I tol' you a long time ago about how niggers is the only people in America who get hung up on them bogus Democratic ideals like the right to assemble. Fuck a right to assemble! You want the women gone? Then bes' you be there to tell their parents to take their crazy asses home! 'Cause you know as well as I do that if anything happens to any one of them you gon' be the man with the pipe up his ass when they start handin' out the blame.'

'Maybe I'll go,' Earl said wearily.

'Maybe hell!' Lawman said with his temper subsiding a bit. 'You better back yo'self up. It's all the help thass comin'.'

'The way I see it I back myself up if I give 'um busfare.'

There was a pause, an empty hole in the air that neither man bothered to try and fill with words. Lawman knew that he was pushing his friend. Earl was definitely not the type of politician or man to throw his weight around. He had won the election and was carrying out the job in the best way he knew how. When he told people something he was giving them his opinion and what they did after that he generally didn't influence. Lawman had never heard him say, 'I told you that wouldn't work,' when something failed, or 'I told you that would work,' when a venture was successful. It occurred to Lawman that the reason the post-operative statements were never needed was because Earl was generally such a forceful speaker and so adept at bringing people over to his train of thought that his policies toward campus political issues were never challenged. But now it was time for Earl to be more forceful. He could no longer advise as though he were objective about the entire project. He had to make people see what he was talking about whether it appealed to them or not.

The problem facing Sutton University's student body was one of face-saving and adventure. There were many people whose departure had been made very quietly. Some of those who stayed were staying because no one wanted to be considered a coward unwilling to face whatever force Ogden Calhoun sent against them. The adventure that the situation was presenting was obvious. Most of the students at Sutton were the post-civil-rights-marches generation of Black students. They hadn't been old enough to take part in the marches on Washington and the march against Selma. They had never been actively involved in the Black revolution on any level. They were still inside the educational womb and their discussions were all hot air and rhetoric based on television revolutionaries and imported upheavals from Franz Fanon or Mao.

Six o'clock looked like excitement from their viewpoint. Chances were that very few of them had ever had a billy club come crashing down on their heads or mace sprayed on them or tear gas choking them and setting their lungs on fire. Lawman knew that it would be no picnic, but he had agreed with Earl when the SGA president had told the men to make up their own minds while the women were asked to leave. The thing he thought he had to impress on Earl was the fact that no one who had never been involved in a confrontation would want to be on campus to pay for resisting arrest or refusing to vacate private property. He decided that he would try and find some clippings that he had cut out of various Black magazines depicting the true possibilities in the picture for those who had some romantic notion about a revolutionary picnic on Sutton's campus when the law arrived. He smiled when it occurred to him that the sight of those pictures might turn Earl's head around.

'When you comin' over here?' Earl asked. 'Hey! Lawman! You still on?'

'Yeah, man,' Lawman said, cutting his daydream short.

'When you comin' over here?' Earl repeated.

'About quarter to three,' Lawman said. 'Where's Odds?'

'Out front buggin' hell outta Sheila last I saw,' Earl laughed.

'Well, I'll see you.'

'Yeah,' Earl said, 'I'll see you.'

Earl dropped the receiver back into the holster. He lit a cigarette and finding it to be the last one in the package he crushed the container and tossed it into the trash. As he stood up to stretch his legs the sound of honking car horns drew his attention to the back window. There were three cars trying to get out of the driveway next to Garvey Plaza. No one could decide who was going to go first. Earl pulled the shade down.

Deep inside he knew that the things Lawman had said were true. Not going to the three o'clock MJUMBE meeting *would* be a cop out of sorts. If he had any responsibility at all to the people in the community and particularly to the women, perhaps it was an obligation to describe Selma, Alabama to them or some of the things that had happened to him as a Freedom Rider.

His hand automatically went to the crown of his head when he thought about the Freedom Rides. He had been only a boy of nine traveling with his college-aged brother. Their first stop had been a small cafe just outside of Charleston, South Carolina. As far as they knew no one, not even the members of the press, had known where they were to stop. But there had been a huge reception waiting for them in the cafe – policeman, rednecks, and Kluxers. Their best move would have been to move on to the next stop, but once they got out of the bus their retreat back into the vehicle was blocked by a stick-swinging, rock-throwing mob. Earl had been kicked to the ground and when his brother had tried to shield his body by crouching over the younger Thomas, a broom handle had crashed into his skull and the last thing Earl remembered was the salty taste of his brother's blood as the red ooze from the gaping wound covered his face.

'I gotta go to that meetin',' Earl decided. 'I'm damned if I know what I'll say. Maybe I'll just recount my own experiences for them, but I gotta do somethin'.'

'Earl?' Someone was calling him and knocking on the closed door to the inner office.

'C'mon in!' Earl said.

It was Odds. 'I wuz on my way over to get a sandwich,' Earl's sidekick informed him. 'I wuz wond'rin' if you wanted somethin'.'

'I'll go,' Earl said reaching for his jacket. 'I need a pack a smokes.'

'Damn!' Odds said, 'you smoke like they ain' makin' no mo' a them things.'

'Yeah,' Earl flashed. 'An' it's gonna get worse befo' it gets better.'

Ogden Calhoun was having a meeting all his own. He had literally dictated the names of the young men that he did not want readmitted to Sutton University. His recommendation to the Board of Trustees had merely stated that certain members of the community would not be readmitted because of activities that endangered the lives and property of the Sutton family. The $8,000 damage (not including labor for replacing damaged equipment) and the takeover of the Thursday afternoon meeting were cited in detail as examples of the activities of these students.

The list of names placed on the desk of Charles Hague, Admissions Director, came as no surprise to either Hague or concerned faculty members who drifted into the Admissions office to find out the particulars of Calhoun's decision.

The list read alphabetically:

Ralph Washington Baker
Everett McAllister Cotton
Roy Edward Dean
Frederick L. Jones

Benjamin Raymond King
Kenneth C. Smith
Earl Joseph Thomas
Jonathan Wise

Those who didn't know were informed that Roy Dean was called 'Lawman' on Sutton's campus, and that Everett Cotton was really the backfield ace 'Speedy' Cotton. Few people had ever heard Earl's private nickname for Ken Smith – 'Odds' – nor had they heard the term 'Captain Cool' from anyone other than Arnold McNeil and a few students. But there was a fretful, worried frown on the face of every faculty member and administrator who saw the list. They had good reason to believe that these eight men would not leave Sutton without a fight.

33

Explosion!

The only member of MJUMBE who was wearing a dashiki for the three o'clock meeting with Sutton parents was Abul Menka. The tall, bushy-headed New Yorker wore a corduroy dashiki with red, green, and black patches symbolizing the three colors of the Black liberation flag. He was sitting alone in the far-left corner of the stage, smoking a cigarette, eyes hidden behind gold-framed sunglasses.

Three members, Ralph Baker, Speedy Cotton, and Fred Jones, were standing huddled in the opposite corner. They wore sports shirts open at the throat and jackets.

Ben King was standing at the base of the stairs that led up to the stage. He wore a pair of blue jeans, a sweat shirt, and a very casual pea jacket with one pocket missing and the collar ripped.

The auditorium was little over a quarter full at three o'clock. Recognizing the twelve-hundred-seat capacity Baker was reluctant to start before so scant a turnout, hoping that there were more people on the way.

In the assembly were women and parents, male students who had remained on campus, and members of the faculty and interested administrators. Earl, from his vantage point between Odds and Lawman, who were leaning against the door in the far rear of the room, estimated a total of maybe one hundred coeds. The interesting thing about their clothing was that few of them were dressed for a normal day's activities. Most of them were wearing traveling clothes.

The gathering stopped its low hum of conversation when Ralph Baker approached the microphone.

'Excuse me,' he began a trifle nervously. 'I am sorry to have added additional stops on people's schedules, but I feel that too many times things are taken for granted by 'student leaders' that would amaze many parents. But this info'mation is never relayed. For this reason the things that have happened here at Sutton this week would seem to be vague an' mysterious. This meetin' is to perhaps clarify a few things fo' parents as to what our strike has been about. Maybe things will then be clearer as to why we are takin' the stands that we have.

'We men of MJUMBE are all seniors. We are representatives of what is mosta the time the mos' stagnant, cautious section of the studen' body. We see ev'ry possible distraction as a possible delay from graduatin' on time.

'Unfortunately there comes a time when the boat mus' be rocked. In this case President Calhoun is indicatin' that we were intent on sinkin' the boat. No one wants ta drown. Especially,' Baker added with a smile, 'if you've been on it fo' three years an' only have one mo' to go.

'We have handed out a copy of our requests and our reasons for askin' that these changes be made. I read once in a magazine an interview wit' a former political leader at Howard University who said, 'It's not enough to hol' a gun at an administrator's head. You have to pull the trigger.' At Sutton we didn' even do that. We called for a studen' strike to impress our sincerity, our unity. We wanned to show how committed each an' every studen' was to these issues.

'President Calhoun tipped the boat over. Not only did he turn away our demands with only token interest, he sent for the police force that is known in this county to be the most brutal and racist. I know, 'cause I'm a native of this county. The police came out an' threatened us wit' their sticks an' their curses. They acted jus' like everyone knew they would act. They acted white.

'There are several ways of lookin' at our request for studen's to remain here at Sutton. It can be looked at as a personal plea from the members of MJUMBE since all five of us will prob'bly be expelled. But that's not our primary concern. Our concern is that only three of our deman's will be instituted. We will only have, as I said, a token response, and our submission to pressure will intimidate those who follow. There will always be studen' leaders on their han's an' knees insteada their feet.

'Fo' that reason . . .'

Anyone present in the room could have testified to the weight that Baker's words were having. Even though he was reading most of the time from a typed sheet and sounded somewhat stilted, the young man was being effective. But just as he began to draw his suggestions to a close and call for the support that most people felt he most surely would have received, an explosion shook the building.

The explosion came from somewhere behind the building, shaking the auditorium with quick, jerking vibrations. Baker raced to a side window even as the first scream was being drowned by the chaos that was unleashed by the frightened crowd. He reached the door just in time to see a school bus engulfed in a shield of flame; tongues of orange and blue fire lunging skyward from the hull of the vehicle.

The crowd pushed through the exits and toward the streets. The first three men to leave the building had turned the corner in the direction of the blast. They could feel the warmth from the charring and smoking metal, see the melting tires allow the skeleton of the vehicle to collapse around the white-hot wheels.

'A plastic bomb,' Odds said surveying the ashes.

'A son-uva-bitch,' Earl Thomas declared.

34

MJUMBE Discovery

It was after five thirty. The men of MJUMBE had watched all but a very few members of the Sutton community depart by car or taxi or bus, through the narrow passages between buildings, around the oval of dead and dying flowers, and through the cast-iron arch with its proclamation, SUTTON UNIVERSITY.

The last two hours had seen their last plan destroyed, seared by flames and as easily pushed aside as a puff of the black whorls of smoke that had been carried away by the brisk winds hurtling across campus from the east.

The revelation by Victor Johnson that a unit of National Guardsmen was camped just south of Sutton was another setback. Somehow pieces of information about a unit of soldiers never hit solidly home until the last station wagon, with suitcases of clothes bulging out of the storage space, had disappeared from view.

There had been no discussion about the bomb or the Guard. No one had said a word except to confirm the fact that when the five o'clock bus left it would be time to arm themselves. When the last of two late buses belched a stream of black smoke and accelerated southward the five men each got up slowly and started to take his position. Baker was trying to make a last-minute call to the SGA office when he realized that the telephones had been cut off for the day. He cursed and ripped the phone out of the wall. He figured he owed Calhoun a favor.

'The barricades up in back?' Baker asked Cotton.

'Both door an' windows,' Cotton said.

'Jonesy an' I decided we'll lay here,' Abul said, gesturing toward the positions facing the oval near the front door.

'Need somebody up top,' Baker said. 'Ben, you got that scope?'

'Yeah.'

'Why don' we have Ben on the third floor with the scope, you an' Cotton on the secon' floor with the two high powers, an' me an' Jonesy down here since we don't have much range?' Abul said to Baker.

Baker nodded and collected his case.

'Rub Vaseline on yo' face when you take yo' positions. It fights mace,' Abul said. 'An' use the handkerchiefs soaked in vinegar to fight the tear gas. It's boun' to get in here once the windows get broken.'

''Bout that time,' Baker pointed out.

The five men picked up their arms and ammunition to depart. There was no fanfare or commotion. Jones had a .38 Special Rossi from Brazil. Menka had a Winchester .22 rifle. Baker and Cotton had identical .30–30 rifles with a case of Norma cartridges and *bandoleras*. King had a 30.06 with a huge track scope. He carried two metal boxes of ammunition. When the meeting broke up he sat at the base of the stairs and put his gun together smoothly and turned, almost anxiously, to the front window where three of the four panes had been reinforced with metal strips. He nodded to Fred Jones and departed.

There was no final word from anyone. All five men knew what they had to do. Abul was tempted to shake hands because it seemed that only in the past two days had he really gotten to know them, really gotten to be brothers to them. He couldn't find a way to acknowledge this bond without seemingly confessing that he felt death near them. He remained flawlessly cool, crouching behind a sofa and lighting a cigarette.

Barricades had also been placed in front of the entrance to Carver Hall. Earl, Lawman, and Odds sat in the front office armed with a bottle of rum and two quarts of Coca-Cola.

There were no guns, no sticks, no knives. They had been drinking since the explosive ending to the meeting with the parents. Their eyes were red, their jokes becoming less and less funny and yet receiving larger laughs, and their underarms were soaked with nervous perspiration, but they considered themselves ready.

Ogden Calhoun was on the line to the security office. Reporters had been running all over campus and a television crew complete with camera was staked out in his outer office. They had been waiting for a statement from him for over an hour and he had been waiting for a call from the security guard for almost that long. Miss Felch had been brewing coffee and making small talk since the reporters had flocked to Calhoun's office from the scene of the explosion. There had been a dictated paragraph at three thirty stating that the explosion was only further evidence that the institution had to be closed. There was less than a word for the next two hours.

'Hello? Jones? This is President Calhoun. I was waiting for . . .'

'I just got here an' listed the things you wanted, sir,' Jones said breathlessly. 'There are only two occupied buildings. One is the fraternity house and the other is Carver Hall.'

'I want you to direct the Guard when they come in,' Calhoun said icily.

'Yes, sir,' Jones mumbled. 'An' stay wit' the Guard unit?'

'Every damn second! I want to know everything that happens in an instant.'

'Yes, sir,' Jones agreed. 'It's ten minutes to . . .'

'Right,' Calhoun cut in. 'Come on over.'

The intercom buzzer went on.

'It's your wife,' Miss Felch said.

'Tell her I'm busy,' Calhoun snapped.

'I told her that, sir, but she's insisting.'

'Then hang the damn phone up an' call the Guard number. Don't take any more calls. Tell the press I'll make a statement when the Guard arrives at the front door. Tell them I'll speak then. I know they'll complain about the lighting an' all, but kick 'em out of my office an' bring me a cup of coffee, please.'

'Yes, sir,' Miss Felch replied in her monotone. 'What shall I say to the Guard?'

'Tell 'em I said to come on.'

As Miss Felch dialed the numbers that would bring National Guardsmen onto the campus of Sutton University for the first time in the institution's eighty-seven-year history, Abul Menka was making a startling discovery on the third floor of the fraternity house. He had gone up to the top floor to demonstrate the use of the handkerchiefs-soaked-in-vinegar to Ben King. What he discovered was that one of the two metal boxes that he had seen on the first floor did not contain the supposed clip of 30.06 shells, but instead a plastic bomb.

'What in hell is that for?' Abul screamed. 'Oh! I get it! You stupid bastard! You're the one who blew up that goddamn bus! You stupid muthafuckuh! Where's the goddamn timer?'

'This is for an emergency!' King declared picking up the bomb in his hands.

'Like the goddamn bus two minutes befo' we coulda stayed on this muthafuckuh with fifty parents an' seventy women. Right?'

'All right! I won' set it!' the huskier man exclaimed, putting the bomb on a table.

'Set it? You think I give a fuck? What do I care? All I know is that you fucked everythin' aroun' today.'

Baker, Cotton, and Jones all seemed to arrive at the third-floor door at that time. They were speechless. Fred Jones started to wipe Vaseline from his face with a towel. He threw down the handkerchief soaked in vinegar and pocketed his .38 Special.

'Hard bombs to fuck wit',' he said softly as he zipped up his peacoat. 'Them's the kind that blew up them Weathermen in New York. Hard to trus' somethin' like that.'

'Where you goin'?' King asked him.

'I'm leavin', man,' Jonesy said in his ever-quiet manner.

'Why? I made a mistake! You never made a mistake? I thought the meetin' wuz gonna flop! I wanned everybody to know that we meant business. All right! I made a mistake! I couldn' go out there an' undo the fuckin' thing jus' because the meetin' wuz goin' all right . . . I . . . look, I took a chance, man! I made a mistake. All right?'

'Fuck you!' Abul sneered. 'A silly-assed one-man power play! We wuz a team! We wudn' fuckin' aroun'. You fucked it all up!'

'Team? You never been wit' a fuckin' team in yo life. Man, you always by yo'self,' King flashed.

Jonesy walked between the two men and looked questioningly at Baker. Baker nodded and followed him out of the door followed closely by Speedy Cotton and Abul Menka.

'Chicken out, muthafuckuhs!' King raged, running halfway down the landing that led to the third floor. 'You all jus' scared a them whiteys! Thass all! You can't hand me that too-disappointed-to-fight story.'

The Black giant evidently had known very little about the point to which he had driven Abul Menka. When King pulled up next to him and pointed an accusing finger in Abul's face the man in the gold dashiki turned and landed a right hand flush in the center of King's face. As his victim stumbled backward, Abul leaped at him, landing punishing blows on the heavier man's face and neck. King tumbled into the corner of the landing covering his face with his arms until Baker and Jones subdued Abul from behind.

King was spitting blood. He made a slight move as though he would attack Menka when he regained his balance, but Baker proffered a restraining hand.

'I wish you would!' Abul declared, shaking loose and adjusting his sunglasses. 'I'd love to beat yo' fuckin' brains out.'

King turned from the four men and walked back up the stairs. 'I'm stayin'!' he shouted as loudly as he could. 'They'll have to kill this stupid Black bastard while they pry yo' asses from between yo' legs!' He shook a fist at them from the top of the stairs. 'Fuck you cats! Fuck you!'

'That nigger is crazy,' Abul said to Baker as they went down the stairs.

'Maybe,' Baker said collecting his gear. 'His mama was raped by a white man six or seven years ago. He hate 'um now. You should see when he git a chance to block one or tackle a whitey. He's a mean muthafuckuh, man. He sees red.'

'I hear tell some is comin' fo' him to tackle,' Menka said pointedly. 'They gonna have U.S.A. on their jerseys. He should play a helluva game.'

'I hope so,' Baker said.

35

Downhill Snowball

Miss Felch never had a chance to stop Gloria Calhoun from entering her husband's office. Mrs Calhoun came through the open door to the outer office and barged by the startled secretary before a word could be exchanged.

Ogden Calhoun was both surprised and annoyed to see his wife intrude on him. He was putting the finishing touches on his press statement and having a last cup of coffee when the interruption took place. He leaped to his feet and held out a warning hand to his wife.

Mrs Calhoun's face was bitten with anger, her dark eyes flashing too much despair to withstand the tears she felt about to boil over and smear her carefully prepared makeup. Her hair was glistening from the raindrops that had started to sprinkle the air.

'I just came to tell you something important!' she declared ignoring her husband's hand. 'I came to tell you that I'm leavin' you tonight. Right now! I swear to God in heaven, Ogden, that if you send those troops down on those boys I'm through.'

'I have no choice,' Calhoun said, rushing to the door to be sure that it was closed and locked.

'That's a lie!' his wife objected. 'That's as much of a lie as anything else that's gone on this week. There is a choice. You've always had some kind of choice. But you're old. You don't want to see. An' now the choice is almost life or death.'

'I have my duty to . . .'

'Stop! God, I hate to think that I'm really hearin' *you* sayin' those sort of things. I hate to think of you callin' on clichés and lies when I'm practically down on my knees askin' you to take a look at what you're doin'.'

'I know.'

'Stop! I said stop!' Mrs Calhoun almost screamed. 'I'm very tired. I didn't come here to argue. I didn't even come here to change your mind. I was leavin' without a word, but when I called to talk to you as usual you were too busy for me.' Mrs Calhoun sat in the chair facing the president's desk.

'Gloria, you don't know all the facts.'

'Maybe not,' Mrs Calhoun agreed. 'But,' she added as she struggled for composure, 'I do know that there are boys out there ready to die for what they believe in. Boys that are takin' a stand that you would have taken when you were their age. But, God that must have been a long time ago. And they have to face this, this death, because you're an old man. Not really old. Not too old to see as I see, but all you have been able to see for a long time has been yourself. Any idea that wasn't conceived by Ogden Calhoun is not a good idea.'

'They're wrong,' Calhoun said heavily. 'You're wrong. We never did things like this. There was communication an' we faced everybody like a man. We sat down an' argued an' fought.' Calhoun was flustered beyond his frayed nerves and late hours. The mask of rock-hard calm had split like fabric stretched too tightly against its subject, leaving him feeling old and tired and open.

'We never did,' his wife snapped. '*WE WHO?* We, in the thirties? *WE WHO?* We, at Howard? For nine years I've watched you fool people and lie to yourself, using Sutton University as an example to show everyone that the same tough man who was fired for speaking his mind about Black psychology is still as tough and as hard to overpower as ever. All I've read about is the history of collective thought you've been in favor of here at Sutton. That's another lie! Everything that you have implemented here that *wasn't* your idea has been used and publicized as though you had conceived it. Threatening students. "My way or the Highway Calhoun" . . . I feel so sorry for you Ogden. And me, too. I feel sorry for me too. Because I never said anythin' though I saw it all happening a long time ago. But I thought you knew you were acting. I never suspected that you believed that liberal façade that you exposed an' the talk about being on the students' side. I thought you knew that you were only on your side.'

'You're wrong,' Calhoun repeated.

'And you really think I'm wrong too,' Mrs Calhoun said, standing up as though she had just had another revelation.

'I know you're wrong,' Calhoun said weakly.

'I'm leaving,' Mrs Calhoun said turning for the door. Her husband didn't look up as she departed. 'Good-bye,' she concluded.

Minutes tick-ticked by. Ogden Calhoun stared out of the window watching darkness engulf the campus. He saw the sparkling shadows of the raindrops dancing across the path of the light outside his second-floor window.

Miss Felch cut into his thoughts by way of the intercom.

'Yes?' he asked, getting up.

'The Guard is here,' Miss Felch said.

'Where are they?' Calhoun asked.

'Their commander is downstairs with Captain Jones. The rest of them will be pulling in in a few seconds.'

'Good. I'm coming out.'

Calhoun straightened his tie in the small mirror on his desk, finished his coffee, and smoothed out his hair with his palm. When he came through the oak door into the outer office Miss Felch was throwing a sweater over her shoulders. Together they went down the flight of stairs onto the first floor and then out into the misty Virginia evening.

Captain Jones was standing on the second step talking to a man in an army uniform. Flashbulbs went off in the president's face. Huge rows of illuminating camera lights were turned on and the night television cameras started to roll.

'This is the Guard commander, General Rice,' Captain Jones said introducing the two men. 'This is President Ogden Calhoun.' Calhoun shook the general's hand and more pictures were taken.

'I'll be very brief, gentlemen,' Calhoun said to the assembly of reporters and photographers and interested by-standers. 'In the past forty-eight hours Sutton University has been the scene of over twenty-three thousand dollars' worth of damage. We have lost ten thousand dollars' worth of equipment in our resident facilities and today, a thirteen-thousand-dollar school bus, formerly used to transport our teams to athletic events, was blown up. The members of the community were asked to leave in order that we might establish a readmission program, but there are certain members of the community who didn't leave. I think, and Captain Jones will correct me if I'm wrong, that the men responsible for the majority of the damage, the Student Government Association heads and members of a militant group called MJUMBE, are the only students who insisted on staying. All other students apparently saw the sincerity and responsibility from my office to bring peace to Sutton. Therefore . . .' President Calhoun was interrupted by the large roar of motors as the six huge transport trucks carrying the Guardsmen wheeled around the oval and pulled to a stop in front of the office. Flashbulbs were fired at the halting trucks. One man from each truck dropped off quickly and trotted through the rain toward the building. '. . . therefore,' Calhoun continued, 'I have summoned the National Guard unit placed at my disposal by the governor, and I am asking them to clear the buildings here at Sutton. That's all.'

Had Calhoun looked up just at that moment he would have seen one last student car leaving the campus. It was a late-model Ford station wagon with Fred Jones at the wheel and Speedy Cotton and Ralph Baker sitting in the back seat as passengers. The other two MJUMBE men were not in the car.

Ben King was sitting in a chair on the third floor of the frat house. He couldn't see through the darkness and mist across the oval to where Calhoun stood in front of Sutton Hall, but he had heard the roaring engines of the transport trucks as they arrived on campus and then idled in front of the administration building. He was readying the 30.06.

Abul Menka heard the trucks entering too. He was standing at the side window of Carver Hall knocking on the glass window, trying to summon Earl Thomas. Abul had turned down an opportunity to ride with Fred Jones and had even got as far as revving up the motor for his own car to leave, but the lights in Carver Hall, just across the parking lot from the fraternity building, made him think of Earl and the reason why he was leaving. He saw no reason for Earl to die because of King's stupidity either.

'Earl,' he was calling. 'Earl!'

The SGA president finally heard him above the transistor radio that was playing on the desk and went over to the window and opened it.

'Abul. Whuss up, brother?' Earl asked.

'This whole thing,' Captain Cool replied. 'Baker an' Cotton an' Jonesy already left. We found a bomb that Ben King had made. He was planning to use it this evenin'. He was the one who bombed the bus.'

'So you leavin'?'

'What the hell?' Abul asked. 'When I realized that whatever those parents saw and felt during that meetin' explosion really *was* our fault instead a jus' somethin' that someone had planted to blame us, it really took the wind outta me ... thass why I came over here to tell you to split.'

'No can do,' Earl laughed without humor, turning his face up into the mist. 'The money you guys bet over the las' couple days is comin' to be collected. My signature was on the bogus check.'

'You don' have ta stay,' Abul complained. 'Man, King fucked everything aroun'. Thass part a the reason the ol' man is sendin' the Guard in. You don' have to pay for *that*.'

'Look, man. I know how you guys got those papers that Baker made up the demands from. Sheila tol' me everything ...'

'What?' Abul asked.

'That Baker took the papers from my desk after she loaned him the key. She tol' me today.'

'I didn't know that ... either,' Abul said sincerely. 'Baker convinced us all that you wuz jus' another bootlickin' ass-kissin'-type-cat.'

'Doesn't matter,' Earl said. 'Somebody had to start it.'

'It was like a snowball, man,' Abul continued blankly. 'One lie led to the nex' one.' Abul looked up again suddenly as the truck engines began to rev again. 'They comin', man,' he declared. 'Why don' yawl c'mon out. Can't you see that ain' nothin' like we thought it was?'

'But regardless, man,' Earl said calmly, trying to peer through the density of the rain now falling heavily, 'the things on that paper was comin' to a head, an' this was the inevitable result.'

'What you're sayin' is that you gonna pay fo' our mistakes. You know that if you had been runnin' things they would a been diff'rent.'

'Maybe. It don' matter now.'

'Move aside,' Abul said climbing through the window. 'I'll wait with yawl.'

There was little room in the cramped office. Odds and Lawman were sitting on the floor because all of the furniture had been propped against the door.

Abul was welcomed. He sat in the middle of the two SGA appointed workers and poured himself a drink. He didn't have time to enjoy it.

The first burst of fire came from the direction of the fraternity house. It was a series of four shots echoing like firecrackers to the men in Carver Hall. The return fire shook them where they sat. There was a repeating-rifle burst, followed by a thundering from guns. The last explosion was a mammoth roar that none of the four men in Carver Hall would ever believe had come from a gun. Abul Menka dropped his glass when he realized the truth.

'They hit the bomb,' He cried leaping to his feet. 'One of those bullets hit the bomb. Oh, God!' he raced to the side window to see the fraternity house being swallowed by flame leaping toward the stairs starting at the top floor and running quickly down the front of the old wooden structure.

Earl, Odds, and Lawman were rooted to the window unable to react. They could scarcely accept the fact that Ben King was somewhere in that building.

Abul Menka was still screaming as he tore the barricades from their prop positions at the door. He threw the chairs behind him in his haste to leave and shoved the desk far enough away from the door to exit. Earl and his companions arrived at the door just behind him, too late to divert him. They stopped. Through the rain they saw his running figure disappear across the parking lot headed toward the fire.

NOW AND THEN

GIL SCOTT-HERON

'A poet and polemicist whose lyrics have inspired and galvanised generations.' *GQ*

The song-poems of this undisputed 'bluesologist' triumphantly stand on their own, evoking the rhythm and urgency which distinguished Gil Scott-Heron's career. His message is black, political, historically accurate, urgent, uncompromising and mature, and as relevant now as it was when he started, back in the early seventies.

'Accessible, intelligent, rhythmic writing which makes poetry seem worthwhile again.' *List*

'Some of the funniest and most literate lyrics in all music . . . From deadpan attacks on racism to withering sarcasm about the Great Society; from Chomskian rants to parodies of media shallowness – every line comes coated in a sardonically witty turn of phrase.' *Time Out*

£9.99

978 0 86241 900 4

DON'T RHYME FOR THE SAKE OF RIDDLIN'
The Authorised Story of Public Enemy

RUSSELL MYRIE

**The only fully authorised biography of Public Enemy,
containing interviews with all the major players**

Public Enemy are one of the greatest hip-hop acts of all
time. Exploding out of Long Island, New York in the early
1980s, their firebrand lyrical assault, the Bomb Squad's
innovative production techniques and their unmistakeable
live performances gave them a formidable reputation.

Urgent, incisive and definitive, *Don't Rhyme for the Sake of
Riddlin'* shows how, in a time of rampant profligacy and
meaningless posturing in hip-hop, Public Enemy is as
important and necessary as ever.

'Public Enemy's is the greatest rap'n'roll story of them all . . .
[Myrie's] book is studded with glittering new anecdotes
[and] hitherto unknown details . . . a terrific account of the
band's early days.' Angus Batey, *Mojo*

'It would take a nation of millions to hold this book back!'
Dizzee Rascal

£9.99

ISBN 978 1 84767 126 4

TRICK BABY

ICEBERG SLIM

A reissue of the cult classic

Trick Baby charts the rise of White Folks, a white Negro who uses his colour as a trump card in the tough game of the Con. Blue-eyed, light-haired and white-skinned, White Folks is the most incredible con man the ghetto ever spawned, a hustler in the jungle of Southside Chicago where only the sharpest survive.

With his partner Blue, an old hand who teaches him the tricks of the trade, White Folks rises to the top of his profession. The cons he pulls off get more and more lucrative and dangerous until one day they go too far . . .

'Slim fully earns his place in the canon of America's greatest.' Helen Walsh

'Slim belongs to the knuckle-duster-in-the-face school of storytelling.' *Sunday Times*

£8.99

ISBN 978 1 84767 431 9

PIMP
The Story of My Life

ICEBERG SLIM
With an Introduction by Irvine Welsh

**Nobody but a pimp could tell this story and no-one ever
has . . . until Iceberg Slim**

This is the true story of the pimp. The story of the smells,
the sounds, the fears and the petty triumphs of his world.
A legendary figure of the Chicago underworld, Iceberg
Slim relates his twenty-five years in the Game. Few
survived – Iceberg did.

'Iceberg Slim does for the pimp what Jean Genet did for
the thief.' *Washington Post*

'One of the most influential writers of
our age.' Irvine Welsh

£8.99

ISBN 978 1 84767 332 9